The Last Shepherd

West Word Fiction

THE
Last Shepherd

MARTIN ETCHART

UNIVERSITY OF NEVADA PRESS RENO & LAS VEGAS

WEST WORD FICTION

University of Nevada Press, Reno, Nevada 89557 USA

Copyright © 2012 by Martin Etchart

Manufactured in the United States of America

Design by Kathleen Szawiola

Library of Congress Cataloging-in-Publication Data

Etchart, Martin, 1960–

The last shepherd / by Martin Etchart.

p. cm. — (West word fiction)

ISBN 978-0-87417-886-9 (pbk. : alk. paper) — ISBN 978-0-87417-887-6 (ebook)

1. Basque Americans—Fiction. 2. Young men—Fiction. 3. Sheep ranches—Arizona—Fiction. 4. Inheritance and succession—Fiction. 5. Basques—France—Fiction. 6. Family secrets—Fiction. 7. Life change events—Fiction. I. Title.

PS3605.T38L37   2012

813'.6—dc22   2012017300

The paper used in this book is a recycled stock made from 30 percent post-consumer waste materials, certified by FSC, and meets the requirements of American National Standard for Information Sciences—Permanence of Paper for Printed Library Materials, ANSI/NISO Z39.48-1992 (R2002). Binding materials were selected for strength and durability.

21   20   19   18   17   16   15   14   13   12

5   4   3   2

Ene amarenko
For my mother

Jainkoa da ene zaintzailea; ez dut deus nahi.
The Lord is my shepherd; I shall not want.

—PSALM 23

The Last Shepherd

« SUMMER 1980 »

1

B A T

Nahi nin—I wanted.

"Now, then," Dad said as he shifted the truck into a lower gear. "Clean out sheep pens. *Bat*—one on list."

And my wanting was something more than the stupid sheep that were ruining my life.

"Paint sheep corrals," Dad said. "*Bi*—two on list."

Wanting chewed at my gut as lightning splintered the air, and I watched a monsoon erase Phoenix. In the valley below, clouds rushed forward like a flock of startled sheep; a coyote-colored wall of dirt pursued them—suburban houses were swallowed, downtown buildings engulfed, and the road we were on devoured.

I hunched down in the truck's passenger seat and pressed my knees up against the dash and picked strands of wool from beneath my fingernails and wanted and wanted and wanted.

"Patch fence around sheep pasture," Dad said. "*Hiru*—three on list."

I tried to shrug out the ache in my shoulders—a "gift" from the 534 sheep we'd unloaded up at the summer *etxola*—sheep camp. The sheep would remain in the mountains, tucked beneath the oak trees, until the triple-digit temperatures of Phoenix broke. Luis and Diego were stuck watching over the flock for the summer. Which gave me three months of freedom to find a way to get what I wanted onto Dad's list.

"Drain sheep pond," Dad said. "*Lau*—four on list."

Thunder rumbled as the first grains of the monsoon's wall of dirt struck the truck's windshield.

"Sharpen sheep clippers," Dad said. "*Bost*—five on list—"

"What number on that list is my going to U of A?"

My father's grip tightened on the truck's steering wheel. The scab on his knuckle cracked open. Blood oozed out.

"Now, then, Mathieu, you know that sheep and the university can't be on the same list."

"Maybe it's time for a new list," I said.

"Mathieu, I can't—"

"It's Matt," I said. "My name's Matt. That's what my friends call me—would call me—if they all hadn't already left for the university."

The downgrade steepened as wind worked its way through the truck. Unsealed windows whistled. Slack door hinges creaked.

"I can't sell the ranch," Dad finally said, as if he were stating a fact that couldn't be changed and not a choice that could. "I want you to try—"

"What about what I want?" I said as my hands clenched into fists.

"Now, the—"

"I hate sheep—I hate the damn ranch—I hate—"

"Enough!"

A gust of wind rocked the truck. It was no use. I would never get what I wanted. Not as long as sheep were on my father's list.

I unclenched my fists and looked down at my empty hands with their stubby fingers like sausage links that had rolled off the plates of my palms. On those fingers, I counted all the things I hated: One—I hated sheep. Two—I hated the ranch. Three—I hated my father. Four—I hated my fingers. And for five, I decided not to just hate my fingers but to hate every part of my Basque hands because the skin was too callused and the palms too fat and the wrinkles too deep. But mostly, I hated my hands because they were just like Dad's and Aitatxi's and Oxea's.

"God's hands," Aitatxi had called them on a Sunday morning nearly ten years before.

"God doesn't even have hands," I said from where I sat on the Farmall tractor eating strips of bacon and watching Aitatxi and Oxea load bales of hay onto a trailer.

Dad had dropped me at the ranch after church. When Aitatxi asked me how church was, I told him, "Boring." When he asked me what the *apeza*—priest talked about, I said, "Adam and Eve and that stupid snake."

And he said, "Sure, no, you learn Basque history." Which didn't make any sense. Then Oxea said that Adam and Eve were Basque, which made even less sense. Then Aitatxi said that it was a scientific fact since they both had Basque hands—God's hands. And when I pointed out that the only thing "scientific" about anything they said was that it was stupid, Oxea replied, "*Ai-ai-ama,* what you know about God? You *gaixua*—poor little one."

"Don't call me that."

"Gaixua—you can no even butt wipe by you-self."

"I'm ten and half," I said. "And you're the one who can't wipe his own butt."

"Sure, no, if God he no have hands," Aitatxi said, "how he make man?"

"Hello? Ever hear of Darwin? We were like evolutionized."

Aitatxi shook his head as he leaned on a bale of hay and picked up his *zakua*—wineskin. He shot a stream of red wine from the leather bag into his mouth.

"Basque hands good for *pilota*—handball," Oxea said. Then he used his right hand to hit a rock into the air.

"What planet are you from?" I said as Oxea reached for the *zakua*. And when the wineskin slipped through his short, fat fingers and dropped onto the hay, I laughed and said, "Nice work with your God-hands."

Oxea glared at me as he picked up the *zakua* and squeezed it until the top popped off; red liquid shot into the air and flowed over his fingers. A piece of bacon caught in my throat, and I coughed. Aitatxi mumbled to Oxea in the Basque language—Euskara. "*Oraitzenzira, ene anea ono haur dela*"—Remember, my brother, he is still only a boy.

Then, with the *zakua* in his hand, Oxea turned and walked into the barn, leaving a trail of wine on the ground behind him.

"Joking," I called after him.

"Oxea, he just showing you his God-hands," Aitatxi said. "They may be no so good for grabbing a thing. But one time they get hold, they no let go."

I was thinking about those God-hands that "no let go" as I looked out the truck's passenger window. The monsoon was closing around us, the brown wall of dirt tightening its grasp, blocking out the world—only a last glimmer of blue still visible overhead.

"Under the seat," Dad said. "Something—for you."

The words, though spoken in almost a whisper, caused me to jump. I hadn't thought I'd hear my father's voice for at least another day, maybe two. That was the way it was with us. Silence always followed a conflict. An angry word would need an hour. A minor disagreement—six to eight. And a full-scale argument, like we'd just had, at least a day of unspoken words, avoided eye contact, and forced indifference. In my family, apologizing was like poking a finger into an open wound; time and silence healed our conflicts.

But today was different. And I knew it as I reached down and pulled out an envelope.

"*Zorionak zuri*—happy birthday, Mathieu."

I grunted in reply, having thought Dad had forgotten the date—May 6, 1980. Forgotten that I was officially twenty.

Inside the envelope was a birthday card. When I opened it, the folded title for the truck fell out. On it, I saw that in place of Dad's name was now mine.

"Now then, that community college over in Glendale has night classes, doesn't it?" Dad said, and actually smiled. When I didn't say anything, he added, "You're going to need your own truck to drive over there after work—"

"I'm dying here," I said as my face flushed with heat, and for a moment I became a different me; I was no longer a boy sitting in a truck beside his father on his birthday feeling as if his whole life was over, as if all the things he'd ever wanted were out of reach, all his choices already made, and that the past, the present, and the future were all the same day to be lived over and over. That boy was gone. And in his place was a man who wanted to make his own list.

But before I could tell Dad this, he sighed and seemed to shrink. His mouth opened but no words came out as he bit the corner of his lip. And I saw that the salt-and-pepper stubble on his face had somehow become just salt.

A few drops of rain splattered on the dusty windshield. They turned into streaks of mud as I noticed the way Dad's sweat-stained T-shirt hung loose on his body and how when he raised his hand a tremble like a breeze through grass ran along his fingers. And I thought of Oxea and the week before he died. How he walked out of the barn, a sheep tucked under his arm as if it were a package he'd forgotten he was carrying. And me laughing at him. And Oxea saying, "*Ai-ai-ama,* Gaixua, you no know nothing." And the *nothing* I didn't know was that in a week Oxea would be gone.

Blowing dust licked at the corners of my window. A few grains of sand slipped through a crack to gather on my pants leg as something heavy and solid settled into my chest.

"Dad I'm sor—"

But before I could get out the words, the monsoon tightened into a fist that crushed my world.

2

B I

I have more memories of my last day of high school than all four years leading up to it. That's because I knew it was the end. And I was prepared.

From the moment I stepped onto campus, I grabbed up all the *hows* I could—how the *I* in the library's sign was crooked, how the dandelions growing behind the gym smelled of canned beets, how the footsteps echoing through the hallway sounded like rushing water, how the rusted lower right corner of my locker was just sharp enough to catch but not tear the skin of my index finger. I tucked those *hows* away as the school bell rang and I hurried to Ms. Whittaker's room and my last English class.

It took Ms. Whittaker a good five minutes to get us all into our seats. Even then, we fidgeted—suddenly having grown too large for the chairs we'd sat in for the last nine months.

"Ya gotta come man," Rich said as he snapped in two every pencil in his backpack.

"Did you even apply?" Mike asked.

"There's a lot of work to do on the ranch," I said.

"Bullshit." Mike rolled a basketball back and forth over his desktop.

"The problem is you're in love with sheep," Rich said. "Ewe oughta just marry a sheep—get it, e-w-e."

"And they accepted you at the U of A?"

"Admit it," Rich said, "You loooooooove sheep."

"There's laws against that sort of thing." Mike tossed the basketball to Rich.

"Not for Basques," Rich said.

I laughed and said, "You guys are sick."

"Quiet please," Ms. Whittaker said, and when that didn't work, she took off her shoe and banged it on the blackboard until we stopped talking. "Now, before I give you back your final papers, I want to read an essay one of you wrote."

A groan went up from the class.

"Haven't we suffered enough?" Rich threw his hands into the air.

"Don't worry, Mr. Clausen, it's not yours," Ms. Whittaker said. "I don't think everyone would be as enthralled about the trials and tribulations of filling a Coke bottle with tobacco spit as you seem to be."

At that, Rich high-fived Mike and me as the boys in class hooted and the girls let out a disgusted "Ewwwwww."

"If you all listen quietly," Ms. Whittaker said through the noise, "I'll let you go early."

That got the room silent.

Ms. Whittaker slipped her shoe back on, picked a paper from her desktop, and began to read.

"On Sunday, May 6, 1973, I turned thirteen and my world changed. Only not in the way I thought it would."

Hearing the words I'd written made me blink as if a bright light had been shined in my eyes. The words confused me—didn't seem to belong to me. But then as Ms. Whittaker kept reading, I couldn't escape what was mine. I slumped in my chair and ducked low and kept my eyes on the front of my desk as if it were the edge of a cliff I was running toward; any moment the ground beneath my feet would be gone and I would be flying through midair.

And then it was over.

I heard voices, chairs scraping over tile, laughter; Mike and Rich arguing about whose truck was faster; someone touched me on the shoulder and said, "Nice story." And then the classroom was empty and Ms. Whittaker was laying my essay on the desktop in front of me.

"Thank you, Mathieu."

And since I wasn't sure what Ms. Whittaker was thanking me for, I kept quiet as I folded the paper into a tight square and jammed it in my pants pocket and hurried to catch up to Mike and Rich so that I could argue that my dad's truck was faster than either of theirs. And later, with all the things

I remembered from that day, I forgot about what I'd written. That was, until the day of my father's funeral when I found my essay in the top drawer of his dresser.

My essay was at the back where Dad kept his black socks. At first, I didn't recognize it for what it was. But then I unfolded the paper and saw my words. Dad must have found it in my pocket when he was doing laundry; after the Skoal can incident, I had been banned from using the washer.

But why had he never said anything about the essay to me?

My eyes moved down to the bottom of the paper: *I watched Oxea swing back and forth, his body ticking off seconds to a birthday that was over before it started.*

I chewed on the corner of my lip. What had Dad felt when he read about me finding Oxea hanging from the oak tree? Did he wish he hadn't sold the last of Aitatxi's sheep? Did he regret creating a world where Oxea no longer had a flock to tend? A world Oxea couldn't live in. Why had Dad wanted to keep that memory?

The essay had just been another English assignment—write about a day that in some way changed you. And so I wrote about the day I couldn't forget—about the ranch and the sheep and Aitatxi and Dad and Oxea. But I hadn't done the assignment right. In my essay, there was nothing about how the day changed me. Because, even though it had, I couldn't say how.

The paper now sat half-open on my Dad's dresser, where I'd earlier tossed it in my rush to get ready. The "A" still puzzled me. I pulled off the tie that Dad used when he stood behind me, hands over mine, saying, "Now, then, around and over the top. Down through the middle and tighten the knot."

Downstairs, I could hear people arriving. The hinges of the porch door squeaked. Boots and high heels clanked along the wood floor. Someone turned on the faucet in the kitchen; pipes groaned before spitting out water. Dirty dishes clattered in the sink. My face grew warm. I should have washed those.

But I hadn't been able to do much of anything since I'd gotten home from the hospital. Although I had no broken bones, not even a cut or scrape, I hurt. Even if there was no medical reason why. The only thing I had to show from the accident was a bruise above my right eye, where my head hit the dashboard. I leaned closer to the mirror and ran the tips of my fingers over the bruise that looked like a kiss from a pair of plum-colored lips.

There was a crash of breaking glass from below, followed by the opening and closing of doors as someone searched for a broom. I pictured Amatxi's blue and white plates hanging on the kitchen wall; plates that she'd brought with her when she came from Urepel, France; plates that depicted men tending sheep and women baking bread; plates that had been there my whole life; plates that as a kid I was not allowed to touch; plates that I hadn't noticed for years. Was one of them gone now? Broken and lying in pieces on the floor?

I shrugged off my father's coat and let it fall to the ground. I began unbuttoning the white dress shirt I'd found in his closet. I started with the buttons on the sleeves that rode a couple inches too high on my arms. Then I worked my way up the front of the shirt to the collar that was too tight to button. I'd hidden the gap there beneath the knot of my tie.

The voices from downstairs grew louder. A woman's voice—Mrs. Hiller's? —said something about "men" and "cleaning." Another woman—Mrs. Carl's?—said, "What a strange house." A man—Mr. Humphrey?—asked, "Who builds a second floor in the desert?" He was answered by a booming voice I recognized immediately: Mr. Steele, my dad's lawyer.

"I guess a . . . a thermal radiation don't rise up over there in them Euro-pee-an countries."

There was some laughter. A man coughed. A baby cried.

I pulled off the dress shirt, balled it up, and tossed it onto the faded green bedspread. Next to the shirt was the cross the priest had given me at the cemetery. Later, once I was alone again, I would nail the cross onto the living room wall, to hang there alongside the crosses of Amatxi and Aitatxi and Oxea and Mom.

The window-mounted air conditioner kicked on to send a blast of cool air over my damp skin. I shivered. Dad and I had replaced the electric fans with the AC units when we moved back to the ranch full time. Before that, on summer nights when the upstairs rooms were too hot for sleep, Aitatxi and Oxea and I slept in the potato cellar.

I once asked Aitatxi why he didn't build a house with bedrooms downstairs like a "normal" person. And he told me that downstairs was for animals.

"That doesn't even make any sense."

"It how it is," Aitatxi had said, and then told me to go feed the chickens.

There was a different kind of animal downstairs now—pacing, waiting. People I didn't really know, none of whom were related to me, none of whom were family. Most had never been in this house before and were here now only because of the death of my father.

I licked my dry lips and swallowed. For the first time in my life I was alone. The thought tightened around me as I stared at the boy in the mirror wearing an undershirt and black pants. The boy's arms seemingly too thin to hold his palm-heavy hands; his eyes too close to tears to see anything clearly. I watched as those eyes moved to the black-and-white photo tucked in the dresser mirror's lower right-hand corner.

In the photo, Dad is about my age. Like me, he has on an undershirt and black pants. He sits in the pasture, back up against the oak tree, barefoot, legs tucked in front of him, elbows resting on his knees. Dad's dark hair is brushed away from his face, and only one of his eyes can be seen as he presses the other to a camera. His mouth is open in a slight grin, white teeth visible.

Who took this picture of my father taking a picture? And what was Dad looking at through the lens? Was it me? Had I even been born? Was it my mother? Had the car that would end her life not reached her yet? What did Dad see? What made him keep this photo? Made it special? Important? After all, it was just of him—alone.

When I looked up from the picture, it was my father—not me—reflected in the mirror. And I thought: if I don't move, don't breathe, he will stay—forever, right there, forever in the glass. But then there was a knock on the bedroom door and I turned my head. And in that instant, Dad was gone.

"Mathieu?" Ms. Whittaker called.

Besides being my high school English teacher, Ms. Whittaker had attended elementary school with my father. Earlier, she'd stopped me in the church parking lot and told me with tears in her eyes that in third grade she gave Dad half a Hershey bar for a kiss behind the library.

"He had the chocolate in his mouth before I could open my eyes," she said and laughed as she wiped tears away. "There has always been something utterly irresistible about the disinterest of you Basque boys."

"Are you all right, dear?" Ms. Whittaker said through the door.

"Be down in a minute," I said.

And as her footsteps retreated, I was again left alone with the memory of breaking glass echoing in my ears.

When the monsoon slammed into us, I forgot about Dad and our fighting and about the apology I was saying; there would be time for that later. The truck shook with energy. I smiled. This was going to be fun.

"Big one," Dad said as a bolt of lightning cut through the brown dirt surrounding us. Electricity crackled in the air.

A tumbleweed flattened itself against the windshield, as if trying to hang onto something solid. After a moment it was scraped away by the wind—thorns scratching over the glass.

"Now, then," Dad said, "time we stopped."

Dad gazed into the blowing dust, searching for a place to pull over and wait out the monsoon. But before he could get off the road, there was a bang like the starting gun at the beginning of a race. At first, I thought it was thunder. But then the truck lurched to the left; Dad pressed down hard on the brakes. The smell of moisture was replaced by burning rubber as the front end of the truck seemed to fall away. Dad's hands slipped from the steering wheel. The back of the truck rose. I tried to grab my father's arm, but my hand closed on nothing as I was slammed forward. My head struck the dashboard, and the world turned from brown to black.

Now I walked downstairs into a sea of black coats and dresses. And even though everyone went quiet at the sight of me, I could still hear their voices: *Here comes that Basque boy, the one who stayed behind, the son who looks so much like his father, except for the eyes—green—those are his mother's, gone so many years now. He's the last Etcheberri—the last shepherd.*

As I stepped from the stairs, the wooden floor moaned. The clock on the mantel ticked. Someone cleared their throat. Then everyone started talking at once as they pressed in around me.

"Your father was a wonderful man . . ."

"I knew him for over thirty years . . .

". . . back when he worked for John Deere . . ."

". . . so like your mother . . ."

". . . remember the time you and your grandfather stole those sheep . . ."

". . . that Oxea was kind of scary . . ."

". . . the world changes fast . . ."

". . . what are you going to do now . . ."

And then Jenny was there with the smell of lemon in her hair, sliding her hand into mine, pulling me toward the door as she whispered in my ear, "I'll save you."

3

HIRU

When I was thirteen, Aitatxi decided to save me. Which to him meant making me an accomplice to his stealing a flock of sheep and taking them on a last sheep drive across the desert.

That first night, as I was pointing out for the hundredth time how bad an idea the whole last-sheep-drive thing was, Aitatxi said, "This great adventure."

"This is grand larceny," I told him.

"Sure, no, I save you, and you no know you even being saved."

"How have you saved me?"

"We save sheep," Aitatxi said. "Sheep, they save us."

"We didn't 'save' the sheep," I pointed out. "We stole them."

"They mine, I take back."

"Actually, they're not yours," I said. "They belong to the guy Dad sold them to."

"You no can sell past."

"Past? I thought we were talking about sheep?"

"Sheep is mine," Aitatxi said. "I take back. *Orai,* you take back what belong a you."

At the time, I didn't know Aitatxi was talking about me taking back my past, reclaiming the memories my father had chosen to forget since my mother's death. Right then, I was too busy trying to figure out a way to convince Aitatxi we should return the sheep and tell the police they got loose on their own and explain how we actually saved the sheep by bringing them back, so we were really heroes and no prison time would be necessary. All I knew that night, as I looked up at a sky full of stars that Aitatxi said were my dead ancestors, was that I wanted to go home.

But now, on the day of my father's funeral, the one place I didn't want to be was home.

As Jenny led me onto the porch, I slipped my hand from hers. Even though it was after six, the sun was still bright on the horizon. The day's heat was warm on my face as I closed my eyes, and orange and red circles of light filled my head.

"Mike says to give you his condolences." Jenny's voice was a cool breeze running through me.

"What does condolences even mean?" I opened my eyes and blinked.

"For my brother," Jenny said as she flipped her long brown hair over her shoulders, "it's a way of saying sorry without taking the time to actually do so in person."

"He must be busy at school."

"Yeah, flunking all those classes takes up a lot of time." Jenny straightened the plaque that hung next to the back door. The word *Artzainaskena* was burned into the wood. "What's this mean again?"

"The last shepherd."

"I like that your home has a name."

"Aitatxi did it." I started toward the empty sheep corrals. As I walked, I remembered one of Aitatxi's stories, not about the last shepherd, but the first.

"He Basque," Aitatxi had said.

"Of course." I rolled my eyes. I was ten at the time and already used to Aitatxi giving credit to Basques for everything worthwhile that had been invented, accomplished, or said in the history of the world.

"Sure, no, Mathieu, he just boy—maybe have twenty year in him."

"Twenty?" I said. "That's not a boy—that's a man."

"Maybe *ba*—yes, maybe *ez*—no," Aitatxi said. Then he went on to tell me how God put the first shepherd and his sheep on top of the tallest mountain in the Pyrenees. From there, the shepherd could see the whole world. God told the shepherd that as long as he watched over his flock, the world would be safe.

"Safe from what?" I asked.

"Wolves," Aitatxi said.

But the first shepherd grew tired of watching the sheep. All they did was "baa" and eat grass. The world below looked so much more exciting. So one night the shepherd decided to sneak away and explore that world. And the moment that he left his flock unguarded, the howling of wolves filled the air. When the first shepherd heard the wolves, he ran back to save his sheep. But it was too late. The flock had been scattered.

"So God, he say, 'Since you do this thing, I make all Basque be shepherd until all lost sheep found and world again safe from wolves.'"

"That stinks," I said. "Why should all us Basques have to pay for what that stupid boy did?"

"No is man?"

"Not anymore," I said. "Who was that shepherd anyway?"

"He name Mathieu," Aitatxi said.

I pushed Aitatxi's story out of my head as I reached the corrals. I wasn't going to be a shepherd. No matter what Aitatxi or God said. Not anymore. I leaned against the open gate and rested my chin on my folded arms as Jenny came to stand beside me.

Although the sheep were gone, the smell of wool, manure, and hay rose in a dusty haze that burned my eyes as I gazed toward the oak tree in the pasture. A coyote rested in the shade of the tree. When the coyote saw me looking his way, he got to his feet and trotted up the hill to where the barbed-wire fence marked the northern edge of our land. Beyond that was desert. The coyote slipped beneath the fence and was gone.

"I love this time of day," Jenny said as she put her head on my shoulder. "Everything gets so soft and blurry."

I couldn't help but smile. Jenny had been laying her head on my shoulder my whole life. The first time was when she was seven and I was nine. Mike and I were sitting on the couch at his house watching cartoons when his little sister came in.

"Get out," Mike said without taking his eyes off the TV screen.

But Jenny didn't. She just sat down next to me and put her head on my shoulder. And together we watched as Tom and Jerry raced with leaking buckets of water around a burning house.

As the sun pressed into the horizon, its dying light ignited the stark white walls of Artzainaskena. The house glowed red as if engulfed in flames.

"I need a ride into town tomorrow," I said.

"Truck still in the shop?"

"Couple more days," I said. Then added, "So when you leaving to go flunk classes like Mike?"

"Dad needs my help at the café."

"They hire people for that—they're called waitresses."

"It's not the same as family," Jenny said, and her body stiffened slightly, as if realizing that mentioning family to someone who had just lost the last member of his probably wasn't such a good idea.

"I'm selling the ranch," I said.

"What?"

"I'm selling Artzainaskena," I said.

"No you're not."

"Yes I am."

"Your dad wouldn't want you to sell the ranch," Jenny said as she took her head off my shoulder.

"He's gone," I said, and my words hung in the air for a moment before falling solid and forever to the ground. "I'm leaving."

"You can't leave."

"You can leave too," I said.

"No."

"Why not?"

"You're an idiot," Jenny said.

"Your dad will be fine—"

"Such an idiot."

"Stop calling me that!" My voice came out louder than I meant as a bitter metallic taste filled my mouth and tears sprang up in my eyes. "I want—"

But before I could tell Jenny what I wanted, her lips silenced me. Jenny's tongue, soft and probing, took away my words—my want—until the booming voice of Mr. Steele pulled her from me.

"Sorry if I'm a . . . a interrupting," he said.

Jenny spun free. I tried to grab onto her arm, but she slipped through my fingers. Her black dress swirled as she turned and walked off.

"You don't have to leave, darling," Mr. Steele said. "I just need a word with . . ."

Jenny walked straight to her Mustang, got in, and drove off.

"I guess she had somewhere to go," Mr. Steele said.

I watched as the trail of dust from Jenny's car dissolved.

"I'm awful sorry about your daddy, son," Mr. Steele said. "He was a . . . a determined man. That's it. Determined. That some kind of Basq-oh trait?"

"I don't know," I said.

"I believe I read that somewhere—along with you people sporting six toes."

"What?"

"Some kind of genetic thing."

"I don't have six toes," I said. Then added, "Do you?"

Mr. Steele let out a dry laugh.

"What the hell—guess I deserved that, son. Guess I did . . . Well, I need to get back to the office. I just wanted to set up a time when we could talk about the ranch and—"

"I'm selling it," I said.

"Hold on, now, son, we need—"

"It's what I want."

"Well, a wanting and a getting ain't a . . . a particularly the same thing," Mr. Steele said. "You ever talk with your daddy about this?"

"He wouldn't sell," I said.

"Now, *wouldn't* isn't exactly the right word."

"I don't see how that matters now."

"Son, in this case, it matters a whole helluva lot."

"Why?"

"The thing is," Mr. Steele said, "the ranch is not a . . . a precisely yours to sell."

LAU

When I was fourteen, about a year after Aitatxi and Oxea's deaths, I asked Dad about cutting down the oak tree in the pasture. The sun was falling away as we sat on the porch drinking iced water—only Dad's iced water had a little scotch in it.

We'd spent the entire day working on the new barn, and I was still try-ing to shake out the tingling in my fingers from the thousand plus hammer blows I'd delivered. The old barn's roof had collapsed a month earlier. One night, the sound of it sent Dad and me running through the dark.

"Now, then, lucky we didn't pen the sheep in here tonight," Dad had said as we picked through the fallen wood.

"How come it fell?"

"I guess time just grew too heavy for it," Dad said.

And I picked up a board and used my foot to break it in two and didn't tell my father that what he'd said didn't make any sense—that "time" didn't weigh anything. Because I knew if I said that, Dad would sigh and look tired in a way that had nothing to do with it being late or his needing sleep, and that would make my stomach feel hollow and my mouth go dry.

So instead I pointed up through the hole in the barn's roof.

"Look, there's Orion."

"The hunter," Dad said.

"How'd he end up getting turned into a constellation again?"

"Now, then," Dad said, and explained how the goddess Diana put Orion into the stars after accidently shooting him with an arrow; and while that didn't make any sense either, it seemed to lighten the heaviness of time for my father. He smiled and talked about building a new barn as we walked back to the house.

A month later, when we started working on the new barn, I figured it was a good time to get rid of something old as well. So I kicked at a loose plank in the porch and told Dad how we could use the tractor to pull down the oak tree.

"Now, then," Dad said, "you know that tree was here when Aitatxi bought this land?"

"It's old," I said. "Besides, everything will be clearer when it's gone."

Unlike what Dad had said about the weight of time, me saying how the tree being gone would make everything clearer seemed like it made sense, but didn't. Everything was already clearer. The old barn that had blocked the view of the pasture was gone. And we were building the new barn off to the side, so that from the porch the pasture and the oak tree were clearly visible. But I knew what I was saying was right and could only hope Dad could see it as well.

Staring out at the oak, he shook his glass so that the ice tinkled. In the growing darkness, the tree looked like something a little kid would draw, with a perfect round top and straight trunk. But that wasn't how it really was. The limbs were gnarled and twisted. The bark thick and cracked. And when the wind blew like tonight, every branch creaked with age.

And as my father was looking at the tree, it changed.

Dad leaned forward. His eyes unblinking, his breaths quick. And I knew what he was seeing. It was like when something appears in the clouds—a face or hand—that wasn't there a moment before. Two dogs at the base of the oak. A *zakua* on the ground between them. A rope hanging from one of the tree's limbs. And Oxea hanging from the rope. But shapes in clouds don't last. And neither did these. The wind moved through the tree and blew the dogs, the *zakua,* the rope, and Oxea away.

At least for Dad.

For me, Oxea would always be hanging from the oak tree. And so the tree needed to be cut down. Nothing would be clear until it was.

"Now, then, your mother used to rock you to sleep in her arms beneath that tree." Dad leaned back into his chair. "Said the sound of the wind in the leaves was like a sleeping potion to you."

"She did?"

"And when Amatxi first arrived in America, she and Aitatxi carved their initials in the trunk."

"I've seen them," I said.

"Didn't Oxea use to tell you stories about Euskal Herria when you two sat in the shade of the oak?"

"He told me that the Mamu makes Bigfoot look like a puppy."

"And Mari?"

"That she is the queen of the genies and flies through the air in a ball of flames," I said. "Which is kind of cool."

"Remember the time Aitatxi put a tire swing on the oak for you?"

"Oxea got stuck in it."

"Now, then, didn't you trick him into sitting in the swing?" Dad looked over at me.

I grinned.

"He told me the Mamu ate bad boys like me because we tasted like chicken."

"Well I don't—"

"And you and Aitatxi had to use the wire cutters to get him out."

"I remember how mad Oxea was," Dad said. "I didn't know Euskara had such words."

"Amatxi told me that there are no bad words in Basque."

"Now, then, your *amatxi* was too sweet to know such words," Dad said. "She used to like to have picnics under the oak tree on Sundays. She'd make *oilaskoa arno zurian.*"

"Chicken in white wine," I said. "And Mom would make strawberry pie."

"You were just a baby—you can't remember that."

"I remember," I said. "Oxea told me he saw you kiss Mom for the first time beneath the oak."

"She kissed me."

"That sounds like something Aitatxi would say."

"It's true. I was very *eder*—handsome back then."

"You mean like me now," I said.

Dad laughed. "Now who sounds like Aitatxi?"

And as I sat on the porch that night with my father, I began to understand what he meant about time having weight. For Dad, the weight of time stored up in the oak tree was an anchor to the past. For me, it was an anchor as well—one that held me to a day I wished never happened. But now I was seeing that the oak tree anchored me to more than just one bad day. As the sun disappeared and the stars came out, we continued talking about the memories of our family, both good and bad, and the tree that held them in place. By morning any thought I had of cutting down the oak was gone.

As the last cars from my father's funeral drove away, I leaned my back up against the oak tree and thought again about the weight of time. Had that "weight" shaped the things Dad chose to do? Not to do? The things he gave away? And those he kept? Like the photo tucked in the corner of his dresser mirror. Dad looking through the lens of a camera. Why was that image worth holding onto with no one but himself in it?

I copied my father's pose from the photo. Knees bent up, elbows resting on them. Hoping that by imitating his body position I could somehow imitate his thoughts. Thinking that if I understood why Dad kept that picture, I would somehow understand what Mr. Steele said: "The ranch isn't a . . . a precisely yours to sell."

The only thing missing from my re-creation of the photo was the camera. Instead, I held the letter the lawyer had given me.

"There are more," Mr. Steele had said. "All of 'em returned unopened."

Isabelle Etcheberri was written in my father's blunt handwriting on the envelope, along with *Gorrienea, Urepel, France.*

"Who is she?" I'd asked Mr. Steele.

"Her name is on the deed to the ranch."

"I don't understand."

"I wish Fred had explained this to you."

"Explained what?"

"It's a . . . a complicated, son," Mr. Steele said. "Best you just read the letter."

"But how can her name—"

"Read the letter," Mr. Steele said as he walked away. "And come by my office tomorrow. We'll a . . . a confer about the situation."

But I didn't read the letter. Not right then. Because by not opening the envelope, for the moment, I still had control of my world. Not much I knew.

I couldn't un-write what was written. I couldn't stop what was coming. But unlike the unseen blowing of a truck's front left tire, I could postpone this change. Stay a little longer in the "before" and put off the "after."

I tried to concentrate on the woman who had the same last name as me. A woman I had never heard of—did not know existed. Who was she? And why was her name on the deed to Artzainaskena? But the only thing I could think about was what Dad had said in the truck: "I can't sell the land."

At the time, I had thought his *can't* meant *won't*. That it was a choice he was making. But it wasn't. Can't meant can't. Dad couldn't sell what wasn't his.

Why hadn't he just told me that? Why had he let me believe he was the one keeping me from leaving? Denying me what I wanted?

The answer to my questions was bitter on my tongue. In my father's eyes, even though I was twenty, I was still just a boy who needed taking care of. And so he'd let me be angry with him in order to in some way protect me from the truth.

I looked down at the unopened letter: Isabelle Etcheberri lay inside.

I spit on the ground, ripped open the envelope, and read: *How are you, my sister?*

$\int$

BOST

I never learned to read or write Euskara, the Basque language. Why would I? There was no one for me to write to. And the only words I'd ever seen written in Euskara were on Christmas, *Eguberri Hun,* and birthday, *zorionak zuri,* cards, or jotted on notepads, *ikusi arteo*—see you later, and *izan ontsa*—be well. Basque for me was a spoken language of words like sheep and chickens, *ardiak eta oilaskoak;* and father and home, *aita eta etxea.* And even though I knew a lot of Basque words, I didn't exactly know how to string them together into sentences. While I could say milk, *esnia;* I want, *nahi dut;* glass, *basoa;* I had no idea how to ask for a glass of milk.

After the first line of the letter, which my father wrote in English, most of the rest was in Euskara. I hadn't known Dad could write in Basque. Until Aitatxi died, the only time my father even spoke Euskara was when he was arguing with his own father. Even if I could have recognized the written form of the words I knew, the way they were put together was strange to me. They were long, jumbled mixtures of *x*'s and *z*'s, with only a few vowels jammed in. And, as far as I could tell, there was not one mention of sheep anywhere.

So the only parts of Dad's letter that I understood were in English. And those were words like "retribution" and "reconciliation," which I guessed either didn't exist in Basque or at least were unknown to my father. Still, I went over the letter again and again, trying to understand what was not understandable: everyone in my family had lied to me; dad didn't really own the ranch; and he had a sister.

Finally, when night blurred the words of the letter together, I got up and walked back to the house.

No lights were on. And as I approached, Artzainaskena's dark frame seemed unfamiliar. It was as if another house had been set down where mine once was. This house's roof was lower, the windows bigger, the outer walls farther apart. Boards creaked as I stepped onto the porch, and for a moment I was ten again and looked around for the reaching arms of the Mamu, whom Oxea promised was always lurking and hiding and waiting. I held my breath. Listened. There was nothing. I was alone. And that scared me in a different way. My body felt light, as if I were dissolving into the darkness, as if the hand of someone stepping through the door, reaching out to touch me, would pass right through my chest. But then I realized that wasn't possible. Because there was no one left to step from Artzainaskena.

An owl hooted from where it was perched in the oak. I could see its silhouette in the light of the rising moon. Then, as if sensing my attention, the owl fell silent. Stars flickered to life in the sky. A warm breeze brushed my cheek. I pushed open the front door.

The smell of sourdough bread and alfalfa greeted me. Years of Saturday morning bread making had baked the aroma of sourdough into the walls; countless trips from the barn had tracked in alfalfa, the flakes slipping between the wooden floor's loose planks, the scent of hay rising with each taken step.

Moonlight fell in streaks through the living room's curtained windows. Cut across the tan couch Dad took his daily nap on. Fell on the arm of the chair I flung my legs over while reading a book. Light spilled over the corded area rug with its wine stain in the shape of a bull's head and onto the clock Amatxi bought in France in 1931. A breeze blew past me and into the house, shifting the curtains and causing the moonlight to dance around the room. In the shadows, I saw Dad reaching down to pick me up when I was three; Mom going into the kitchen to get my bottle; Amatxi sewing on the couch while Aitatxi and Oxea sat drinking *arno gorria*—red wine, and playing a card game of Mus. But then the breeze died, the curtains settled, and the shadows turned back into tables and chairs.

I stepped inside and closed the door behind me. Without turning on a light, I moved toward the kitchen. Moonlight fell through the sink's uncovered window and over the workingmen and women of Amatxi's blue and white plates. I counted the plates, seven, still hanging, still whole.

I didn't need the note Ms. Whittaker had left to lead me to the dish of tuna casserole warming in the oven. I dropped the lawyer's letter on the table and used a hot pad to retrieve the food. Then I grabbed a carton of milk from the fridge and headed to the cellar.

At the top of the cellar's stairs, I turned on the light switch. I hadn't been in the cellar since the summer Aitatxi died. Particles of dust swirled around the room's lone bulb. Below me, cardboard boxes crowded the floor. As I started down the wooden steps, the air cooled, and I became aware of the thin layer of sweat that covered my body. I shivered.

When I reached the bottom step, I sat down and placed the carton of milk on one of the shelves lining the wall. Once, jars of Amatxi's blackberry preserves filled the shelves so that the whole wall shined as if it were made of dark, wet stones. Even now, the empty shelves sagged like they still held jars instead of cobwebs.

I scanned the cardboard boxes in front of me as I shoveled tuna casserole into my mouth and washed it down with gulps of milk. Every spring when I was a kid, burlap sacks of potatoes dug from Aitatxi and Oxea's small garden were set on the cellar's cement floor. The sacks would lie one on top of the other like discarded bodies. By the following Christmas, all the sacks would be empty, the potatoes gone. Now, in place of swollen sacks were swollen cardboard boxes.

I set the unfinished plate of food aside and opened the closest box. *Photos* was written on its side in the sure letters of my Dad's handwriting. I pulled back the cardboard flaps and began digging through the pictures. I didn't have a clear idea of what I was looking for, just something to explain the day and help me understand the existence of Isabelle Etcheberri.

Some of the pictures were stuck together, and I couldn't get them apart without tearing off pieces of the images they held. Others were sealed in individual envelopes with phrases scribbled on their outside.

In *Mathieu At Six,* I found a picture of a grinning me wearing a cowboy hat with my arm thrown around the neck of a sheep as if it were my trusty steed. In *Wedding Day,* there was a black-and-white photo of Aitatxi and Amatxi. He is sitting in a carved, dark wood chair. She wears a simple white wedding dress with a ring of flowers in her hair; she stands beside him with her hand not on his arm but the chair's. Neither is smiling. Inside *Easter*

Morning was a picture of Mom and Dad with Amatxi and Aitatxi. They are all sitting at a picnic table in front of the oak. The tree's trunk shoots through the middle of the picture, separating the two couples. Everyone looks so young. Even Aitatxi. He is holding Amatxi in his arms in a way I never saw him do, pulling her into his body. Mom has her hand lying on the table; Dad's hand is on top of hers. I figured Oxea took the picture because he was not in it and also because it was slightly out of focus. Oxea and any sort of technology not associated with sheep never mixed.

When I'd looked through all the photos and found nothing to do with Isabelle, I stood up and waded farther into the room. I stopped at the boxes labeled with misspelled words. The letters were written in Aitatxi's childlike scribble. I kneeled in front of a box with the words *My Bother* on it.

The first thing I pulled from the box was Oxea's marriage certificate. His wife's name had been Pascaline. She died before I was born. In fact, I hadn't even learned of her existence or that Oxea was married until after his death. That was just another thing my family hadn't talked about. Silence made for many secrets.

Beneath the marriage certificate was a wedding photo, and in it I saw Oxea's wife for the first time. I frowned. She was all wrong. When I had learned Oxea was married, an image of his wife popped into my head. My Pascaline was thick and sturdy. The kind of woman who could throw a bale of hay into the back of a truck. But Oxea's Pascaline was nothing like that. She was about half his size and had long hair that looped in rolling curls down to her waist. Nothing about her spoke of life on a ranch. The wife I'd given Oxea was much more practical. But then my face warmed as I realized that, even for Oxea, there were reasons other than practical ones to marry a woman.

In the photo, Oxea towers over Pascaline. His figure would be imposing if it weren't for the goofy grin on his face and the way his beret sits crooked on his pumpkin head. He looks so happy and a bit drunk, like he has already had two or three glasses of wine. His new wife is grinning too. Her mouth is too large for her face, as her white dress is too large for her frame. In contrast, Oxea's dark suit is too tight. His muscles bulge against the seams. Together, the two of them reminded me of kids playing at dress-up.

The next item in the box was a death certificate issued in Colorado. *Pas-*

caline Etcheberri, 34 years of age, cause of death unknown. What was she doing in Colorado? Hadn't she lived here on the ranch? With Oxea and Amatxi and Aitatxi? What happened? And how could a cause of death be unknown?

The muscles of my jaw tightened. More questions without answers. I dropped the death certificate back into the box. Why hadn't I ever brought Dad down into the cellar and gone through the boxes with him? He could have explained the meaning of the photos. He could have told me the story behind each of them.

But would he have? Would he have told me about his sister?

I pushed the box at my feet to the side and moved deeper into the cellar. I had no more time for reminiscing or regret. There was only one piece of the past I was interested in and that was the piece both messing up my present and stealing my future.

Piled against the back wall of the cellar I found Amatxi's boxes. Her name, *Dominica,* was written on the boxes in handwriting I didn't recognize. A friend? Neighbor? Someone I didn't know had written her name in flowing letters. I opened a box labeled *Urepel* and remembered Aitatxi telling me that *urepel* meant "warm water" in Euskara. And I couldn't help thinking how strange it was that he and Amatxi had chosen to leave a place with so much water that their home was named after it for a desert where water was only abundant in mirages.

The first thing I found in the box were letters of transit, dated June 7, 1932. Beneath the letters was a black-and-white photo of a girl about ten years old standing in front of a white house. On the wall behind the girl is a wooden plaque that says, *Gorrienea.* On either side of the plaque hang what look to be rows of peppers. I turned the photo over and saw written in Amatxi's tight, fragmented hand, *Isabelle, 1921.*

Next, I found a bundle of unopened letters. There were about twenty, and they had a piece of nylon string tied around them. I used my teeth to pull apart the string's tight knot. As the knot gave, the letters fluttered onto the cement. I gathered them up and saw that all the envelopes were addressed in Amatxi's handwriting to *Isabelle Etcheberri, Gorrienea, Urepel, France.* I also saw that all of the letters had been returned unopened.

I didn't bother opening the letters now, as I knew they would be written in Euskara and therefore unintelligible to me. So I retied the string around them and was placing the bundle back when I saw one last letter sitting in the bottom of the box. The handwriting on this envelope was different— thin lines spelled out the names *Mathieu and Dominica Etcheberri*. I picked the envelope up and saw that it had been opened. The sheet of paper inside was crumpled and there was a slight tear in the upper left-hand corner. On the bottom, the words in Euskara were smeared as if by spilled water.

I looked again at the envelope. The postmark was July 15, 1933, and the sender's address matched the address on Amatxi's returned letters. Only the name of the sender was different. *Isabelle Etcheberri* was gone. In her place was *Isabelle Odolen*.

6

S E I

That night I dreamed of the Mamu.

I was standing on the edge of a cliff, so close that I had to lean back to keep from falling. But I didn't step away. There was something I needed to see. What, I didn't know. But I could feel it pulling at the center of my chest, causing my heart to race so that I was not sure if I was excited or scared. Below, the cliff's broken face fell away to disappear into clouds that hid the world from me. A breeze moved through the clouds, causing them to shift and reveal green trees, the red tops of houses, the white backs of grazing sheep.

Then I heard a Basque *irrintzina*. Oxea told me shepherds used the call to signal to each other across the Pyrenees.

"Ai-ai-ai-ai-ai-ai-ai-yaaaaa!"

The cry came from another cliff, directly across from me. There, the land was different, thick with trees that formed an unbroken wall of green.

Out of that wall stepped the Mamu.

Like man before he was man. Mountainous and wild. Face cut with scars. Teeth chipped with age. Dark hair matting his body. Tree-limb arms hanging down to end in short, thick fingers.

The Mamu never changed. He was the same now as he had been when I was a boy. Time moved around but not through him. He was forever.

The Mamu threw back his head and again let loose his *irrintzina*. It echoed through the chasm between us. And as it died, the Mamu stood motionless, looking at me, waiting for me to answer him with my own *irrintzina*.

But I didn't.

Instead I said, "*Ez*—no."

The Mamu cried again, "Ai-ai-ai-ai-ai-ai-yaaaaa."

I cupped my hands to my ears and said, "I don't believe in you anymore."

The Mamu shook his body as if my words were drops of water that could be thrown off.

I yelled, "I don't want you."

At that, the Mamu turned his head to the side as if confused—as if I was speaking a language he didn't know.

"I'm a man now," I said. "Go away."

For a moment, the Mamu didn't move, perhaps hoping I would change my mind. But I didn't. Finally, the creature's shoulders slumped; he lowered his massive head, walked back into the wall of trees, and was gone.

And I thought: the Mamu was the thing I needed to see and put behind me. A childish thing that a man doesn't have in his life. And that was what I was now: a man. Sending him away only proved it. I could go. Leave this place. But then something new stepped from the trees.

I bit the corner of my lip. Had I failed? Was the Mamu returning? But then I saw that it wasn't the Mamu who emerged this time but my father.

He cupped his hands to his mouth as he called to me. But the wind had picked up, and it blew his words away.

I wanted to call back—"Dad, I'm sorry." But I knew that it was no use. My words, like his, would be lost in the distance between us.

Still, my father kept calling. And from the forward nodding of his head, I could see that he was saying three words. But what they were I couldn't tell.

I leaned over the cliff's edge, trying to hear what he was saying. At my feet, rocks tumbled into the clouds as rain rose. A single drop struck me again and again in the middle of my forehead. The smell of lemons floated over me as I opened my eyes to find Jenny poking her index finger against my skull.

"What the hell!" I sat up in bed.

"Get your lazy butt up." Jenny walked over and jerked open the curtains. Sunlight flooded my bedroom.

I pulled the bedcovers to my chest.

"You know I'm naked under here."

"Good for you," Jenny said.

"How'd you get in?"

"Door was unlocked," Jenny said.

"Oh, yeah, I forgot."

"Did you also forget that you asked me for a ride into town this morning?"

"No . . . I just thought . . . you know . . . after yesterday and all . . ."

"It was a kiss—not a marriage proposal," Jenny said. "Now get up."

"Throw me my pants."

Jenny grabbed my Levis off the floor and tossed them to me. Then, while I slipped them on under the covers, she picked up the leather-bound book off my desk.

"What's this? Your diary?"

"It's a journal."

"Kind of like a guy's purse is a backpack?" Jenny said. "What do you write in this thing anyway?"

"Stuff," I said, as I stepped out of bed still buttoning up my pants.

"Wow, deep." Jenny set my journal back down and moved over to run a finger over the books lined up on my bookshelf. She snagged a copy of *For Whom the Bell Tolls* and then put it back in a different spot.

"You're messing up the order," I said and returned Hemingway to his place.

"What order?" Jenny asked. "Bradbury is next to Grey—Asimov by Tolkien—"

"It's by time."

"When they were written?"

"When they were read." I pointed to the far left of the shelf where Dr Seuss was cluttered in with an assortment of Hardy Boy mysteries and Edgar Rice Burroughs Tarzan adventures. "Those are all pre-Tolkien."

"Pre-Tolkien."

"*The Hobbit* is the first book that I know exactly how old I was when I read it," I said. "Eleven years, four months, and twenty days."

"And yet you can't remember to lock the door?"

"Ha ha," I said.

"So tell me, what were you doing at eleven years, four months, and twenty days?"

"I was under the oak tree in the pasture picking up acorns. I'd come up with the idea of growing oaks and selling them to buy a bike."

"Which has nothing to do with Tolkien . . ."

"It will, if you'll be quiet long enough for me to tell the story."

Jenny used an invisible key to lock her lips closed.

"It had rained the night before. The leaves on the ground were wet. The air thick. So that when I breathed it felt like my lungs were filling with water. I had just taken a big gulp when Dad walked up and said, 'Exhale.' And I did. Only no water came out. But Dad still slapped me on the back like I was drowning and handed me the book he was holding, which I knew was a bribe even before he told me he was going on a business trip and wouldn't be home for Thanksgiving."

"Did you tell him that?"

"I didn't say anything. I just kept rolling an acorn over and over between my fingers, thinking about that bike—seeing myself on it—pedaling fast—riding away. I spent the rest of that Thanksgiving reading a book about a hobbit who didn't want to leave his home when all I wanted was to leave mine."

Oh," Jenny said. And stepped closer, her hair falling over my bare chest, light on her face. Looking confused. As if I wasn't really Mathieu Etcheberri. Or at least not the Mathieu Etcheberri she knew.

I stepped away. Retrieved a shirt from atop my bed.

"Do you think the diner's busy?" I headed for the door. "I'm starving."

Downstairs in the kitchen, I called Mr. Steele.

"You seeing the world in a little different a . . . a resolution today, son?"

I set up an eleven o'clock appointment with the lawyer just as Jenny began honking her car's horn. I found her waiting for me outside with the engine running.

"You want your usual for breakfast?" Jenny asked as I climbed in.

"I want eggs Florentine with a splash of mint jelly."

"You'll get three pancakes and two sausage."

"Boring." I fiddled with the radio before settling on an Eagles song. "I want to try something new."

"You ever have mint jelly?"

"Can't remember."

"Which means no." Jenny merged onto the main road leading into town. "And you don't like spinach."

"What's that got to do—"

"There's spinach in eggs Florentine."

"I'll have my usual then."

"Idiot," Jenny said.

When we reached the diner, it was empty. What passed for the breakfast rush was over. I took a seat at Dad and my's usual booth. On the wall behind it was a painting of a longhorn bull standing alone amid a desert landscape. The bull was red and white and there was a saguaro cactus that appeared to be growing out of the animal's rear. Dad said the artist must have had a couple of scotches while painting.

"Don't burn the mint jelly," I said.

Jenny stuck her tongue at me as she went through the swinging door into the kitchen.

There, I heard her talking to her father. I couldn't make out what they were saying, but the rhythm of their speech was quick and overlapping. Nothing like with Dad and me. Our conversations didn't involve talking as much as silence. In fact, the last time we'd had breakfast at the diner, we didn't speak two complete sentences to each other. We didn't need to. I knew when my father's eggs arrived that he would cut them into tiny squares and pour on Tabasco, and that he would drink two cups of coffee—no cream, one sugar—and that when he cleared his throat and pulled a toothpick from his shirt pocket, it was time to leave, and the tip would be three dollars and fifty cents. A nod of his head meant for me to notice something. A touch on the arm was to signal me to slow the shoveling of food into my mouth. And a smile and nearly inaudible grunt said that it was a good meal.

Now, with Dad gone, there would be the need for more words in my life to get tangled and confused, be misunderstood and unknowable. Right then, chewing on the nail of my index finger, I longed for my father to be there and, with nothing more than a silent frown, tell me to stop biting my nail.

When Jenny came back through the swinging door, she was holding a plate with three pancakes and two sausage links. She set it down as she slid in opposite me.

"You just going to watch me?" I asked.

Jenny picked a sausage link from my plate and took a bite out of it.

"Happy now?"

I couldn't help smiling as I slathered butter on my pancakes and soaked them in syrup.

"Dad says he's going to put in all new booths and retile the floor." Jenny handed me a napkin as she took a tube of gloss from her pocket and rubbed it onto her lips, making them moist and shiny. "He thinks it will draw in more customers. But I told him we already have all the customers in town. And that, if anything, he should build a bigger kitchen. And maybe offer some different kinds of food—like Italian."

Was the gloss what made her lips taste like strawberries? The way they had the day before when she kissed me. Did I kiss her back? I couldn't remember. And what did my lips taste like to Jenny? Dirt and wool?

"Or maybe Mexican," Jenny said. "Why do you keep staring at my lips?"

I set down the bite of pancake I was about to put in my mouth.

"That pancake is not burned," Jenny said.

"I have to go see my lawyer." I stood up.

"You have a lawyer?"

"I don't know how long it'll take," I said. "I can get a ride home."

"Dad needs help with the lunch shift, anyway."

I walked to the door. But before leaving, I turned back. Jenny was still sitting in the booth. She had one elbow on the table and my fork in her hand and was running the tines through the syrup on my plate, as if she were writing something in the sticky liquid. Her hair hung down so I couldn't see her face, and right then she didn't look at all like the girl who'd spent her life laying her head on my shoulder but a stranger I'd never met.

Jenny looked up to see me watching her. She flipped her hair back and sat up straight—like I'd caught her doing something that I wasn't supposed to know about.

"Just go," Jenny said.

"You don't have to wait."

"Go—I'll be here when you get back."

Only she wasn't. But I didn't know that as the diner's door clanged shut behind me.

7

ZAZPI

Outside, the white-hot sun had already burned the color out of the town's buildings. I cut across Miller Avenue and headed down Cotton Lane. Sunlight glared off of store windows, making it impossible to see through the glass, hiding what was inside. The oily smell of soft asphalt rippled up from the street. My eyes watered as I quickened my pace.

The law office of *Mr. Thaddeus Steele, Esq.* was next to the Dairy Queen, and even though it was only three blocks from the diner, my armpits were ringed with sweat by the time I pushed open the door. Cool air splashed over my face. I blinked as I stepped into the darkness of the room. From that darkness, Mr. Steele's voice boomed.

"So you make any sense out of that crazy Basqu-oh language of yours, son?"

"Some," I said, not able to admit that I couldn't read the Euskara of my father's letter.

As my eyes got used to the room's light, I saw that Mr. Steele was sitting at a large metal desk eating a Dennis the Menace Peanut Parfait. The desktop was covered with peanuts that had rolled off Mr. Steele's ice cream. On the wall behind him was a giant black-and-white map of Phoenix and the surrounding area. Green and red pins were scattered over the map seemingly as randomly as the nuts over his desktop.

"I found this," I said as I placed the black-and-white photo of the young Isabelle on the desk. "It's the woman from the letter."

"Go-ri-in-ah?" Mr. Steele leaned over and peered at the photo.

"Gor-e-en-ya," I said. "I think my dad told me that it's the name of our family house in the Basque Country."

"I advised Fred to just be a . . . a candid about the situation with you, son," Mr. Steele said, waving the red plastic ice cream spoon in the air. And I thought about telling him that my father's name was Ferdinand, not Fred. But then I wasn't sure why that would matter now, as the person who had used both names was gone.

"He never said anything." I looked for a place to sit, but Mr. Steele occupied the room's only chair.

"Well, you know your daddy."

I did. Or thought I did. But then it was turning out that my knowing had some pretty big pieces missing.

"He kept insisting that he could take care of this—that his sister would see the light, so to speak. But hell, she never even opened one of his letters."

I didn't know what to say to that. In fact, I didn't know what to say to anything as I stood there shifting my weight from one foot to the other, uncomfortable in front of a stranger who knew more about my family than I did.

"But old Fred wouldn't listen to my a . . . a consultation." Mr. Steele began picking the peanuts off the desktop and popping them into his mouth. "Let's hope you didn't inherit his Basqu-oh hard head."

"This woman," I said, "Isabelle—"

"You mean your aunt, son?"

"What do you know about her?"

"All I know is that her name is on the deed to the ranch."

"But how can that be?"

"You'd have to ask her," Mr. Steele said. "But good luck on that. I tried to call her once—your aunt—never mentioned that to Fred, not that it mattered. Turns out she don't even have a phone up in that a . . . a village she lives in."

"Urepel," I said.

"Is that how you say it?"

"Dad's parents were from Urepel."

"And this Isabelle Etcheberri still is," Mr. Steele said.

"Her name is Odolen now," I said.

"Huh?"

"She changed her name to Odolen," I said.

"Odolen?" Mr. Steele clicked the tip of his red spoon against his front teeth.

"It means 'in the blood' in Basque," I said.

"It means she got married in any language," Mr. Steele said as if that fact had some great importance.

"Does that change anything?"

"Logistically—no," Mr. Steele said.

"But the ranch is mine."

"Legally, son, it ain't." Mr. Steele sighed and pursed his lips together and tossed his empty ice cream dish into the trashcan. "The law's a funny thing. Sometimes a thing you think is yours lock, stock, and barrel can be taken away. Just like that. Trust me, son, I know all about loss."

And I guessed Mr. Steele wasn't talking about me losing my father or the ranch, but about his wife. The one who cleaned out his bank account and left without even a note. The wife that he never mentioned and was now only a whispered rumor in the diner. Gone for over a year. Jenny told me that her name was Ruby, and she left because her husband was too cheap to give her money to visit her family back East, and so she took it and left him flat-ass broke.

When I came home and told Dad what I'd learned about Mr. Steele and his wife, he said not to believe everything I heard—especially about families.

"Why not?"

"Because families are like trees," Dad had said.

"What?"

"Now, then, you only ever see half of a tree—the trunk, the limbs, the leaves," Dad said. "The roots the tree grew from—what made it the way it is—are hidden underground. It's the same with families. You never really know what causes a family to turn out the way it does."

Which, at the time, made no sense at all. But now that I was learning all about the hidden roots of my family's tree, it was becoming clearer.

"You need to move forward, son," Mr. Steele said. "You can't let yourself be held down by the past."

"Past?"

"You ready to a . . . a seize the future?"

"Future?"

"Taking control of your a . . . a destiny?"

"Destiny?"

"Or do you want to live like your daddy did, waiting for the a . . . a pro-verbial other shoe to fall?"

"Fall?"

"It's your choice, son," Mr. Steele said as he began tapping the plastic red spoon on the metal top of the desk. "What's it going to be?"

Mr. Steele looked at me like a teacher waiting on a student to give the obvious answer to a simple question. Only the answer wasn't obvious—not to me anyway. The ranch? Future? Destiny? Falling? I needed help, but Dad wasn't there to give it to me.

The sound of Mr. Steele's spoon tap tap tapping on the desk worked its way into my head and became a stick hitting the trunk of a tree. I was eight, and it was the summer I wandered too far from the mountain *etxola*—sheep camp. One moment, I was walking down a well-marked path, banging a stick against the trunks of trees, listening to the "baaing" of nearby sheep. And the next, the sheep were silent. The path gone. I found myself standing on a rock, looking down into a valley that stretched into the horizon. The day turned cold. I dropped the stick I was holding and turned to head back the way I'd come. But where there'd once only been a few trees, now there was a forest. The path I'd taken was swallowed up by it. My heart beat quick as the world around me swelled. I began to run along the tree line, search-ing for a way in, yelling for my father. I needed help—I needed him. But my voice was too small to carry over the tops of the trees. Finally, exhausted, I gave up and collapsed crying to the ground.

And then Dad was there, alfalfa on his skin, whispering deep words to me as he lifted me in his arms and carried me back to the path that led home.

Standing there in the lawyer's office, I once again felt the world swelling, becoming too big for me to make sense of. I couldn't find the path.

"Tell me what to do," I said.

Mr. Steele grinned. I'd given him the right answer.

"There is one other a . . . a option, son," Mr. Steele said. "It's called a quit deed."

"Quit deed?"

"We get that aunt of yours to give up her rights to the ranch," Mr. Steele said.

"How?"

"By going over to that Gorri—whatever, knocking on the door, and convincing her to sign on the dotted line."

"I have to go to France?"

Mr. Steele chuckled.

"Now, son, I don't expect a boy like you to travel halfway across the world to a strange country and persuade a hostile relation to do something she will obviously be a . . . a reluctant to comply with," Mr. Steele said.

"But then how?"

"I'll go."

"You?"

"That's right," Mr. Steele said. "All you need to do is sign the quit deed yourself."

"But the ranch is all I have."

"Don't you want to go to the university, son," Mr. Steele said.

"The university?"

"Fred and I, well, we had lots of talks about you wanting to further your a . . . a educational horizons."

"Sheep and the university can't be on the same list," I said.

"As far as you're concerned, no, they can't," Mr. Steele said. "Now, in exchange for you giving up any legal rights to the ranch, I will provide you with funds a . . . a sufficient to cover your tuition."

"I don't understand."

"You don't have to, son, you just have to sign," Mr. Steele said.

"But what if Isabelle Odolen won't sign this quit deed?"

"Well, then I guess I'm a . . . a screwed," Mr. Steele said with a laugh. "But you don't need to worry about that, son. Once you sign the quit deed, you're free."

"Why are you doing this for me?"

"Let's just say, out of a . . . a remembrance for your father," Mr. Steele said, and his chair squeaked as he got to his feet and walked over and threw his arm around my shoulder. "I just wish I could have assisted Fred while he was still . . . well, here."

And even though hearing Mr. Steele say that made me sad for Dad, I was also relieved. It was over. I was free. I would have stayed on the ranch, kept it going, done what my father wanted, if he were still alive. At least that was what I told myself. But Dad was gone. Although the thought was like a punch to my gut, I knew I couldn't change it. I also knew Mr. Steele was right. Maybe not about the "destiny" thing, but there was a future I wanted, and it had nothing to do with sheep.

I exhaled, emptying my lungs of the stale breath I seemed to have been holding since the day of the crash. The office's air conditioner rattled on: cool air washed over my face. I licked my lips and enjoyed the way they tingled. Suddenly, the whole world was clean and new—I was clean and new. Now, instead of thoughts of broken fences to be fixed and flocks of sheep to be tended, my head filled with entrance exams to be taken and class schedules to be arranged.

In the fall, I would start at the university. And I could go there without feeling guilty because losing the ranch wasn't my fault. In the end, the home I thought was mine wasn't really mine to lose.

I grabbed the photo of Isabelle off the desk and stuck it in my back pocket as Mr. Steele moved me toward the door.

"What about the flock?" I asked.

"Flock?"

"The sheep—are they still mine?"

"I don't want your sheep, son," Mr. Steele said. "Hell, you can have yourself a giant Basqu-oh barbecue for all I care."

"I think I'll just sell them," I said.

"Wise decision, son," Mr. Steele said. "Now while I draw up the quit deed, I'm going to need you to find the original deed to the ranch."

"You don't have it?"

"Fred always insisted on a . . . a maintaining it," Mr. Steele said, and then grinned. "I think just having it made your daddy feel like he was somehow in control. Even though you and I both know he wasn't."

"I'll look for it when I get home."

"Good." Mr. Steele pulled open the door. "The sooner we can a . . . a conduct this exchange, the better for everyone concerned, son."

And with a slight push, Mr. Steele sent me out the door and back into the light.

_8_

ZORTZI

The word _monsoon_ comes from the Arabic _mausim,_ which means "a season." I found that out while doing a science report my junior year of high school. I also learned that a monsoon can't officially happen until the dew point is fifty-five or higher. Which, in Arizona, isn't usually until around the first week of July. Any monsoons before then aren't really monsoons—just thunderstorms.

I explained all this to my father on a May day while shearing sheep, after he looked at the thunderclouds building to the south and said, "Now, then, monsoon's a coming."

When I ended my tutorial, Dad put down his shears and pointed to a coyote trotting along the edge of the pasture.

"Now, then, you see that thing over there," Dad said. "What is it?"

"Huh?"

"That animal," he said. "What do you call it?"

"Come on."

"Name it."

"Fine," I said, "a coyote."

"You sure?" Dad said. "Because I thought they were only called coyotes between September and October."

"I was just telling you what I learned in school," I said as I got the next sheep in position to shear.

"I appreciate that." Dad clicked on his shears. "But there are some things you don't have to be taught—you just know."

I was thinking about what Dad said as I stepped out of Mr. Steele's office. What things should I have just known? That I didn't own the ranch? That

Dad had a sister? Were there clues I had overlooked? Not seen? Not wanted to see? Or was it just different for me? Unlike Dad, would I have to be taught everything I learned? Did I have no natural instinct passed down to guide me? No Basqu-oh traits to show me the way?

A bank of clouds floated in front of the sun. Cooled the day's heat to a simmer. And even though it was only May, a monsoon was coming. Dad had taught me that.

I looked down the street—not the way I'd come, but in the opposite direction toward I-10, the highway that led to Phoenix and all those places beyond. But like always, the road was obscured. A mirage blurred the horizon in wavy lines of heat. Created a shining lake that spread out over the desert. The ribbon of asphalt rippled beyond the water. Today, that water appeared closer than ever. All I needed to do was make a good sprint, and I could be splashing through the mirage, toward the highway and the world beyond. I tensed the muscles in my thighs as a pair of high school girls stepped out of the Dairy Queen, each holding a swirl of vanilla. They smiled as they walked past. And I smiled back and started off. Not toward the water. Not yet. But back to Jenny and the diner.

The overcast sky dimmed the sun's glare on the store windows so that I could now see the people inside, buying things, talking, laughing. I moved across the street. The smell of orange blossoms from the line of trees in front of Garcia's pink and yellow Tienda de Flores spun around me.

I jumped from the asphalt of the street onto the cement of the sidewalk. I wondered what Mike was doing at the U of A right then. Going to class? Ditching? Sleeping in late after a night out with friends?

I could see the diner at the end of the block.

In a few months, what would I be doing? Moving into a dorm room? Choosing my classes? Reading books I'd never thought to read? And would all this be just a memory to me? Something from another life that seemed to have happened years ago, to another person who was no longer me?

I was going to the University of Arizona. The very idea of it made me smile as I pushed open the diner door. The place was again empty. Whatever there had been of a lunch crowd had come and gone.

"Jenny?" I called toward the kitchen. But instead of Jenny walking through the swinging door, her father, Mr. Krawski, stepped out.

"She's gone," he said as he flipped the towel he was holding over his shoulder and took a seat at the counter.

"Gone?"

"She left her keys for you." He pulled a cigarette out of his shirt pocket and lit it. "Said she'd call you later to get her car back."

"Where'd she go?"

Mr. Krawski shrugged.

"Just said she was leaving."

Even though Mike had been my best friend since grade school, this conversation was the longest I'd ever had with Mr. Krawski. He wasn't one of those parents who you called by their first name or the kind who asked about how your classes were going at school or if you thought the high school football team was going to win Friday night. Most of the time growing up, I wasn't even sure he knew I existed. When I'd come over to the house, he never said a word to me or looked in my direction. And when I would say, "Hello, Mr. Krawski," he would just wave a hand in the air and go back to reading his newspaper or watching whatever sporting event was on TV. To me, he was Mr. Krawski, and would always be, no matter how old either one of us got.

I stood near the diner's front door, watching him blow clouds of smoke into the air. The smoke filtered down around him.

"Sorry about your father," Mr. Krawski said. "He was a good customer . . . friend."

I swallowed. My throat was dry and the smoke was causing my eyes to burn as I thought of the funeral—not my dad's, but Mrs. Krawski's. I was fifteen, and no one I knew had died for two years. In those two years, I'd almost been able to forget that death existed, that people wouldn't always be there, that time could run out before you said the things that you wanted to say but didn't. At the church, I had stared at Mr. Krawski as Father Bill talked about what a good wife and mother Mrs. Krawski had been. Mr. Krawski wore a gray suit, not black like everyone around him. And he wasn't crying. Not like Mike and Jenny. He was just sitting there looking straight ahead, looking at the coffin that held his wife, seeming to look but not see what was right in front of him. And then he turned and his gaze moved across the aisle and through the rows of people to me. My skin tingled, and

I remembered Oxea and Aitatxi and their two funerals. And as if sensing my thoughts, Mr. Krawski dropped his head at our common understanding of the holes death left in you—bottomless and unfillable. Holes that if you spent too long looking into would swallow you. Then Mr. Krawski turned back to the priest and the coffin. Or maybe he didn't see me at all and just lowered his head because his wife was gone.

Mr. Krawski leaned an elbow on the diner's counter. His shoulders slumped casually forward, and the sweat of work matted the hair on his head. And while Mr. Krawski wasn't my father, he was a man about the same age, and so I said, "I'm going to the university."

Mr. Krawski looked at me as he blew out a stream of smoke and said, "I wish you could talk Jenny into going."

And then he put out his cigarette, handed me Jenny's car keys, and disappeared through the swinging door.

When I got back to Artzainaskena, I found the deed to the ranch. It was in a metal box on the top shelf of Dad's closet along with a John Deere coffee mug, a couple of green pens, and my father's company nameplate— *Fred Echbar*.

I tossed the box onto the bed as I flipped the nameplate over and over in my hand. I'd almost forgotten that until I was thirteen, I had been someone else—Matt Echbar.

When Dad had started at John Deere, he changed his name from Ferdinand to Fred, and our name from Etcheberri to Echbar. He said he did it to fit in. But Aitatxi told me Dad did it to forget. "Sure, no, he think only of what coming and forget what already come." And, even at thirteen, I understood his wanting to do that. For my dad, the past held a wife who had been hit by a car only moments after she had been smiling while having her picture taken. But Aitatxi said that in forgetting the bad, Dad also forgot the good. Then Aitatxi told me it was my job to help Dad remember.

And I did.

The man known as Fred Echbar, the one who was always going out of town for work, wore a suit and tie, and wanted nothing to do with sheep, had been gone for over seven years. Ferdinand Etcheberri, the shepherd, took his place.

I tossed the nameplate onto the bed and turned to the metal box. It was unlocked.

The paper of the deed was yellowed and cracked and smelled like sour milk. Mathieu and Dominica and Isabelle Etcheberri were written on it. But not my father's name. There was no mention of him. My grandparents had left the ranch to a daughter I had never even heard either of them mention. How did that make Dad feel? Having his father give what should have been his to a sister who wouldn't even read his letters?

These questions swirled through my head and caused things I was sure of to become unsure. The past wobbled like a mirage. And in that unsteady horizon, I found a memory taped to the metal box.

The tissue paper was folded into a square no bigger than a stamp and attached to the inside lid. Had Dad put it there? The tape cracked as I pulled the tissue free. It was so light that for a moment I thought there was nothing in it. Then I unfolded the tissue and watched as a single lock of wheat-colored hair fell onto my lap.

I brought the lock of hair up to my nose and breathed in my mother—a tinkle of laughter, a cool hand against my brow, soft words murmured in the dark: "*Tun gulan bat, tun gulan bi, tun gulan hureran, er-or-i.*"

Who had clipped it from her head? And when? When she was a baby? Cradled in her own mother's arms? Or later, after everything changed, and she was gone? Dead. Lying in her coffin. I remembered the wood, shiny and dark, and the rough feel of Dad's jacket on my cheek, and the shaking of his body as he cried.

I pulled the lock of my mother's hair away from my nose and tried to drop it into the metal box, but the hair stuck to my moist skin. I shook my hand to get it off, but it clung there. I wanted it gone. I scraped the tips of my fingers over the box's edge, pressing down until it hurt and the lock of hair fell back into the box.

But even with it gone, I still felt like I had just stepped off a rollercoaster—my thoughts jumbled, the ground unsteady. I folded the deed up, stuck it into my back pants pocket, and started to close the metal box. That was when I spotted the worn ball tucked in the box's corner. I picked it up. It was about the size of a golf ball and covered in sheep's skin. I smiled. The ball held a different kind of memory.

Pilota. I remembered what Aitatxi said when I found the ball in a kitchen drawer. I was ten and had asked him where the racquet for the ball was.

"*Ez,* no is for racquet," Aitatxi said. "You play the *pilota* with you *eskua*—hand. Like this way."

Aitatxi took the ball from me and led me outside. He walked to within about twenty feet of the barn, then threw the ball into the air and smacked it with his hand. It ricocheted off the barn wall and almost hit me in the head.

"Cool." I ran to retrieve the ball from the dirt. And, in imitation of Aitatxi, I threw the ball into the air and struck it with my open palm—pain shot up my arm and I let out a yelp.

"You *eskua* no is ready for *pilota,* Gaixua."

"Don't call me that," I said as I wedged my hand between my legs and tried to squeeze out the pain.

"Sure, no," Aitatxi said. "You is poor little one."

Aitatxi took my hand and looked at the red welt in the center of my palm.

"Good beginning for *pilota,*" he said. "You hit ball two maybe three hundred time again, then hand it no hurt no more."

"Forget that." I could feel each pulse of my heart in the hand I'd used to strike the ball.

"Sure, no," Aitatxi said. "What I think? You *gaixua,* you too little for *pilota.*"

"I'm eleven."

"*Gaixua.*"

"If I learn this pee-low-ta, do you promise not to call me *gaixua*?"

"Sure, no."

"Ever?"

"You play the *pilota,* you no be *gaixua.*"

"Swear?"

"Sure, no." Aitatxi picked up the ball and started teaching me. And even though I learned how to play *pilota,* first with Aitatxi and later with Dad, Aitatxi never stopped calling me "*gaixua.*"

I dropped the ball back into the metal box and closed the lid. *Gaixua.* For years I hadn't thought of the name Aitatxi called me. Poor little one—the same name I'd given to a sheep on that last sheep drive. The name that, right then, with dusk slipping through my father's bedroom window, was settling into me. And I knew if I didn't move, didn't change things, I would be *gaixua* forever. So I grabbed the box and shoved it up onto the closet shelf and rushed out of my father's room, closing and locking the door behind me.

As I headed downstairs, I was thinking about going back into town, getting something to eat at the diner, and finding Jenny. I would tell her about the university and try and talk her into leaving as well. I moved across the living room and was reaching for the front door when someone knocked from the other side. I was smiling as I opened the door, thinking it was Jenny, and was greeted by the dark figure of a man.

"Mr. Steele?" the man said. The setting sun lit up the porch. In the brightness, I couldn't see the details of the man's face as he took off his hat. He shielded his eyes as he reached out, blindly searching for my hand to shake. "Horace Beechnut—we are going to make a killing."

9

BEDERATZI

Aitatxi told me that after God created the Basques, he gave them *pilota* to remind the Eskualdunak of who they were.

"How can you forget who you are?" I asked as I pushed the grocery cart down the cereal aisle. We were at the Bashas' market in Phoenix, and Aitatxi had just asked the butcher if he had any blood sausage.

"No," the butcher said. "Same as last week, next week, and every week."

"I check other week," Aitatxi said with a wave of his hand. "Maybe you have then."

I was twelve and dreaded going to public places with my *aitatxi*. Especially the grocery store, where he would ask every store clerk for items that clearly no store in America would have. I could see the clerks ducking and running whenever Aitatxi approached. So I was glad for his talk of *pilota*. If I could just keep him focused on that while we completed Dad's grocery list, I might be able to escape the store without further embarrassment.

"Sure, no," Aitatxi said. "Peoples forget who they is all time now. You ask them, who you is, and they tell name. But no even know what name it mean or where it come from."

"So God gave Basques handball so they wouldn't forget their name?"

Aitatxi was throwing boxes of sugary kids' cereal into the cart that were clearly not on Dad's list. His favorite was Sugar Pops. I once asked him if they had the cereal in the Basque land. He said no, but he was sure a Basque-American created it.

"*Ez*," Aitatxi said. "What you head made of stone? God, he gave Basque they hands so they no forget they world."

Aitatxi stopped and held up his large, flat palm for me as if the mere sight of it was proof of what he said being true.

"I thought we were talking about *pilota*?"

"You hear, but you no listen," Aitatxi said. "God, he gave *pilota* so Eskualdunak, we have something good to do with hands."

"You are giving me a headache," I said.

Aitatxi grabbed onto my right hand and pressed it between his palms.

"Hand is beginning of all thing," Aitatxi said. "You see, you hear, you smell—but you no touch something with hand, you no know. Ball, it round like world. It have no start, no end. You grow up, you learn how a make own ball for *pilota* out of wool and sheep skin. *Baina* each time when you play *pilota* and hit ball with *eskua*, you touch whole world. You know who you is."

"Oh," I said, pulling my hand free from his, "so this was all like some big life lesson? Wow—I get it. I'm supposed to make my own world. Earthshaking news."

"*Zer?*" Aitatxi said. "What? Make you world? You no barely can make you own bed. Now you think you make world—*ai-ai-ama*. Sometimes, I no know how you thought. Now go ask that pretty little *neska* if maybe they have some pickled pigs feets today. *Fite. Neska,* she I think maybe like you. *Ba.* Go."

If, like Aitatxi said, the hand was the beginning of all things, then my beginning with Mr. Beechnut was short and confusing. When he found my hand, he gave it one quick pump and released it before my fingers could even close around his. Then Mr. Beechnut opened his briefcase and pulled out a sheet of paper.

"Good to finally meet you." Mr. Beechnut handed me the sheet. I recognized the pattern on the paper from Mr. Steele's office. It was a smaller copy of the one tacked to his wall. Only instead of green and red pins, this paper had green and red circles. And the largest of these circles was around the words *Etcheberri Ranch*.

"Always like to put a face with a voice," Mr. Beechnut said. "Now, based on the schematic you faxed over, I've pulled together some numbers for the property."

"I, uh, don't—"

"I think you're going to be impressed with—"

"I'm not Mr. Steele."

"Excuse me?"

"I'm Mathieu Etcheberri," I said just as the sun dipped a little lower and the light faded to a soft glow and I could see the logo, *Westside Reality,* on the pocket of Mr. Beechnut's white shirt. Underneath the logo were the words, *Finding New Homes Is Our Specialty.*

"Oh." Mr. Beechnut seemed to lose his balance for a moment as he stumbled back a step. He lowered his gaze—sweat glistened on his bald and sunburned head. "My mistake."

"I can call Mr. Steele—"

"Wrong address." Mr. Beechnut snatched the paper from my hand. Then, with his head down, he turned and rushed off the porch steps.

"Are you sure—"

"Never mind." Mr. Beechnut hurried toward his white Cadillac. He only looked back once: shoulders hunched, eyes cut low, regarding me like a coyote that I'd caught sneaking up on a flock of sheep. The coyote's eyes holding a mixture of apology and anger as he slinked away with his tail between his legs, as if to say he never meant any harm, wouldn't have snagged a young lamb if I wasn't there; he was harmless—really, harmless. Only I'd learned otherwise. Coyotes were never harmless. They killed things. Had to. In order to survive.

This Mr. Beechnut said he was going to make a killing—no, he said, *we are going to make a killing.* Was that "we" he and Mr. Steele?

As Mr. Beechnut slid into the driver's seat of his car, Ms. Whittaker raced up in her green station wagon. She came to a skidding stop next to the Cadillac: gravel popped beneath her tires and a trailing cloud of dust covered both cars. Mr. Beechnut's Cadillac pulled out of the cloud as he turned around and headed back toward the main road

"Tell me you haven't had dinner," Ms. Whittaker said as she stepped from the station wagon with a casserole dish covered in aluminum foil.

"You didn't have to do that," I said.

"A boy has to eat," Ms. Whittaker said as she walked up the porch steps. "Who was that pulling away?"

"A guy from Westside Reality."

"That's the company the Armstrongs used to sell their place," Ms. Whittaker said. "You thinking of selling the ranch?"

"Uh . . . ," I said. "I think he was lost."

"People are always getting lost in the country—I blame it on poor signage."

I followed Ms. Whitaker inside to the kitchen. There, I sat down at the table while she plated up some of the casserole.

"It's got beef and noodles and a bit of everything in it." She placed the plate with a fork on it in front of me. "And something new."

"Cinnamon?" I said as I took a bite.

"Nutmeg." Ms. Whittaker handed me a napkin. "Milk?"

I nodded and she went to pour me a glass.

"I can swing by the store for you tomorrow."

"I know how to shop," I said.

Ms. Whittaker laughed as I took the glass of milk from her.

"I'm sure you do." She sat down at the table across from me. "Just wanted to help."

"Dinner's enough."

And Ms. Whittaker laughed again.

"Sometimes you are too much your father," she said. "He wasn't big on taking help either."

I wondered what Ms. Whittaker could have helped my father with.

"He sure did like to talk though," she said.

"My dad?"

"He was always telling me things about sheep and the ranch, and of course, you."

"Like what?"

"Like how your name means 'new house' . . . or is it 'new home'?"

"Both," I said. "*Etche* means house or home, and *berri* means new. So *etcheberri* can mean either new house or new home."

"That doesn't seem quite right, does it?" Ms. Whittaker looked out the kitchen window. She slipped her left hand into her right and held it against her chest. "You can choose your house but not your home—that chooses you. And, sometimes, well, the two have nothing in common."

I wasn't exactly sure what she was talking about, so I didn't say anything. Besides, I was still stuck on my dad liking to talk and his telling her things.

"But now that I think about it, the name fit him," she said. "Your father was kind of a new house stuck in an old home."

Again, I wasn't certain what Ms. Whittaker meant or even why she was talking so personal about my father. Even if he did tell her things, Ms. Whittaker didn't really know Dad. Sure, they had gone to grammar school together and she was my high school English teacher, but that didn't mean she knew him. In fact, the only time I ever saw them together was at church. And then it was only to say hello at Mass and talk about how big I was getting or maybe the weather—nothing about houses and homes—just small talk. Except for that one time I saw them. When they weren't talking at all.

After Mass, Rich, Mike, and I were playing hide-and-seek. I was running, looking for someplace to hide before Mike counted ten, when I came around the corner and found Dad and Ms. Whittaker. They were out back where the leaves from the mulberry trees had been raked into mounds perfect for hiding. They were just standing there, in plain sight. Not talking. Just looking at each other. I stopped at the church's corner, breathing hard, cool air on my cheeks, the smell of rotting leaves making me light-headed. Dad brushed a lock of hair off Ms. Whittaker's face. She touched his arm. And then they saw me. And Ms. Whittaker stepped away. And Dad said, "Now, then, Mathieu, ready to go home?"

"Home is where the heart is," Ms. Whittaker said as she got up from the kitchen table. "Only the heart isn't always home. Finished?"

I nodded and she took my plate. She hummed a melody as she washed it in the sink. I couldn't name the song, but it sounded familiar, something my father had hummed once. An old song. The kind married people danced to. And I noticed how she was swaying from side to side in time with the melody. Her blue and white dress rocking back and forth against her calves. And I realized that I had never seen Ms. Whittaker in anything but a dress—at school, church, even here on the ranch. Her high heels clicked on the floor as she stepped to the cabinet and pulled out a towel. I half expected her to do a twirl with it, but she didn't.

"Sorry," Ms. Whittaker said as she began to dry the plate, "but I forgot to bring dessert."

In the shadows of the kitchen, her features blurred. The set of her eyes, the curve of her nose, the line of her mouth, became those of a girl as she flipped her hair to the side and did a dance step back to the sink.

"You and my dad," I said. "You were—"

"Friends," Ms. Whittaker said as she clicked on a light, and a fifty-year-old woman with pink rouge settled in the lines of her cheeks smiled down at me. But even in the light, a bit of the girl from the dark remained. I saw that girl in the way Ms. Whittaker patted dry her hands on the kitchen towel, then gently folded it before laying the towel on the counter. With a laugh she said, "You know, in some ways your father was married to this ranch—and it was a prearranged marriage." Then she pressed the back of her hand against my cheek as her face grew serious. "Just know, you don't have to make the same choice, Mathieu."

10

HAMAR

Morning sunlight broke around the top of the barn. It moved down the wall and over the paint that the *pilota* ball had pockmarked with a thousand round circles. In front of the wall, the hard-packed ground was like cement, and when I scraped the toe of my shoe over it, no dust rose. Even though where I stood was still in shadow, a thin layer of sweat coated my body. I rolled the ball in the palm of my right hand. The crowing of roosters that had once accompanied my early morning games was gone. The last rooster had been sold with the chickens three years earlier. Now, the only sound was that of the cooing mourning doves huddled in the barn's rafters.

Aitatxi told me that the key to *pilota* was getting the eye and the hand to work together.

"Sure, no, what see and what feel need be same thing."

I had to keep my eye on the ball and trust that my hand would be where it needed to be. Dad taught me that the engine that got me into position was footwork and that little steps were better than big ones. Little steps would enable me to quickly change direction. Big steps would cause me to lunge and knock me off balance.

"Now, then, anticipate where the ball will go," Dad said. "If you wait to react, it will be too late. You need to feel it in your gut."

And so I learned to ignore the sensation that a nail was being driven through the center of my palm with each strike of the ball. And to not give into the stitch that clawed at my side. The burn of dust in my eyes, the ache of my back, the shortness of my breath—there would be time for those later. While I was in the game, the ball was the world.

As I tossed the ball into the air and smacked it with my *eskua,* the pain that shot up my arm brought me fully awake.

The sound of the ball ricocheting off the wood barn was like a hammer blow. Startled doves flew from the rafters. I pivoted to my right, keeping my eye on the unsure bounce of the ball off the dirt. I reached behind me as I stepped into position and whipped my arm forward to contact the ball out in front of my body.

Even though I was only playing against myself and couldn't win or lose, I still scrambled over the dirt as if I were two people: each trying to outmaneuver the other, determined not to be the one who missed, straining to make the final strike.

On the tenth blow, the ball hit a hole in the dirt and took a sharp bounce to the left. I tried to adjust, but my swinging hand met only air as the ball sailed past me to roll across the dirt and stop at the feet of Mr. Steele.

"Now that there was some animal-like movement, son," Mr. Steele said as he reached down with a slight grunt to pick up the *pilota* ball between his index finger and thumb. He held the ball at arm's length, like it was covered in blood and not dirt, and pushed back the wide-brimmed straw hat he was wearing. "Is this sheep skin?"

"My *aitatxi* made it."

"Hmmm, he was a . . . a clever man that ahh-ta-chee of yours."

"He wouldn't have liked to hear you say that." I gazed up at Mr. Steele from where I leaned over with my hands on my knees catching my breath. My hair fell in front of my eyes and through it Mr. Steele appeared to float like a parade balloon. For some reason, my heart was beating as if I were still playing *pilota,* running to strike the ball, and I noticed that behind Mr. Steele the gates of the empty sheep pens hung open. I was sure I had shut them the day before. But now they were all unlatched.

"I meant it as a compliment, son," Mr. Steele said.

"Coyotes are clever, and Aitatxi didn't care much for coyotes."

"Then how about a . . . a industrious?" Mr. Steele grinned as he tossed me the ball. I straightened up to catch it. "Your grandfather, and his son for that matter, Fred, were both industrious. Now that's a word whose connotation can't be a . . . a misconstrued."

"I found the deed."

"You don't say? Well, then we can—"

"So what are you and Mr. Beechnut going to kill?"

"Excuse me?"

"Mr. Beechnut said you were going to make a killing."

"That's just a figure of speech, son."

"I know what it is," I said.

The sun cleared the top of the barn. Mr. Steele shielded his eyes and stepped back into the last bit of shade hugging the barn. There, for a moment, he seemed to disappear.

"Mr. Beechnut is none of your concern, son," Mr. Steele said. "So why don't you concentrate on more important things—like getting ready for the university."

For some reason, I couldn't look Mr. Steele straight in the eye. So I gazed over his shoulder, up the slope of the dry pasture, to where the oak stood. The grass was dead. The flowers wilted. Nothing had been watered since the accident. Only the tree, whose deep roots tapped into groundwater, was still green.

"You're right," I said, and tried to smile. "Sorry."

Mr. Steele pulled out a paper from his pocket.

"No need to apologize, son," he said. "You've been under a great deal of a . . . a duress. But all that will be over once you sign this here quit deed."

Mr. Steele handed me the paper along with a pen. I didn't bother trying to make sense of the thick typing on the page, but scanned down to the bottom where there were two names printed with lines for signatures—mine and Isabelle Odolen's.

"Thank you for helping me." I leaned over and pressed the quit deed to my thigh to sign. The pen was slippery with sweat between my fingers. The tip pressed to the paper for me to sign.

"It's the least I can do for Fred."

Mr. Steele's words stopped me.

"My father's name was Ferdinand—not Fred," I said as I looked up at Mr. Steele, surprised at how hot the sun was on my face.

Mr. Steele didn't say anything to that. He just leaned against the barn wall and slid a pack of cigarettes from his pocket.

"My wife's name was Rebecca," Mr. Steele said as he tapped a cigarette out, hooked it into the corner of his mouth, and lit it. He took a long pull on the cigarette and held the smoke in for three of my breaths before letting it trickle up over his face. "But I always called her Ruby. We had plans—a future. But in the end . . . well, it didn't matter what I called her. What mattered were the things she didn't tell me."

Mr. Steele put the pack of cigarettes back into his pocket.

"I knew your father's name was Ferdinand. Hell, I was his lawyer. But I always called him Fred. And he never told me he preferred otherwise. Then again, there were a few things he didn't tell you about either. Now weren't there, son?"

Mr. Steele spit the cigarette onto the ground and let it smolder there. And then, maybe because Mr. Steele knew the answer to the question he asked better than anyone, or maybe because I didn't understand why Dad kept so many secrets, or maybe because in the light of day Mr. Steele looked so pale and soft and out of place on my ranch, or maybe just because the heat was getting to me—instead of agreeing with him and putting the past behind me and moving into that new future I wanted so badly, I pulled the pen from the quit deed, stood up straight, and said, "I could stay."

"You ain't no shepherd, son," Mr. Steele said as he stepped out of the shadow to grind the cigarette butt beneath his shoe.

"I just—"

"Face facts." Mr. Steele snatched his hat off his head and smacked it against his thigh. "You are not capable of running this place by yourself."

And he was right. I couldn't. Not alone. I didn't even want to try. It was just the idea of Mr. Beechnut and Westside Realty and Mr. Steele and what they would do to the ranch. Even though I wanted to leave Artzainaskena behind, I hadn't really thought of it being gone. The house bulldozed. The oak tree uprooted. The pasture sectioned into lots. I had just thought the ranch would be here. Forever. Waiting for me. Like always.

"Time for you to wise up, son," Mr. Steele said. "I am giving you an opportunity here. Your aunt—she's not going to give you nothing. Understand that. My way is the only way. I told that to Fred, but he wouldn't listen—"

"You made this offer to my father?"

Mr. Steele blinked and swallowed. The question seemed to surprise him more than anything else I'd said. He raised his hat into the air and for a moment I thought he was going to hit me with it. But instead, he put the hat back on his head and narrowed his gaze at me as if seeing me for the first time.

"Yes I did. I a . . . a provided him the same way out I am providing you. Only he didn't take it."

"Why not?"

"I don't know, son," Mr. Steele said. "Maybe it was his Basqu-oh hard head. But he didn't want my help. And if you don't want it either then fine. Stay here with your sheep and write letters like Fred did—letters that will never even get read. Or better yet, why don't you just jump on a plane and go knock on your aunt's door and ask her to give you the ranch."

"Maybe I will."

"Go to France?" Mr. Steele said and followed it with a belly laugh. "You ever even been out of Arizona?"

"I've been to Colorado."

"Colorado's not exactly a foreign country, son," Mr. Steele said. "But be my guest. And when you come back with your tail between your legs, I'll a . . . a renew my offer—only at half price. Then we'll see who's clever."

And with that, Mr. Steele turned and walked away.

Right off, I wanted to run after him and apologize and tell him he was right and take the deal and thank him. But I didn't. I just stood where I was and watched him get into his Buick and drive off.

When he was gone, I looked down at the quit deed in my hand and thought about what my father had said about taking little steps. I wished I had listened to him. Because I had just taken a big step—lunged. And in doing so, again knocked my world out of balance.

JJ

HAMAIKA

According to Oxea, the Mamu was always on the prowl for naughty boys. According to Aitatxi, the Mamu was everything Basque—both good and bad. According to my father, the Mamu didn't exist.

Oxea told me that the *lamiak* were little people with birdlike feet who danced on the top of your head while you slept and "scramble egg'd" your dreams. Aitatxi told me that the *lamiak* crept into houses every night, cleaning and putting things in order, in hopes of earning the privilege of becoming human. Dad told me the *lamiak* didn't exist.

I wondered if that was the way it was with every family. Did each member look at the same thing and see it in a totally different way? And if so, which way was the right way?

Oxea would have said my going to the Basque land was crazy. I was still a *gaixua*. "Five maybe ten year, then you go. It still be there." Aitatxi would have smiled and said, "It like heaven. You go, you no come back—no ever." Dad would have told me not to go.

And Mr. Steele, well, he didn't say anything. He just froze my bank account.

When I drove to town to find out how much money I had for my trip, Mrs. Price, the bank teller, informed me that the account was in probate and wouldn't be settled for another month, maybe two.

"Is that normal?" I asked her.

"Nothing is normal about death," she said.

Oxea would have bounced Mr. Steele's head on the ground a few times until he "got thinking right way" and gave me my money. Aitatxi would have shouted at Mr. Steele, first in Euskara, then in English. "*Hau enea da eta nahi dut gileat.* It is mine and I want back." Dad would have gotten a new lawyer.

But I didn't do any of those things. Instead, I went to the diner for breakfast.

The place was crowded and my usual booth was taken. So I sat at the counter and waited for Jenny.

"You get all your lawyer stuff taken care of?" Jenny asked as she walked past me carrying two plates full of bacon and eggs with biscuits and gravy on top.

"Not all of it." I watched her slide the plates in front of Fred Mitchell and Jake Crooner.

"You forgot the Tabasco," Jake said.

Jenny pulled the bottle out of her apron pocket and pretended to hit Jake over the head with it before placing it on the table.

"Brought your car back," I said.

"I was about to file a police report." Jenny piled up another table's dirty dishes. One of the plates looked like it had been dipped in ketchup.

"Your dad said you were going to call me."

"Been busy—working girl, remember?" Jenny loaded the plates into her arms. She started to back through the swinging door into the kitchen. "What'll it be? Crêpes suzette?"

"French toast," I said.

"You hate French toast." Jenny stopped with the swinging door resting on her hip.

"I'm going to France."

"Idiot—they don't eat American French toast in France."

Then she disappeared into the kitchen. I waited for her to come back out. But she didn't. So I got up and went into the kitchen. I was greeted by George Strait singing, *That woman I had wrapped around my finger just come unwound.*

A radio sat on the countertop by the cook grill. Behind the grill, Mr. Krawski flipped strips of bacon, and I got the feeling he had been dancing to the music right before I walked in. There was something about the way he was standing—his weight shifted to the left—that made me think of a two-step cut into one.

"Jenny?"

With his spatula, Mr. Krawski pointed toward the back room.

I slid past the rumbling ice machine in the hallway as newly formed cubes fell in a crackle. A knocked-over mop leaned across the back room's doorway. I moved it out of the way and stepped through.

Cold air from the freezer slid along the cement and up my pants leg. A fan buzzed on the ceiling and swirled together the smells of fresh produce and garbage as a faucet dripped onto the stack of dishes in the sink. I recognized the ketchup-dipped plate on top. The door leading out to the alley was ajar and light fell through the open gap to cut across the floor. I followed the light to Jenny leaning up against the garbage bin, crying.

When I saw her, I stopped, my hand still on wood of the door, my body still half inside. My chest tightened and I began shifting my weight from one foot to the other as if someone had lit a fire under my feet. The urge to return to the cool darkness of the diner's back room pulled at my gut. But I ignored it and stepped outside. The door swung shut behind me.

Jenny must have heard the door click as it closed because she straightened up and used a corner of her apron to wipe her eyes.

"Why are you crying?"

"I'm not," Jenny said.

"I'm not that big an idiot," I said.

Jenny laughed at that, and the sound of her laughter made the tightness in my chest loosen.

"When do you leave?"

"I have to sell my truck first."

"You need money?"

"No," I said. "Just enough to get my truck out of the shop."

"I'll put it on your tab," Jenny said as she tried to walk past me to the door.

"Hey." I reached to grab onto her arm, but Jenny pulled it away from me. "You mad at me?"

"Why would I be mad at you?"

"Why would you lie to me?"

Jenny kept her eyes down as if studying the dirt.

"I talked to your dad," I said.

"That's none of your business."

"Why won't you go?"

"I might." Jenny raised her eyes, moving them right past me to gaze up into the sky. "Now."

"Good. You should."

"Idiot." Jenny shoved her hands against my chest so that I stumbled backward.

"What's wrong with me wanting to go to school?"

"Go to school," Jenny said. "Won't help—you're too big an idiot to learn anything."

"Why am I an idiot?"

Jenny stomped her foot on the ground.

The heat of the sun was on my neck as a breeze blew a strand of Jenny's hair across her face; it carried the scent of lemons on it. A car horn honked in the distance. Jenny's eyes brimmed with tears. Her strawberry lips glistened. And I knew. Jenny's crying. The way she looked at me. The kiss the day of the funeral. Her head always on my shoulder. They all came together.

"Shit," I said, "I am an idiot."

And I leaned forward. But before my lips could find Jenny's, I doubled over with pain as she sucker punched me in the gut.

12

HAMABI

Females scare me. They always have.

Even before my teenage years when I realized that the difference between boys and girls had nothing to do with dresses and everything to do with what was under those dresses, girls made my stomach all shaky. It was the same feeling I got when I had the flu—right before I threw up.

In the beginning of high school, as the girls' dresses took on new and exciting dimensions, the shakiness became a steady tremble. It was like I'd swallowed a block of ice and had no control over my body's reaction to it. When I was around the opposite sex, I folded my arms across my chest and locked them in place. But even then, I could still feel the tips of my fingers twitching.

By my senior year, as the girls threatened to become women, I gained some control over my body. Still, I never really trusted them—or myself—when we were in close proximity. There was always the outside possibility that a girl might actually touch me, and at that "contact," a good chance I would fall onto the floor and go into spasms.

Maybe it was because I was only two years old when Mom died—hit by a car that didn't even slow down. And even though my mother had no choice in the matter, she left me. And so I learned that women leave.

Maybe it was because after Amatxi passed away, I was raised by silent men who moved through a world where when something had to be said, it was almost never a good thing. And so I learned to fear a woman's need for words.

Maybe it was because Dad didn't remarry. I never even saw him kiss a woman other than my mother, and time had faded that memory, so I was no longer even sure it was real. And so I learned that being alone was how a man should be.

Or maybe it was just because I was an idiot like Jenny said.

After she punched me, which hurt way more than I would have expected, Jenny walked back into the diner. After she was gone, I sat with my back up against the dumpster and waited for the pain to subside.

I didn't think a lot about why she punched me. Just that she'd punched me. That was enough. The why, I was sure, was way beyond my understanding.

When I could stand up straight again, I walked around the outside of the diner to the front. I still had Jenny's car keys in my pocket and needed to return them. I thought about chucking them into the dumpster, but then as Jenny had just proved she was a "violent" woman, I didn't want to risk it. I would leave the keys on a table in the diner and go.

I eased open the diner door and peeked inside to see if the coast was clear. Jenny was there, sitting on a stool, counting money onto the counter.

"Get in here," she said when she saw me.

I strolled in like I was doing her a big favor by just being there.

"I called the shop," Jenny said. "The insurance covered most of the body work, but you still owe two hundred and eighty-five dollars. I'm giving you three hundred because you probably don't have any food at home."

"I got food."

"You got a passport?" She jammed the wad of cash into my hand.

"Where do you get those again?"

"Talk to Mrs. Fickle." Jenny got up and moved around the counter.

"Thanks for help—"

"Don't," she said and walked into the kitchen.

I waited until the swinging door was still before leaving. Then I walked over to the garage and paid the repair bill. I asked the mechanic who'd worked on my truck if he knew anyone who might want to buy it. In response, he offered me $1200.

"It's worth more than that," I said.

"Don't forget—I seen exactly what was busted up," the mechanic said.

When I asked if that included the $285 I'd just paid to have it fixed, he laughed and said, "Hell, if I'd known I was going to buy the thing, I'd have used new parts."

I told the mechanic he couldn't have the truck for about a week, and he took fifty more bucks off his offer. When I told him I needed half up front, he took off another fifty.

The truck was parked on the side of the shop. When I came around the corner, sun glared off the truck's fresh white paint job. I shielded my eyes. Even though it was old, the truck looked pretty good. And not like it had recently been wrecked. Or that someone had died in it.

My heart started beating big as I pulled open the driver's door. I had to take two or three deep breaths to get my heart to shrink back down before I could slide into my father's seat. How long ago had the accident happened? Months? Weeks? Fifteen days. I glanced over and seemed to see a shadow of myself in the passenger seat. I tried to catch Dad's smell in the cab, but it was lost in the odor of the truck's new paint.

As I curled my fingers around the steering wheel, I saw my father's hands. And I remembered how I used to measure mine against his. I was fourteen when our hands matched up perfectly for the first time. Dad and I were sitting with our backs against the barn after a game of *pilota*. When I raised my open hand and threw down the challenge, Dad pressed his hand against mine and there was no difference between them. Which was not what I wanted. I tried to make my fingers stretch just a little farther. But it was no use.

"Now, then," Dad said. "Soon."

Then he tossed me the ball and we sat for a while. Occasionally, I commented on the game we'd just played—fixing my mistakes and pumping up my good shots.

By sixteen my fingers were half an inch longer than Dad's. By seventeen I quit measuring.

I turned the key in the ignition. The truck kicked into life.

I drove down Eucalyptus to where Rosario's Mexican Restaurant used to be. Dad and I would eat there every Friday. But then Rosario fell in love with a migrant worker and moved to Mexico—a country she informed us she had never been to.

After a year of being nothing, the place became Fickle Travel.

When I walked in, I noticed that the faint scent of refried beans still hung in the air. Other than that, there was nothing of Rosario left. The walls had been painted banana yellow, and on one, hula girls in grass skirts danced their way across. On another, the Leaning Tower of Pisa was being carried in the tusks of an elephant. Mrs. Fickle, in shorts and a Phoenix Suns T-shirt, sat in a wicker chair behind a patio table she was using as a desk.

"Where are you off to, young man?" Mrs. Fickle asked, and I noticed the pair of chopsticks she had wedged into the thin bun of her hair.

Mrs. Fickle never remembered who I was—even though she'd known me all my life. I'd gone to school with her son, Carl, who ate his boogers all the way through the sixth grade. After that, he probably still ate them, but no longer in public. Now, Carl was going to some Ivy League school out East. I heard he was studying to become a microbiologist. Maybe he could figure out why his boogers tasted so good.

"Paris, I think," I said as I took the wicker chair opposite her.

"*Oui,*" Mrs. Fickle said. "Paris is beautiful in the summer."

"Okay."

"First class or coach?"

I shrugged. I'd been on an airplane only once in my life, and that was to fly to Colorado for Oxea's funeral. I had no idea of cost. But I did know that after I repaid Jenny and bought some food for the house, I'd only have about $700 left. And I didn't know how long that would have to last me.

"There's a special," Mrs. Fickle said. "Round-trip to Paris with a connection in New York for eight hundred seventy-five."

"Coach," I said.

"That is coach."

"Can you get me to Paris for five hundred?"

"Sure." Mrs. Fickle smiled. "But not home."

She probably ate her boogers as well.

"How about some other city in Europe?"

"Ah, an open adventure," Mrs. Fickle said. "How exciting—Stockholm, Hamburg, Athens, Oslo—"

"Just Europe."

"You know how big Europe is, Mathieu?"

So she did recognize me.

"Let's try this again," Mrs. Fickle said. "Exactly why are you going to Europe?"

"I have to see someone."

"And where does that someone live?"

"Urepel, France."

"So that's where you need to go?"

"It's near the Spanish and French border—I think."

Mrs. Fickle pulled out an atlas.

"I don't see it."

"It's real," I said.

"Tell you what, Mathieu," Mrs. Fickle said. "Why don't you let me work on this, and I'll call you at home later."

And with that she got up and led me to the door.

"How exciting this must be for you—traveling the world. When do you want to leave?"

"As soon as I get a passport," I said.

Mrs. Fickle sighed and went back to her desk to get a pamphlet.

"They might be able to express deliver it for you."

"Thanks." I pushed open the door to leave. "Oh, uh, say hi to Carl for me."

"I will," Mrs. Fickle said. "And I'm truly sorry about the loss of your father. He was a unique individual—a good shepherd."

As I drove home, I thought about what Mrs. Fickle said about Dad. How she'd called him a "good shepherd." My father's life summed up in a label. Was that how people thought of him? As just the guy who took care of sheep?

When I got home, the phone was ringing.

"There's a round-trip flight to Madrid for four hundred and fifty-seven dollars," Mrs. Fickle said without introduction. "You have a six-hour layover and change planes in Atlanta. Altogether it's going to take you about twenty-four hours of travel time and you lose a day, but it's within your budget."

"If I take a parachute can I just jump out as we go over France?"

She didn't laugh.

"Once you arrive in Madrid, you'll take a train to some place called Bill-bow. From there, I need to get you into France and then up to where you want to go. I'm still working on that."

"Sounds like a long way."

"Europe isn't next door," Mrs. Fickle said. "And I found that Err-a-pel place. It's a tiny village way up in the Pyrenees. Appears charming. Of course, I still haven't figured out how I'm going to get you there, but stop by tomorrow and we'll work out the details."

"Okay," I said. "Thanks . . . and Mrs. Fickle, uh, what did you mean when you said my dad was a good shepherd?"

"Just that he took care of his flock," Mrs. Fickle said.

"Oh, the sheep."

"No, Mathieu—his family."

13

HAMAHIRU

I made a list of things I needed to get done before I left for France.

(1) Get passport.

"Smile," Mrs. Fickle said as she took a photo of me. "Foreign countries like happy tourists." Then I drove into Phoenix and turned in the paperwork. The lady behind the desk at the state travel office said it would take at least a week for me to get my passport. When I asked her if there was any way to get it sooner, she said, "Yeah, drive to DC. Next."

(2) Check on sheep.

I drove up to the *etxola*. Dad had paid Luis and Diego through the summer, so that was set. But since I hadn't seen or spoken to either of the shepherds since the accident, I thought I better go up. Besides, I knew Dad would have wanted me to. The sheep were the same as always. They ate, went "baaa," and continued on as if nothing had happened. Lucky sheep. Both Luis and Diego told me how sorry they were about the loss of my father. Then Diego reached over and touched my head, right where the bruise from the crash had been, and said, "*Mi dios.*" I don't know why he did that. There was no trace of the bruise anymore, and I hadn't said anything about it.

On the way up to the sheep camp, I drove past the "spot" without even knowing. It wasn't until I saw a mile marker that I realized it was behind me. And I felt guilty because there had been no icy-chill sliding down my spine when I passed over the place my father died. Coming back down the mountain, I made a point of looking for the "spot." But I couldn't find it. There was no broken glass. No twisted metal. Everything was swept up or blown away. Like it had never happened.

(3) Talk to Jenny.

While I didn't exactly talk to Jenny, I did spy on her. Every morning, I parked across the street and watched as she moved past the diner's front window. I don't know if Jenny saw me or not. I was hoping she would. But if she did, she didn't make any sign of it. No little wave to invite me in for breakfast. Not even a flicker of a smile to tell me that—while I was still an idiot—no more punches would be thrown. So I just sat in my truck waiting to be forgiven for something I wasn't even sure I needed forgiving for.

(4) Tell Mr. Steele he was an asshole.

I decided to do that when I got back. I pictured myself waving the signed quit deed in his face and saying, "Who's clever now, asshole." The fact that I hadn't exactly figured out how I was going to get my aunt to sign over the ranch to me didn't stop me from imagining different scenarios of my triumphant return. A couple of times I even had Mr. Steele crying.

(5) Pack.

Mrs. Fickle told me I would need clothes for warm weather, cold weather, wet weather, and dry weather. "And every other kind of weather possible." When I asked what other kind of weather was possible, she said, "You've never been to Europe." I jammed most of everything I owned into a backpack, including the journal I hadn't written in since the accident. I didn't intend to write anything on my trip either. I had decided to leave a number of blank pages to mark the time from when Dad died until I left for U of A. I would start writing again when I got to Tucson. Until then, the empty pages held what I wanted to say.

I had another reason for bringing the journal that had been a Christmas present from my father. When I first saw it under the Christmas tree, I thought it was a gag gift. The tag on it said, *From Santa Claus,* and I was thirteen. When I pulled off the wrapping paper and found a book with no words in it, I was sure there'd been some kind of Christmas-exchange mistake.

"What am I supposed to do with this?" I asked Dad as he unwrapped the compass I got him. I would later point out how the compass would be very useful for a camping trip that I wanted to take in the White Mountains.

"Now, then, why don't you write something in it?"

"Why would I want to do that?"

"I don't know," Dad said. "Maybe to remember things."

"Remember what?"

"Not so much what as *who*."

"Oh," I said, my face going red at having almost forced my father to actually say *who*.

I slipped the journal under the couch and grabbed another present to open. Later, while cleaning up, I retrieved the book and took it to my room. There, I wrote about Aitatxi and Oxea and Mom and Amatxi and many other *whos* in my life.

I would take these *whos* in my journal with me on my trip to Urepel, France. My whole family coming along. The idea of it made me feel less alone.

After I was packed, I went down into the basement and grabbed the bundle of letters Amatxi had written to her daughter. I stuffed the unopened letters in with my clothes. I did it just in case Isabelle Odolen didn't believe that I was who I said I was. She probably didn't even know I existed. How could she? I was counting on there being some mention of my birth inside one of the unopened letters. At least I told myself that was why I was bringing them, but I had another reason—revenge. I blamed this woman for my father's death. By not answering his letters, she had forced him—and me—to stay on the ranch. Isabelle Odolen was the reason we were driving down the mountain that day. And I would find a way to use that against her. I saw myself throwing the letters onto the floor at her feet, watching as she crumpled to her knees before the truth of what she had done, weeping and begging me for forgiveness—which, I would refuse to give her, unless, of course, she signed the ranch over to me.

On June 1, I woke up early. Took a shower. Combed my hair. Got dressed. Then, just before I left Artzainaskena, I stuck the black-and-white photo of Isabelle in my back pocket. Then I locked the front door and drove into town.

I dropped the truck off at the shop, got the rest of my money, and waited for Ms. Whittaker to pick me up and take me to the airport. While I was standing on the curb, the mechanic who had bought my truck came out and handed me the birthday card my father had given me.

"Found it wedged down in the seat."

I slipped the card into my ticket sleeve as Ms. Whittaker pulled up. I threw my backpack into her station wagon and climbed in.

"You ready for your adventure?" Ms. Whittaker asked.

I shrugged.

"Is there anything you need me to do while you're away?" She turned onto the highway leading to Phoenix.

I wanted to say, "Keep Mr. Steele away from my ranch." But instead I just shrugged again.

"How long do you expect to be away?"

"Don't know," I said. My return ticket was open-ended. "Couple weeks."

"That should be plenty of time to visit your homeland," Ms. Whittaker said.

I didn't think of where I was going as my "homeland." It was just where I had to go because of Isabelle Odolen. But everyone in town thought that, because of my father's death, I wanted to reconnect with my family's origins. And I let them.

"Your father always talked about visiting the house where his mother was born," Ms. Whittaker said, and then sighed. "Poor Ferdinand, he never got the chance."

I wanted to ask Ms. Whittaker why? Why hadn't he gone? He could have done what I was doing years ago. Should have. He had the chance. And if he had gone, everything would have been different—better. We could have sold the ranch. I could have gone to the university with my friends. Dad would not have been driving the truck when the storm hit. The tire would have never blown.

But my father chose not to. Why did he make that choice?

I clenched my teeth and slid down in the seat. I felt my chin jut forward the way Dad told me Mom's did when she was angry. He laughed at me when he caught me doing it—which only made me angrier. And I'd push my chin back into place. But now, I kept my chin where it was, because I was angry, and because there was no one left in the world that knew me well enough to see that.

Ms. Whittaker talked the whole hour and a half it took to get to the airport. I grunted a couple of replies to her questions, but for the most part kept silent. When we pulled up to the drop-off curb, I took a hundred dollars of the money I'd gotten for the truck and handed it to Ms. Whittaker.

"Give this to Jenny," I said. "Tell her I'll pay her the rest when I get back."

I started to push open the passenger door when Ms. Whittaker leaned over and kissed me on the cheek.

"Your father would be so proud of you."

Which only made my eyes watery and confused me as I grabbed my backpack. Would it always be that way? Just the mention of him knocking the wind out of me? I waited until Ms. Whittaker drove off before using my shirtsleeve to wipe my eyes.

And as I stood there with people rushing past me, hurrying to catch flights to places I'd never been, my skin tingled like it had just been scrubbed with a stiff brush. I was leaving, going farther away from the ranch than I'd ever been. A taxi honked, a driver swore, a traffic guard blew his whistle, and I smiled and joined the flow of people into the airport.

Checking in was easier than I thought. After I paid the remainder due on my plane ticket, the guy at the counter looked at my blank passport, winked, and said, "Virgin."

On the plane, I settled into a window seat and went over the itinerary Mrs. Fickle had put together for me. Somewhere over the Atlantic I was going to lose a day, so I would arrive in Madrid at 6:52 A.M. on June 3. From there, I had to catch a train to Bilbao. Next a bus to San Sebastián. Then another bus over to Biarritz, France. There was no bus that actually went to Urepel, so I had to take one to some town called Aldudes. For the remainder of my trip, Mrs. Fickle said, I could catch a taxi.

The whole journey from Phoenix to Urepel would take me two days and include two planes, one train, three buses, and a taxi.

Using a pen, I gave each segment of my trip a number. I checked off number one—catch flight to Atlanta. I put the itinerary into the pocket of the seatback in front of me, where I left it for about a minute. I pulled out the itinerary and went over the steps again. Put it back in the pocket. Forty-five seconds later, I read the steps quietly to myself. Back in the pocket. Out to memorize the steps. Returned to pocket for what I swore would be the final time. That lasted ten seconds. This process continued until the plane pulled away from the gate.

I told myself that if I just followed the steps, I would be fine. But to make sure, I decided to go over them once more before takeoff. Only this time, when I reached for the itinerary, my ticket sleeve came out of the seatback pocket as well, and the birthday card Dad had given me fell from it onto the floor.

I picked up the card, wishing I'd left it behind in Ms. Whittaker's station wagon. The front was a blue sky with the summer-corn words—*Happy Birthday Son.*

I opened the card as the plane taxied onto the runway and read what my father had written: *Mathieu, Hope this truck takes you where you want to go. Love Dad.*

And, even before the plane left the ground to rise into a sky as white as a blank sheet of paper, I realized that my memorizing the steps of the itinerary was useless. Everything ahead of me was yet to be written.

14

HAMALAU

Over the two weeks leading up to my leaving, I worked on my foreign language skills. I figured I might need them to communicate with the locals. I didn't speak French, but had taken Spanish for one semester in high school; I got a C for not being able to conjugate irregular verbs. I wasn't that worried though. Luis and Diego told me what they called *frases necesarias*. For meeting girls, *Hola mi vida*—Hello my life. And *Te doi un chinga*—which they wouldn't translate for me but said was good for getting into a fight. Still, just in case I needed to do something beyond meet girls or get into a fight, Ms. Fickle gave me a Spanish phrase book.

I also decided to brush up on my Basque in anticipation of Isabelle Odolen. Did she even speak English? And if not, how was I going to explain to her what I wanted? But then again, her not speaking English might be a good thing. Maybe I could get her to sign the quit deed without knowing what she was doing. I thought that was a pretty good idea, but Dad didn't. And he told me so. It was amazing how much clearer my father's voice was now that he was gone. And how much more he now seemed to want to talk. The Dad in my head offered unasked for advice on every part of my life. Selling the truck—*bad idea*. Going to Basque land—*worse idea*. Wearing jeans on the plane—*inappropriate dress*. Not brushing my teeth before I left—*inappropriate hygiene*. And Jenny? Well, that was for me to figure out. Thanks Dad.

As for my Euskara, well, I knew how to say, yes—*ba*, and no—*ez*. Obviously, I knew house—*etxea*, and sun—*eguzkia*, moon—*ilargia*, stars—*izarrak*. Along with an assortment of farm animals: dog—*zakurra*, sheep—*ardiak*, pig—*txerria*, chicken—*oilaskoa*, and cow—*behia*.

I also knew a few phrases, most having been taught to me by my *aitatxi,* such as: *Ttipia eta itsusia. Bildots gaixua*—Small and ugly. A runt lamb. And, *Zazte ardien bila*—Go get the sheep (or "sheeps" as Aitatxi said). *Mendia heltzen da urrats bat aldian*—Take the mountain one step at a time. And the always useful, *Harrapatu aritz ona*—Look for the good oak.

The biggest problem was that all the Basque I knew, I'd learned through parroting. Well, that and the fact that ninety percent of it was related to sheep. I only ever repeated words or phrases that were told to me, and never created any original sentences. Why should I? Everything I needed to say about life on the ranch had already been said. I just needed to memorize it. But now that I was traveling to another country, it seemed a good time to try and learn some new language skills. So I worked on putting my Basque words together to create sentences such as:

"How do I get to Urepel?"

"How much is this?"

"Where is the bathroom?" (On the ranch, at least for peeing, the bathroom was pretty much anywhere you were standing.)

And, "Can you help me?"

Only I didn't know all the words for any of the things I wanted to say. And, on top of that, I wasn't exactly sure what order to put the words into for them to make sense. I might know how to say, *joaiten gira*—let's go. But I didn't know which part was "let's" and which part was "go." In the end the best I could hope for was that the general meaning of what I was trying to say would come through.

So "How do I get to Urepel?" turned into "*Nola egin Urepel?*" Which was something like "How do I make Urepel," only without any mention of "I."

And that was one of my better sentences.

I finally gave up on trying to figure out how to say, "Can you help me?" While I knew the words for help—*lagundu,* you—*zuk,* and me—*ni,* it was the "can" I couldn't figure out. I did know how to say "want"—*nahi.* And so I created what I thought might be, "Want you help me." But, besides possibly getting me slapped, it just didn't sound right.

The whole time I was going over the Basque words I was familiar with, there were two that kept echoing in my head: *bihotza*—heart, and *isileko*—

secret. Alone, each was just a word, but when combined into *bihotz isilekoa*, they became a symbol to me of my father. Dad had a *bihotz isilekoa*—secret heart. In it, he kept pieces of the past, present, and future hidden from me. And that made the beating of my own heart less sure. If I hadn't really known my own father, how could I know myself? Did I have a secret heart as well?

Lying in bed at night, I listened to my heart beating. Solitary. Alone. The sound of it comforting. I was only me. There was nothing hidden. Nothing unknown. And yet, sometimes, right before sleep, I would catch the beat of a second heart, like an echo, chasing after the first. It would follow me into dreams I couldn't remember. By morning the second heart would be gone. And there would be only one heart beating in my chest. But still, the memory of that *bihotz isilekoa* stayed with me.

I was asleep when we landed in Madrid. A bald guy who had gotten on the plane in Atlanta woke me up.

"You snore, kid," the bald guy said as he gathered up his belongings.

The Madrid airport wasn't that different from the one in Phoenix—lots of people in a hurry to get somewhere other than where they were. I hadn't been in many large crowds, other than high school football games, and there I'd basically known everyone bumping into me. Here, I didn't know anyone. Having so many people moving in different directions was confusing. To keep from getting lost, I stuck close to the bald guy.

As I followed after him, I stretched out my legs and arms; the muscles were tight and sore, like I'd been digging ditches all day instead of just sitting on a plane. I passed beneath a sign with suitcases and a stick figure holding a stamp; the word IMMIGRACION was printed on it. That led to a hallway that opened onto the baggage carousel. Beyond the carousel were three podiums about fifteen feet apart. Behind each podium stood an immigration officer. The officers were dressed in what looked like oversized Boy Scout uniforms.

Travelers lined up at each podium waiting to get their passports stamped. After retrieving my backpack, I got into the middle line behind the bald guy. Our line moved fast. A middle-aged woman, who looked like an overstuffed chair in her tight blue suit, handed the officer her passport.

He said something to her in Spanish. She opened her orange purse and the head of a dog popped out. The officer laughed, gave the dog a pat, stamped her passport, and waved for the next person in line to step up.

As I got closer to the podium, I pulled out my itinerary to again check on the time my train left Madrid for Bilbao—9:00 A.M.. Same as the past twenty times I'd looked. The clock on the far wall read a quarter after seven. I changed the time on my wristwatch to match. Even though it was nearly two hours until my train departed, my stomach rumbled. What if I couldn't get a taxi? What if the train station was far away? What if there was traffic? Or an accident? My gut churned with gas. And I burped just as the bald guy, who had reached the front of the line, turned to me and said, "Go ahead, kid. I can't find my passport."

The bald guy began going through his suitcase as the immigration officer motioned me forward with a flick of his finger. I walked up and, with a smile, handed him my passport. Up close, the officer's mustache became visible—a line of black pepper flakes running through the middle of his upper lip; it was so thin that the slightest flinch while shaving would have wiped it away.

The officer flipped open my passport and reached to routinely stamp it, but then stopped. He looked from my passport to me and said my name aloud, "Mathieu Etcheberri."

I nodded.

"Etcheberri," the officer said again as he ran the tip of his tongue along the tiny grains of his mustache. Then he cut his eyes to either side, and I got the feeling that if he'd been able to catch the attention of one of the officers at the other podiums he would have called them over. But the officers were busy stamping their own traveler passports.

"Is there a problem?" I asked in English.

The officer didn't answer me. He just stamped my passport and returned it. I thanked him in English and turned toward the exit. As I walked away, I couldn't help but glance back. The officer was still watching me. The bald guy was now in front of the podium, having found his passport. He held it out, but the officer didn't seem to notice; his attention stayed on me as I moved through the exit and out into the cool morning air.

Sunlight was creeping into the city, turning buildings a bloody orange. I shivered. A dove fluttered in front of my face. The scent of dust hung in the air. For a moment, it reminded me of the ranch. Then a truck drove by and a wave of diesel fumes washed over me. I coughed at the black smoke that swirled around me. Stamping my feet on the pavement for warmth, I went to get my jacket from my backpack.

"What was that about?" I heard the bald guy say, and turned to see him standing with his suitcase.

"I don't know," I said as I pulled out my jacket and set it on the pavement while I rezipped my backpack.

"What's your name, kid?"

"Mathieu."

"I meant your surname."

"Huh?"

"Your last name."

"Etcheberri."

"Be careful with that." The bald guy nodded knowingly. "That's the kind of name that can get you into trouble around here."

Before I could ask him what he meant, he climbed into a taxi and was gone.

15

HAMABORTZ

Another taxi followed right on the bumper of the one the bald guy took. The driver leaned over and said, *"Adonde?"*

I grabbed my backpack and scrambled into the taxi.

"La estacion de train," I said.

Then as the taxi jerked into motion, I realized I didn't have my jacket. I turned to see it bunched up on the pavement. The sun moved higher. Light struck my jacket so that it glowed like a lost lamb huddled on the ground for protection. And that glowing lamb took me back to a night years before.

I was eight. Dad was away on one of his business trips, so I was staying at the ranch with Aitatxi and Oxea. They each had four glasses of *arno gorria*—red wine at dinner, and by midnight the house was shaking with Oxea's snoring. My room was right next to his. It was like being inside a wooden box and someone banging on the outside with a hammer.

Finally, I decided to go into his room and, like I'd done on other nights, push him onto his side. He still snored that way, but not so loudly—more like water tumbling over stones. Only, when I opened my bedroom door, instead of having to feel my way in the dark, I was covered in light.

For a moment, I couldn't tell where the light was coming from. Then I looked downstairs. Moonlight poured through the living room's windows. Instead of going to Oxea's room, I was drawn to the stairs; there the wooden steps shined as if polished in light; my feet splashed darkly as I descended.

When I reached the ground floor, I hesitated. I could still return to my bedroom, throw the blankets up over my head and drown out both the noise and the light. But I didn't. Instead, I ran and jumped onto the couch.

Kneeling on the seat cushions, I looked out at the full moon that hung low over the pasture.

It was December, and the coolness of the night seeped through the glass and onto my face. My breath misted the window, and I thought, *I am the only thing awake on the whole ranch.* Then I saw the sheep in the pasture. They were standing just beyond the oak tree on the slope of the hill—glowing.

The sensation of having just missed something crept over me. If only I had woken a moment earlier, run down the stairs instead of walked, while the moon was lower, resting on the grass of the pasture, I would have seen the sheep grazing on the moon, witnessed their swallowing pieces of the light that now shone out through their wool.

I touched the window; it was slick with the moisture of my own breath. I thought about waking Aitatxi and showing him the glowing sheep. He would have a story to explain it to me—something old and Basque and not quite understandable. But instead I repositioned myself on the couch, not willing to look away and again miss something. Oxea had stopped snoring. The house was quiet. I yawned and rested my head on my folded arms. The moon moved higher. A few sheep lay down on the grass. My eyes flickered shut, and then, sometime before morning, the sheep lost their light.

I never told Aitatxi or Oxea about the glowing sheep. I almost forgot it ever happened. Until I saw my jacket lying on the pavement, glowing in the morning light.

I thought of asking the driver to stop and go back. But I didn't know the Spanish words to get what I wanted. Besides, a new worry was pushing the jacket out of my head; I didn't have any pesetas to pay for the taxi. I had forgotten to exchange money at the airport and so only had American dollars. What if the driver wouldn't take it? What if he called the police? What if that immigration officer showed up? His watching eyes filled my head as the gas bubbles in my gut began to gurgle.

To distract myself, I looked out the taxi window at Madrid. But I couldn't really see the city through the window's small frame. All I saw were corners of red-bricked buildings and the blurred faces of other passengers in cars and kids running to and from places beyond my view.

And that was when I knew I shouldn't have come.

I should have stayed home. Apologized to Mr. Steele for being a hard-headed Basq-oh. Taken his offer. If I had, I could be getting ready to leave for the university, and not traveling to a place I'd never been, to find people I didn't know, and who didn't know me. Jenny was right—I was an idiot. I closed my eyes and imagined her head on my shoulder and the smell of lemons in the air. The taxi came to a stop. My eyes flew open. The driver pointed to the meter. I handed him a twenty-dollar bill. Fled.

The rest of my journey to France went smoothly. Except for the fact that my train left a half hour earlier than I thought and I almost missed it when I had to keep stepping out of the ticket line because the gas bubbles that had been multiplying inside me started rushing toward the nearest exit. As if a dividing line were drawn around my midsection, the gas split into two groups. One headed up, the other down.

I stepped out of the ticket line when the first bit of gas broke out. But as the departure time of my train to Bilbao got closer, I had to let nature take its course. I stayed in line and kept my gaze straight ahead. I only flinched a little when the woman behind me said, "*Dios mio!*" Then with a hand-kerchief covering her nose, she made a run for clean air. Luckily by then I was at the ticket window. With one last expulsion, I ran to catch the train.

After that, everything went better. At least until I puked out the train window. Once all the gas found its way out of my gut, it was replaced by a painful hunger. Unfortunately, I chose to satisfy that hunger with a paella that included shrimp still sporting their eyes.

The bus ride from Bilbao to San Sebastián truly was uneventful. At least once I got on the right bus. I had not planned on visiting either Zaragoza or Santander, but both towns, and a night spent sleeping on a bench, somehow made it onto my itinerary.

In San Sebastián, I made sure I found the right bus. And once I took my seat, I fell asleep and didn't wake up until we reached the border.

As the bus came to a stop, my eyes fluttered open to see a group of sol-diers in green army fatigues standing outside. The morning was still gray and the smoke from their cigarettes matched the light. All of them had handguns strapped to their belts.

When two of the soldiers boarded the bus and started checking passports, I sat up straight in my seat. As they moved steadily down the row toward me, I started to sweat. This time I didn't smile when I was asked to show my passport.

"*A donde va?*" the first soldier asked me.

"*No entiendo,*" I answered, not because I didn't understand that he was asking me where I was going, but because I was worried if I answered one question in Spanish, the man might think I spoke the language and so ask me more questions that I really wouldn't understand. So I decided to let him think I didn't speak Spanish up front. Only it might have been smarter to do that in English.

"*Entiendes,*" he said back to me, and I thought he was correcting my Spanish, but then I realized he wasn't.

His handgun was only inches from my face, and I saw that the handle was chipped and the barrel scratched, which gave me the impression that the gun had been fired—a lot.

"*Su apellido es Basco?*" he asked.

I recognized the word *apellido,* Spanish for name. And since I had been called a Basco before, I guessed he was asking me if my name was Basque. After the earlier exchange in Spanish, I thought it best to try and answer the question in Euskara. I had listened to Aitatxi on more than one occasion announce that he was Basque, so I was pretty sure of how to say it.

"*Ba, eskualduna niz,*" I announced. Yes, I am a Basque.

The gasp of a large group of people is kind of like a balloon popping. One moment the bus was full of air; the next it was really hard to find enough for a single breathe. Everyone looked away from me. Except for the soldier. He focused solely on me as he grabbed my arm, pulled me to my feet, and began dragging me toward the bus's door.

Two rows from the exit, the second soldier on the bus stepped in front of us. He placed a restraining hand on the chest of the first.

"*Es un Americano,*" the second soldier said.

"*Es un Basco,*" the first soldier replied.

The second soldier shook his head, placed a hand on the first soldier's shoulder, and leaned in and whispered something in his ear. The first soldier's head dropped, and I saw tears running down his cheeks. He let go of my arm. The second soldier removed my passport from his hand and gave it back to me.

"*Vete*," he said and turned me around. Then he pressed the tip of his handgun between my shoulder blades and gave me a push. I stumbled back to my seat.

The soldiers exited; the bus rolled forward.

"That was stupid," said a guy sitting in the seat behind me. His breath was warm and stale on my neck, and there was the clip of a British accent to his words.

"What did—"

"Don't turn around."

And I felt like I was in some kind of spy movie.

"After ETA killed that Guardia last week, you're lucky you're a Basque-American."

"But I don't have anything to do with ETA."

"A stupid Basque-American at that," the voice said with a dry laugh. And then the breath was gone and the bus bounced on.

16

HAMASEI

The bus to Aldudes was late.

I huddled at the station for four hours, waiting. A woman with both the look and smell of my *amatxi* (stinky cheese and rose water) was my only companion. The woman wore a black shawl over her head and worked a rosary through her fingers as her lips moved in silent prayer.

Fear that the bus would come and go without me stopped me from visiting one of the nearby cafés. I wanted to ask the woman when the bus would come. But again, fear kept me silent. I didn't speak any French. And after what had happened at the border, I was afraid my speaking Euskara might send the woman screaming down the street. Or maybe she would just reach over and smack me with her rosary.

Sitting on the bench, I had time to think over what had happened. First with the man at the airport telling me to be careful with my name. Then with the soldier at the border—*Es un Basco.* And, finally, the man on the bus whispering to me about ETA.

I knew what ETA was—the Basque terrorist group that wanted an independent homeland. I had read about ETA in the newspaper articles given to me back home. Whenever there was any mention of Basques in the paper, everyone at school pointed it out to me. Unfortunately, the only articles for the past five years had been about ETA.

"You guys do anything but make bombs?" Rich had asked when an explosion in a Madrid café killed twelve people.

"Yeah, guns to shoot fools like you," I answered.

In Arizona, ETA didn't have anything to do with me. I was an American who just happened to have a Basque name. ETA was an ocean away. In a world where the Mamu roamed and Mari flew in flames and the *lamiak* snuck through windows. All of them were just characters in a made-up story. None of them real for me. Until now. Now I was in that "made-up" world, where having a Basque name could get a gun pressed between my shoulders. I would have to be careful in this world and try to go unnoticed until I understood its rules. So I didn't ask the woman who smelled of stinky cheese and rose water what time the bus to Aldudes would come. I just sat and waited.

A little after 5:00 P.M. the bus arrived. I got on and began my climb into the Pyrenees.

The bus passed through small towns where I saw copies of the house Aitatxi had built in Arizona repeated again and again: clean white walls and red-tiled roofs. Many of the houses had rows of red peppers hanging out front. There were names on the houses: *Xalbador, Biperrenea, Mendianea,* and I wondered if there was another Artzainaskena among them, but I did not see one. I pictured the families inside the houses, sitting down for dinner, glasses of red—*arno gorria* and white—*arno zuria* wine on tables crowded with lamb and cheese and bread. My stomach growled in protest of my imaginings, and to stop it I pulled out the photo I had in my pants pocket. Isabelle stared out at me from the black-and-white version of the passing houses. Did Gorrienea still look the same? Was it even still standing? What if I couldn't find it? What if Isabelle was gone? Dead like my father? What if I'd come all this way for nothing?

I put the photo back into my pocket. It was too late for thoughts like that now. Maybe I was stupid, like the guy at the border said. A stupid Basque-American who didn't belong in this place. But the Basque part of me was also stubborn. I would get what I wanted. No matter what obstacles I had to overcome. That was a Basq-oh trait Mr. Steele hadn't counted on.

As we rose higher into the mountains, the bus twisted its way through streets that were built before things like buses existed. On these streets, I saw versions of Aitatxi and Oxea: men in black coats with matching berets. Amatxi was also there: women in below-the-knees skirts with dark shawls tucked around their shoulders. They glanced my way as the bus passed. And I shrank into my seat, not wanting to be noticed again.

And always there were sheep: in the roads, on the hills, wedged between the buildings, shut up in corrals. The towns changed, the road moved on, but the sheep remained.

It was dark by the time we reached Aldudes. The driver didn't make any announcement. He just stopped at the far end of the town and opened the door. The few remaining passengers filed out.

I grabbed my backpack and followed the old woman from Biarritz toward the exit. When I was on the last step before the door, I stopped and turned back toward the bus driver.

"Is there a taxi stand?"

The driver was surprised by either me or the question or both.

"American?"

I shrugged apologetically.

"*Je ne parle pas Anglais,*" he said.

"Taxi?" I said again. Not that that word was the French word for, well, a taxi. I just figured if I said the word enough the meaning would somehow become apparent to the man.

The driver shook his head.

"Urepel?" I said.

The driver pointed along the road we were on. In the beam of the bus's headlights, I could see where the pavement turned to dirt as the road continued up the mountain.

"Kilometers," he said and held up seven fingers. That didn't really help as I had no idea how long a kilometer was.

"You take me?" I pointed at the road, then used my hands like they were on a steering wheel.

He shook his head.

"*Marche.*"

"Taxi?"

"*Marche,*" he said, and moved two fingers from his right hand back and forth to demonstrate walking.

Realizing that I had gotten all the help out of him I was going to, I thanked the driver in English and stepped off the bus.

The night was cool and damp. And as I stood there watching the bus turn around and drive back through Aldudes, it started to rain. I couldn't feel the drops hitting my face, but moisture appeared on my skin, as if it had come from me and not the sky. I looked up the road that led to Urepel, lowered my head, and began my *marche*.

I wished I had my jacket. It was a dumb wish because there was no hope of it ever coming true. Not like my wishing for a million dollars, which also might not—okay, probably not—come true, but still there was a chance because that wish was in the future. I could win the lottery. Or marry a rich girl. Sell the ranch for way more than it was worth. There were all kinds of million-dollar possibilities in the future. My jacket, on the other hand, was in the past. And my wishing for it was useless and wouldn't make me any drier. But I wished for it anyway. In fact, as I trudged along with the backpack's straps cutting into my shoulders, the vision of my jacket grew clearer. I noticed details about it that I hadn't before—how the flaps of the pockets were turned up at the ends, and how the faded logo of a rearing horse was missing a hind leg. The off-white collar, the silver buttons of the front, the frayed threads of the sleeves—I could see them all as my jacket sat on the pavement outside the Madrid airport, glowing in the moonlight.

The road steepened. After a few hundred yards, I had to take a break. I leaned up against a tree whose trunk was almost white. Decaying wet leaves thickened the air—like under the oak tree back home. I ran a hand over the tree's trunk; it was as smooth as glass and nothing like the gnarled bark of the oak. I wiped my hands off on my pants legs and started walking again.

I made it a couple hundred yards before I doubled over, gulping for air. I couldn't get a good breath. My lungs seemed to be getting one liter of air when they needed eight. Not that I knew how much a liter was any more than I knew how many kilometers were in a mile. Ten? Four? One? Stupid metric system. I tried to remember what Mr. Hathaway said about it in high school math class, but could only picture a chalkboard covered with numbers that didn't add up. I had always disliked math. Now I hated it. I continued on.

My thighs burned. The rain fell harder. Heavy drops splashed on the dirt road and turned it to mud. My feet began to slip out from under me. To keep from sliding backward, I leaned forward and dug my toes into the slope.

I thought about turning around and returning to Aldudes for the night.

Or better yet, just laying my backpack in the middle of the muddy road, climbing onto it, and sledding my way down.

The moon was rising. In its light, I saw off to my right a low wall made of stones. I went over and sat down on it. Even though I was in the open, exposed to the falling rain, I didn't care. I needed a moment's rest.

The wall was made up of hundreds of stones gathered and carefully put in place. It had probably been built to keep in a flock of sheep. That was impossible now, since much of the wall had fallen down. Long empty gaps broke up what was left of it. Beyond the wall, a crumbling house sat in the middle of a pasture. Dark windows stared out from the building. Someone had once looked out those windows. Back when the house had been a home. What had he or she seen? The sheep? The solid wall that held them in? Were they happy with what they saw? Or did they dream of a wider pasture, more sheep, a bigger house? Or were their thoughts even farther away—on another place, where city lights replaced the stars?

I went back to the road and struggled on.

I don't know how long I walked. The rain kept falling. The toes of my feet began to ache. Ten more steps. Five. Three. One. Then I saw the church.

The steeple rose in a sharp point that pierced the moon. I passed a sign that said UREPEL. The road squeezed its way between the back of a large white building and the fronts of smaller shops whose heavy shutters were closed against the rain. On the surrounding hills there were lights. I assumed they were houses. Sections of darkness separated them. And I wondered how I would I ever find the home I was looking for.

I moved on toward the church.

As I neared it, I saw crosses. Some of them were as tall as me. Others were short and didn't look so much like crosses as small trees with thick trunks and rounded tops. Beneath the crosses, sitting on raised slabs of rock, were stone-encased caskets. A low wall surrounded the area, and I leaned over it to see flowers scattered among the graves.

The little cemetery butted up against the side of the church whose wooden doors were ajar. Since the rain was still falling, I didn't hesitate to enter.

Inside, only a hint of moonlight made its way through the stained-glass windows. The light slid over the church's whitewashed walls. Overhead, the dark ribs of the second- and third-floor balconies rose in rings. In front of me, honey-colored pews led to an altar on which candles burned—their light too weak for me to see the face of Jesus looking down from the cross.

Even though the inside of the church was cold, it was at least dry. I could stretch out on a pew. Rest. I shrugged off my backpack. It hit the wooden floor with a thud that caused the pew closest to the altar to rise up and transform into a bent-over woman. She shuffled toward me down the aisle.

I strained in the half-light to see her more clearly, but it wasn't until she had almost reached me that I realized I knew her. She was the same old woman I sat by in Biarritz. No taller than my waist. The same woman who rode with me on the bus. But how had she gotten here before me? No one had passed me on the road. The smoke from the candles was making me dizzy as the woman poked her left index finger into my chest.

"*Zer ari zira hemen?*" the woman asked.

As the woman waited for me to answer a question I had not understood, I saw that the shawl she wore was brown not black, and realized it was anchovies—not cheese—that mixed with her rose water.

I handed the woman the photo of Isabelle in front of Gorrienea.

"*Nor zira zu?*" The woman looked at the photo. Who are you?

And I knew that she was asking who I was. But I was unsure of how to answer her. So I remained silent. And, as if my silence was answer enough, the woman nodded. With the photo in her hand, she moved past me to the church's entrance. I followed. The woman pushed open the door and pointed to a light on a nearby hill.

"*Etxea,*" she said. House.

"House?" I said. "Is that the house in the picture?"

"*Joan,*" the woman said, and gave me back the photo. Go.

I nodded a "thank you," picked up my backpack, and stepped back into the rain.

The name on the house the old woman pointed to was the same as that of the photo—Gorrienea. Only the peppers were gone and the plaster of the outer wall was chipped and peeling. And there was a stream, which had been beyond the borders of the photo, running in front of it. The water bounced and gurgled as it flowed down the slope toward town.

A cow mooed and stuck its head out of the first-floor window. The animal gave me a quick look as if to say, "Get out of the rain, you idiot," and then retreated. But I didn't move. The cow in the house was something I hadn't expected. Hostility, anger, denial, yes, but a cow in the living room? No. But then again, hadn't Aitatxi told me that downstairs was for animals? *It how it is.* Had Isabelle Odolen brought the cows inside to get out of the rain? Were there other animals in there as well? A pig sitting on the couch? Chickens on the shelves?

I jumped across the stream as images of the animal kingdom inside the house made me giggle. I was so tired that everything right then was either comedy or tragedy. Animals in the house—comedy. The rain falling off the roof in a sheet that I had to step through to reach the front door—tragedy. The water slid down my back and into my pants. The chill it sent through me caused my legs to twitch and my teeth to chatter.

When I knocked on the door, it swung open. At first I thought about the cow—how it could have gotten out and wandered off into the hills. But then I saw that the door led to a narrow stairway heading up to the second floor. The door I was at had no connection to the cow. And for some reason that struck me as another tragedy. I was familiar with cows, knew how to treat them, and was pretty sure how they would treat me. Aunts, on the other hand, were foreign to me.

"Hello?" I called, but got no answer.

Light fell from the second floor onto the top of the stairs. I went up a few steps and tried to get a look onto the next level, but all I could see was the upper shelf of an open cabinet made of dark wood. Rows of heavy wine glasses and stacks of folded green and red napkins filled the shelf. I returned to the bottom, propped my backpack against the door, and started again.

As I went up, my shoulders grazed the walls on either side, and the wooden stairs sagged under my weight. More of the second-floor cabinet came into view. I saw a *lauburua* carved into the cabinet's front—the four heads of the Basque cross forming a pinwheel that looked like a good breeze would set spinning.

Then I saw them, hanging on the wall next to the cabinet—Amatxi's seven blue and white plates. And for a moment I was not walking into a house in France but one in Arizona. Having gone in a circle. Stepped through a door. Walked up some stairs. And ended up right back where I started. The plates, like always, hanging on the kitchen wall. And on the plates men still tended sheep, women still baked bread.

As I stepped onto the second floor, my face was flushed with heat. A roaring fire danced in the fireplace. And the girl from the photo danced in front of the flames. Only older, but not old enough—not to be that girl. Her black hair flew. Flames licked the air. She spun. Arms clinging to something pressed to her breast. Her charcoal dress flying out. Smoke filtering up around her. As if she had just stepped out of the fire. Was still smoldering.

Then she saw me. And stopped.

Her eyes were wide and wild. Her chest heaving. Streaks of gray were now visible in her black hair. Not a girl at all, but a woman in her forties or fifties, holding a stuffed teddy bear in her arms. The girl-woman smiled, dropped the teddy bear onto the floor, and rushed toward me. I tried to back away, but wasn't quick enough. She fastened her arms around my waist and pressed her face to my chest.

"*Zu hemen zira,*" she said, her words excited and fast. "*Banakin jinen zinela. Aspaldian hemen nintzan.*"

She pulled me toward the fire. Basque faces with hooked noses and berets were carved into the wood of the mantle. I tried to free myself, but her grip was like a knotted rope. I couldn't get loose. Not without force. And I didn't want to hurt her. Finally, in desperation, I told her to "let go of me" in Euskara. "*Utznezazu ni hemendik.*"

But the girl-woman didn't let go. Instead, she began to spin me in circles, each one moving me closer to the flames. The heat burned my cheeks. Singed the hairs of my arms. Smoke came from my damp clothes. She was going pull me into the fire—take me back with her into the flames from where she came.

"*Utznezazu ni hemendik—orai!*" I said and struggled to get free. Let go of me—now.

"That very bad Basque," a woman's voice said, thick with a French accent. At the sound of the voice, the girl-woman stopped. And I turned to see the real girl from the photo, Isabelle, now a graying woman, holding a shotgun leveled at my face.

"*Utzazu hori joitera, Edita,*" Isabelle said. And the girl-woman released me, picked her teddy bear up off of the floor, and went back to her dancing. "*Ba,* what doing in my house, American?"

When I tried to tell her who I was, my swollen tongue stuck to the roof of my mouth. The heat of the fire was making me light-headed. Sweat dripped into my eyes. I wanted to step away from the flames, but the gun kept me from moving. And then I had the photo in my hand—only I didn't know how it got there. I wanted to give the photo to her, to show Isabelle Odolen that I knew her—or at least of her. That I wasn't an American stranger, or not *that* kind of American stranger. But my arm remained limp against my side. And then it didn't matter because the fire took me. It shot up through my chest and into my head where it exploded to burn the world black.

17

HAMAZAZPI

I woke to voices.

When I opened my eyes, the world remained dark, as if all the light had been drained from it. The voices grew louder. They came from below. A man and a woman arguing in Euskara. I tried to remember what had happened—where I was, how I got here. There had been a dancing girl from a fire. A woman with a shotgun. I was in a bed. In a room whose air smelled of damp wool. There had been a ladder. The girl from the black-and-white photo. There was a blanket over me, rough on my skin. I was naked underneath. Were the dancing girl, the woman, and the girl from the photo all the same person? Or were they three separate people? I couldn't get it straight in my head.

I focused on the voices. I recognized the woman's: Isabelle Odolen. But the other voice, a man's, like breaking stone, was new to me. Their words came fast, overlapped, and rose through the floor.

The taste of garlic was in my mouth. There had been hot food in my throat. Hands pulling off my wet clothes. The dancing girl—no, not a girl, a woman; she tucked something next to me. I turned my head; the tip of my nose grazed soft fur. I ran my fingers over short limbs and glass eyes. It was the teddy bear the girl-woman had been dancing with.

And then there was light—blinding and bright.

It shot up from the floor as a trapdoor opened into the room. The hulking shape of a man climbed through.

I shut my eyes against the hulking man and the light and gripped onto the teddy bear.

The floor creaked as the man walked over. The odor of sweat and wine covered me as he stood next to the bed. I kept my eyes closed, listening to his labored breathing—as if each breath took thought and effort. Ten, twenty, and then the breaking stones again.

"*Mutil*," the man chuckled. "You just boy."

There was a long silence as if the man was waiting for me to deny what he said. But how could I? Right then, I *was* just a boy, one who had woken to a noise in the night and was unwilling to open his eyes in fear that his seeing would make the monster real.

"Nothing but boy."

The odor of sweat and wine lifted as the man turned away. Footsteps retreated; the door closed; the light went out. I was again alone.

The voices from below grew silent.

And in the silence, I remembered the walking and the rain and the house. Isabelle helping me upstairs. The girl-woman singing to me in Euskara: "*Tun gulan bat, tun gulan bi, tun gulan hureran er-or-i.*"

I wanted to run. To find my clothes and escape. But what if the hulking man was there? Waiting for me downstairs? Sitting in the dark? Breathing.

Besides, I couldn't leave now. Not after I'd come this far. I rolled onto my side. In an effort to get the man from my head, I thought of my father. When I was a boy, he was the one who chased away the Mamu from under my bed. Who drove the ghosts from my closet. And thinking of my father took me back to "that day." The monsoon, the tire blowing, my world turning upside down. Only I changed all that. Altered what took place. Reworked the ending.

I don't tell my father, "I'm dying here." In place of that I say, "Pizza."

"Huh?" Dad says.

"Let's get pizza on the way home."

"For your birthday?" Dad says. "You sure that's what you want?"

"That way we'll have time to play a game of *pilota* before it gets dark."

"*Pilota?*" Dad says.

"Afraid?"

"Now, then, just because it's your birthday, Mathieu, don't think I'm going to let you win."

Dad smiles, and I smile, and the heaviness in my chest lifts, and it is my birthday, and it is a good day.

I played the new version of "that day" in my head and, with the teddy bear tucked under my chin, let it lead me into sleep.

In the morning, I again heard voices from below. This time they spoke in French and were accompanied by canned laughter. I opened my eyes. Sunlight fell through a small window and filled the room I now saw was the attic. Boxes were stacked against walls that sloped up into the flat ceiling. I found my backpack at the foot of the bed.

I pulled on some clothes and went to the trapdoor. For a moment, I was afraid I wouldn't be able to open the door—that I was a prisoner—the crazy American relative kept locked in the attic. But when I pulled on the door's steel ring, it rose to reveal a small ladder leading to the house's main floor. With the girl-woman's teddy bear in hand, I climbed down to a hallway. There, black-and-white wedding pictures of couples I'd never seen covered the walls. Nobody in any of the pictures was smiling.

The hallway led back to the main room I'd entered the night before. I lingered in the doorway. The room smelled of smoke, and I saw that the fire was still burning and the girl-woman still dancing in front of it. A color TV sat on the kitchen table. There was some kind of French game show on. The host kept shouting, "*Oila!*" On a side table were stacks of *TV Guide* magazines and piles of French crossword puzzles. Isabelle was at the stove. Eggs popped in grease.

When the girl-woman spotted me, she again rushed over and wrapped her arms around my waist.

"Can you please let go of me . . . please?"

"Her name Edita," Isabelle said as she flipped the eggs in the pan. "She not speak the English."

"Then how do I get—"

"Edita, *txauri jatera*," Isabelle said. Come and eat.

Edita released her hold on me. She took the teddy bear I had brought down for her and sat with it at the table. Isabelle slid a plate of eggs in front of her.

"How many eggs for you want?" Isabelle said to me.

"I don't know—"

"You very *mehe*—skinny," Isabelle said. "I make for you three."

She cracked the eggs into the pan.

"Do you have a bathroom?" I asked.

Isabelle gave me a smile that made me feel like a little kid who has said something both amusing and annoying at the same time. She pointed to a door off to the side.

"Thanks," I said and hustled to use it. When I stepped back into the kitchen, I found a plate of four eggs waiting for me at the table, and Isabelle using a cleaver to chop chunks of meat from a ham bone.

"You eat ham?"

"Okay." I took a seat next to Edita. She smiled and had her teddy bear give me a kiss on the cheek. "Is she your daughter?"

"What other person she be?" Isabelle tossed the ham into the same pan she'd fried the eggs in. The ham sizzled.

"I didn't mean—"

"She special."

"I can see that," I said, and again caught that smile on Isabelle's face. I needed to just shut up, so I went about eating my eggs. The eggs had been cooked in bacon grease, and I could taste the saltiness on their brown edges.

Isabelle took one of the blue and white plates down from where it hung on the wall.

"Amatxi put those same plates on our wall at home," I said.

And without a glance toward me, Isabelle slammed the plate into the sink where it shattered.

"Coffee," she said, and it wasn't a question. She placed a cup in front of me and filled it. Then put a pitcher of cream and a sugar bowl on the table as well.

I didn't drink coffee, but I thought right then would be a good time to start. So I dumped in three spoonfuls of sugar and added cream until my coffee took on the familiar shade of hot cocoa. Only that wasn't how it tasted. I added a couple more spoonfuls of sugar. Tried it again. Then decided I was too young for coffee and just let it sit there.

"By the way, um, I'm Mathieu Etcheberri—your neph—."

"*Ba,* I know you." Isabelle took a piece of ham out of the pan and placed it on Edita's plate. She cut the meat into bite-size pieces for her daughter.

"So, how my brother?"

"My father died a few weeks ago," I said.

Isabelle stopped cutting meat and looked out the kitchen window. Everything became still. Even Edita seemed to hold her breath.

"Say how," Isabelle said with her eyes still on the window.

"In a car accident," I said. "We were on the way back from dropping the sheep off at the *etxola* when—"

"Then he died well," Isabelle said with a nod and went to the stove and grabbed the pan. For a moment, I got the idea she was going to hit me upside the head with it. But instead she dumped the remaining piece of ham onto my plate.

"Eat or we late," she said and turned to Edita. "*Garbi zite.*"

Edita got up from her seat and, with her teddy bear in tow, danced her way to the bathroom.

"Where are you going?" I asked.

"We going," Isabelle said as she cleared the table.

"We?"

"*Ba,* five minute," Isabelle said as she dried her hands on a towel and followed after her daughter.

18

HAMAZORTZI

The inside of Urepel's church looked larger in the daylight. The smell was larger too. Incense and perfume mixed with sweat and wood polish. Saints, hidden the night before, now filled the stained-glass windows that lined the walls and circled the altar. All the saints had swords and shields and lambs at their feet, and were reaching, kneeling, and praying as they looked to Jesus on the cross.

I pushed up against the second-floor banister. Women and children were in the pews below—my aunt and cousin among them. They sat in the fourth row. The only people I knew in the church, and, yet, I didn't know them at all. The cousin who was both young and old and spoke to me in an Euskara I didn't understand. And the aunt who held answers to my present, my past, and my future.

Isabelle had a black veil over her head that draped down onto her shoulders. Edita wore a yellow dress and was having a lively conversation with her teddy bear. I watched the two of them for a long while, thinking they might look up at me, to check on how I was. But they never did.

When Isabelle had informed me we were going to church, I asked her why?

"It Sunday," Isabelle said as we exited Gorrienea. She took Edita's hand and cut across the grass to the dirt road I'd taken the night before.

"Really?" I ran through the itinerary in my head. Number eight was arrive at Urepel—Friday, June 3. But that was before I lost a day traveling in Spain. It didn't seem possible that I had been in Arizona just four days ago. Or no, it was actually three. I lost another day somewhere over the ocean.

At the rate I was going, I would lose a month by the end of the week. Which didn't make any sense, but I still believed it possible.

Men in black coats with berets in hand filed up the church's stairs. They lined the banister on either side of me. At first, the men seemed to be copies of each other: pale skin, hooked noses, and wild eyebrows. But then I saw that they were of varying heights, weights, and ages; and that the younger men weren't wearing coats, just white, long-sleeved shirts. As the men shot glances in my direction, I noticed that some of the faces were rounder than others, some of the noses not as hooked.

Then I saw him, leaning over the third-floor balcony, looking down at me. And even though I'd only had a glimpse of his hulking shape the night before, I knew him. His dark eyes were like muddy pools of water—thoughts concealed beneath the surface; his head, a blocky square, sank into rounded shoulders whose muscles strained against the fabric of his black coat as his meaty hands gripped the banister. And even though he wasn't noticeably taller than the other men in the church, he loomed larger.

There was a look of disgust on his face, as if the whole world smelled bad, and I smelled worst of all. But why? I did not even know his name. Did he know mine? And why was I here? Isabelle had not said anything about who he was. But I guessed. There was a hint of him in the slope of Edita's shoulders.

Unable to match the hulking man's gaze, I looked away. And that was when I noticed the boy beside him. The same rounded shoulders strained against his white shirt. A patchy beard struggled to take hold on his face. The hulking man's son? And if the hulking man was Edita's father, was this boy Isabelle's?

Unanswered questions soured my stomach. I needed a way to understand who these people were. But how could I? In a normal world, my family would have been the ones to help me. But normal was gone, and what I had of family abandoned me the moment we entered the church.

"*Emaztekiak eta haurrak bakarrik,*" Isabelle had said as she stopped me inside the church's door. And while I understood what she was saying to me, "Women and children only," I wondered at her speaking Euskara. After last night, that was a risky way to talk to a guy who spoke "very bad Basque."

Maybe she didn't want anyone to know I was a foreigner? Maybe she was embarrassed by my not speaking the language of my family?

"*Gizonak,*" Isabelle said and pointed to the stairs. Men.

Then she led Edita into the church and left me to find my way up the staircase to the men waiting for me above.

My attention moved from the hulking man and his son back to the women and children below. The pews were nearly full now. I guessed it was pretty much the entire population of Urepel. I spotted the old woman from the night before. She was on her knees praying with the same brown shawl over her shoulders. Isabelle was in the pew in front of the old woman; she too on her knees, working a rosary through her hands while Edita was slumped to the side, having fallen asleep.

The men standing on either side of me struck up a conversation in Basque. They talked over me as if I were a fence post. At first, I couldn't make sense out of what they were saying. But then I heard a word that I knew: *ardiak*—sheep.

I listened more closely.

"*Aurten goizik mostudu ardien ilea joiteko Pariseat Udaberrean.*"

I still couldn't understand everything. But I began to recognize phrases.

"*Ilean preciua goititu da lenahgu baino?*"

"*Galdut prezeoin erdia.*"

It seemed that the guy on my left had wanted to take a spring vacation in Paris, so he chose to shear his sheep early—before wool prices rose. He had sold his wool for half of what he could have gotten for it now and was complaining to the guy on my right about his bad choice. I smiled and thought what Aitatxi always said. And then I repeated it aloud, "*Ez arnoa bizidunik, ez andre bizardunik.*"

The two men went silent and looked at me as if I were a ghost that had suddenly materialized. My face reddened. I wanted to explain what I meant by saying: *Two things to avoid: sparkling wine and bearded women.* To tell them the phrase was what my aitatxi had said whenever a bad choice led to a bad result. "Sure, no," Aitatxi said, "you drink a much the sparkling wine, sometime you get the bearded woman." But while I could repeat a saying in Euskara, there was no way I could explain it in the language.

Luckily, the priest took that moment to enter. And the men's attention turned from me. All the women and children below stood up as the priest walked down the center aisle.

The Urepel priest looked a lot like Father Bill back home. Only I was pretty sure Father Bill didn't speak French like this priest did when he gave his blessing from the altar. And while I couldn't understand what was being said, the movements of the Mass were the same as back home. Just my knowing when to stand, kneel, and sit relaxed me.

During the homily, when a girl in the front row flipped her brown hair over her shoulder so that it brushed the top of the pew behind her, I thought of Jenny. She flipped her hair every Sunday. In summer, she wore sleeveless dresses with floral prints—daisies and roses spilling over the fabric. In winter, it was lacy sweaters that couldn't have offered any real warmth but looked soft to the touch. During Mass, she would flip her hair over her shoulder and turn and flash me a smile. And her smile would make me smile. On the occasions when she wasn't at church, I felt unsettled—like I did now. The Mass incomplete without her presence. Then, as I was wishing Jenny was here to flip her hair, a girl stole into church.

She had a red shawl over her head. I watched as she went to the middle row of pews. There, the women opened a space for her. And the girl slipped in as we knelt for the Eucharistic prayer. The priest blessed the wine as she slid off her shawl to reveal wheat-colored hair. The woman next to the girl leaned over and whispered something to her. The girl turned and looked up at me. And when I saw how her chin narrowed to a point like mine and how her green eyes caught the light, I almost called out to her—because I knew her. I had seen her in a photograph. Not the black-and-white photo I brought to Urepel. But another. In color. Only it couldn't be. Because the girl in the photograph—who is forever leaning out a pickup truck, waving, hair flying, green eyes flashing—that girl was dead.

I watched as this girl's eyes moved past me to the hulking man's son. He was watching her as well. And when their eyes met, she dropped her head as if caught doing something she wasn't supposed to and quickly turned back to the priest. That was when I noticed that everyone was standing while I was still on my knees. I scrambled to my feet as the collection plate was passed from man to man, each dropping a few coins onto it. When it got to me, I realized my pockets were empty. My money left with my backpack at the house. All the men along the banister were looking at me, and I wasn't exactly sure what to do. I tried to hand the plate to the guy next to me, but he wouldn't take it. Then the man who had made the bad shearing choice slipped a coin into my hand. I dropped the coin onto the plate. The men nodded their approval. It was time for Communion.

As the men moved toward the stairwell, I was carried along. They poured onto the wooden steps that creaked beneath their boots. At the bottom, the men pooled at the back of the church and waited as the women rose, pew by pew, to flow into the center aisle and up to the altar. There, the women fanned out seven wide. I watched as the first seven dropped to their knees and the priest began a steady stream of "*Le corps du Christ,*" followed by each woman's "Amen." Knees cracked, rosary beads clinked, feet shuffled. The next seven women knelt. Isabelle, Edita, the girl I knew but had never met—they all received the Eucharist. And when the last woman had said "Amen," the men surged forward.

Again I was carried along. But as the altar got closer, something stiffened inside me and caused me to brace my feet against the tide. I felt a surge of panic. I didn't belong here—I wasn't part of this Communion. I tried to back away from the altar. But the wave of black coats behind me was solid. My feet slipped on the floor's tiles. I lost my balance. Fell forward onto my knees. The priest stood over me, lowering the Eucharist to my lips: "*Le corps du Christ.*" Instinctively, I said, "Amen" and closed my eyes and opened my mouth and tasted the salt of the wafer as it was placed on my tongue.

After Mass, I tried to find the girl in the swirl of people exiting the church. But she wasn't there. Outside, I saw her cutting across an open field, her red shawl flying behind her like the tail of a kite caught in the breeze. Green pastures rolled up the hills and into a line of trees above which hung a layer of haze from the previous night's rain. Sheep dotted the grass between whitewashed houses with their Arizona-like red-tiled roofs.

I started to go after the girl when Isabelle grabbed hold of my arm.

"We need go," Isabelle said.

"Who is that girl?" I pointed.

"She your cousin," Isabelle said.

"My cousin?"

"From your mother's family," Isabelle said.

"My mom has family here?"

"*Ba,* everyone have family," Isabelle said. "Come, it time for visit the dead."

19

HEMERETZI

When I was thirteen, I stole the picture of my mother that Dad kept in the top drawer of his dresser. In it, Mom is only a little older than I am now. I was only two when both she and the photo were taken. She leans out a pickup truck and waves her hand. Her blonde hair flies like she is racing forward. But the truck's door is open and she is stepping out, so it must be the wind. I wish I had told her to stop, to get back into the truck where she would be safe. But the only words I knew at that time were "Mama" and "Dada." My mother's face is turned to the side, something catching her green eyes. Does she see the car coming? Or is it me, lying there in the grass where my father placed me while he took the photo. Whatever she sees is changing her expression. It is taking away her smile. The camera clicks at the moment between now and then.

My mother is buried at Saint Anne's Catholic Cemetery in downtown Phoenix. There are two angels on her headstone, which reads, *Helena Etcheberri 1935–1962 Loving Mother and Wife.* My father is buried next to her. There are no angels on his headstone, which reads, *Ferdinand Jean Etcheberri 1933–1980 Loving Father.* Amatxi and Aitatxi are a short ways off: *Dominica Etcheberri 1895–1963* and *Mathieu Etcheberri 1892–1973.* Oxea, whose headstone says *Martin Etcheberri,* is buried next to his wife, Pascaline, in Denver, Colorado. The rest of my relatives, I discover, are buried in the little cemetery next to the church in Urepel.

As we walked around the side of the church, I was thinking about the girl who was my cousin. It was strange to keep having people I didn't know existed popping into my life. How many more were there? Did I have other cousins, aunts, and uncles that no one had bothered to tell me about?

Edita took my hand and led me into the cemetery where the air smelled of wet stone. There seemed to be even more crosses than I remembered from the night before. At first, they made the cemetery appear crowded, as if there was no more room for anyone else in Urepel to die. But then I noticed it wasn't the cemetery that was crowded, but the graves themselves. Beside flowers, there were plaques and pictures covering every inch of space on and around the headstones.

Edita weaved us between the graves, stopping at a group nestled up against the church's outer wall.

"This your family." Isabelle used a handkerchief to wipe moisture from the headstone of Henri Etcheberri. "He your Aitatxi's brother. He fall from cliff when saving lamb."

Isabelle moved to the next headstone as Edita gathered wild flowers and laid one on each grave.

"This his *aita*—Ferdinand," she said. "He have the pneumonia but still go for work in field. They find him holding handle of plough."

Next headstone.

"Your great aunt, Beatrice. She make the dinner for whole family before she lie down for last time."

It went on this way as Isabelle moved from headstone to headstone and informed me of how all my ancestors died in some sort of creepy family history. When she was done, Isabelle put her hands on her hips and smiled.

"*Ba*, you see," she said. "Like your father, they all die well."

"What's that supposed to mean?"

This earned me one of her smiles. Only this time I wasn't aware of what I had said to deserve it.

"*Odo bizitzea gogorra da, ondo hiltzea gogorrago*," Isabelle said.

"I don't know what that means."

"Living well hard," Isabelle said, "dying well harder."

That sounded like something Aitatxi would have said. And if he had said it, I would have told him it didn't make sense. Who cared how you died? You were dead. So it really didn't matter how you got that way. But I didn't feel like arguing with my newly found aunt, so instead I turned to the only headstone she had not commented on.

Joseph Etcheberri was born in 1928 and died in 1950. The top right corners of his gray headstone had broken off; a crack ran down the face of the stone; green algae worked its way to the base and an oval frame holding what I assumed was a black-and-white photo of Joseph. It was up against the headstone, as if someone had just placed it there—temporarily. The photo looked like it might have been taken the day before, and not thirty years earlier.

Joseph seems to be seated in the photo, though I couldn't tell that for certain as only his face and shoulders are visible. Still, there is something about the image that looks staged, a studio shot, and I imagined him sitting for it. His black jacket is open and his white collared shirt spread wide. There is a bit of James Dean in his look—young and confident. Joseph's dark hair has the same wave in it I have in mine. He appears to have tried to tame it with a brush. But like me, didn't quite succeed. He is not smiling in the photo. And it is hard to tell what he is thinking, if anything. He seems to be merely waiting to be told what to do. Maybe to smile. If so, he never was, or else the picture was snapped too soon, before his smile came.

I did the math. When he died, Joseph was only two years older than me.

"How did he die?" I asked Isabelle as a stiff breeze pressed her dress to her body.

"Joseph go for America," she said, and then turned to Edita. "*Zikinzten aituzu zure eskiak.*"

"Did he die there?"

"*Ba,*" Isabelle said, and began using her handkerchief to clean Edita's hands.

"What happened?"

"He alone." Isabelle straightened the collar of her daughter's dress.

"Did he die well?" I asked.

"No," Isabelle said. "He do not."

And with that, she took Edita by the hand and began retracing our steps to the cemetery's gate.

As I followed Isabelle and Edita, we passed a group of women gathered at the far end of the cemetery. I recognized them from church. Some had been sitting with the girl who was my cousin.

"Where are my mother's parents buried?"

"Her family there," Isabelle said, waving a hand in the direction of the women.

"And that girl from church, how was she related to my mother?"

"She daughter of mother's cousin."

"What is her name?"

"Maria Mendia." Isabelle stopped and kneeled to retie the laces of Edita's left shoe.

"Are any of those women my cousins as well?"

"Some yes, some no."

"Maybe I should introduce myself to them," I said.

"*They* know you." Isabelle got to her feet. "Come, we go for bar now."

"But it's only eight in the morning."

"We late."

20

HOGEI

Urepel's bar turned out to be located in the large white building I'd seen the night before. As soon as I entered through the double red doors, I thought of my high school gym back home. Most of the space was open, and there were folding bleachers along the far wall. A bar made up of a table, some chairs, and lots of liquor and wine occupied a corner.

Basque music was playing from a portable radio that sat on a folding chair. And even though I couldn't understand what was being sung, I knew the rhythm of the words. Edita broke free of Isabelle to dance to the music. I watched as she spun round and round, clutching her teddy bear to her chest, while Isabelle got some *arno gorria* and handed me a glass of the red wine.

"*Zure ozarria,*" she said, clinking her glass with mine. To your health.

More people entered the building. I recognized most of them from church, which gave me an odd sense of knowing these people without knowing them at all. The two men who had been on either side of me at Mass nodded a "hello" as they walked by.

"Did you know who I was right away?" I asked Isabelle.

"*Ez,* but then picture . . . and I know friends who been America. They tell about you."

"Me? What did they say?"

"You got mother's eyes—father's nose."

"Then why did you—"

"*Nola zira,* Isabelle?" A little man with a cherry-red nose swept off his beret and gave her a kiss on each of her cheeks. How are you?

"*Ontxa,*" Isabelle said. Fine.

"This the American king?" the little man asked, looking at me.

"You mean kin, Jacques," Isabelle said. "And yes, this Mathieu Etcheberri."

"*Oui,* I tell you, I Jacques Igorri," the little man said, and threw his arms around me, and gave me a kiss on each cheek.

"He your fifth cousin from father's family," Isabelle said.

"*Oui,* I tell you, good a Etcheberri in Urepel once more," Jacques said in a heavy French accent. "Sorry, my English no so good."

"That's okay," I said. "*Ene Euskara ez da hain huna ere.*"

Jacques seemed to get a big kick out of my saying my Basque wasn't very good either and waved over some people who also turned out to be related to me. For the next hour, I met second, third, fourth, fifth, and "unspeci-fied" cousins. None of them really spoke English, so our conversations were mostly composed of nodding, with the few Basque phrases I knew thrown in. My "newly found" cousins all nodded approvingly when I spoke Euskara—though I think there was also a bit of chuckling at both my choice of words and pronunciation. I didn't care. A few days ago I'd had no family. Now I had more than I could count. The only thing that seemed strange was that every relative I met was from my father's side of the family.

"Where are all my mother's relatives?" I finally asked Isabelle.

"They here," she said.

"Can I meet some of them?"

Isabelle gave me her smile and said, "They want meet you, they will come."

I was going to ask her to point out some of my mom's relatives to me when a couple of men started yelling at each other in really bad English. In fact, I wasn't even sure it was English until one of the men yelled, "Pig, pig, pig!" And the other yelled back, "Mine, mine, mine!" Even after I realized they were using a language I actually spoke, I had a hard time figuring out what they were fighting about. I knew it involved a pig, ownership of the pig, a bet, and some kind of stone that somebody was either carrying or throwing, or as one of the men said, "progressing over ground."

"Why are they trying to speak English?" I asked Isabelle.

"So they understand what other say," she said.

"I don't even understand them," I said. "Why don't they argue in Euskara?"

"That worse," Isabelle said.

"I don't see how."

"*Ba,* that man, he wear his beret high on head—he from Biscaya."

"So?"

"That man, he from Zuberoa," Isabelle said and gave a nod of her head as if that explained everything.

"I don't understand."

Isabelle sighed as if my lack of intelligence was a huge disappointment to her.

"The Biscayan, he from Spain—no speak French. The Zuberoan, he from France—no speak Spanish."

"Don't they both speak Euskara?"

"*Ba,* but no speak same Euskara."

"There is more than one Euskara?"

"My brother he teach you nothing?" Isabelle said. "*Euskal Herria zazpiak bat*—seven provinces they one. Four in Spain—three in France. Because of that thing, they many ways for speak Euskara."

The two men had somehow come to an agreement and with arms around each other's shoulders were now sharing a bottle of wine.

Isabelle got that smile of hers—for once not aimed at me—as she said, "*Hitz berak, hitz ezberdinak*—the same word, they different word, so we no can understand each other. It make each have small world. Good thing we have wine."

And with that, Isabelle went and got us each a third glass of *arno gorria.* I met more relatives from my father's side of the family and danced with Edita for a bit. Then Isabelle said it was time to go home to make the noon-time meal. And that was when Maria Mendia walked into the building.

"I think I'll stay for a while," I said.

"We eat one hour," Isabelle said and held her index finger in the air to make clear the point.

"Got it," I said.

"*Bat*—one."

"I'll be there."

Isabelle led Edita toward the door. When she passed by Maria, neither of them exchanged a glance.

The room was getting warm and my head was a bit fuzzy as Maria slid through the people toward me. I got the sense that she was going to walk right up and kiss me on both my cheeks. But then, a few feet before she reached me, she veered off and joined the group of women I'd seen in the cemetery.

I stood watching Maria for a while, drinking my wine, thinking about my mother. Dad told me she had lived in Urepel until she came to America. She was sixteen when she met my father in Arizona. Two years later, they were married.

And now I was here. Among people who had known my mother. But no one was talking about her. It was almost as if she never existed. And maybe it was because I wasn't used to drinking wine, at least not that early in the day. Or maybe it was because I felt like ever since I'd arrived in Urepel I'd been carried along like a leaf in a stream. For whatever reason, I decided that if my mother's relatives weren't going to come to me, then I would go to them. So I set my glass of wine down and went over to the group of women.

The women facing me fell silent—smiles fading as I walked up. Those with their backs to me, which included Maria, turned to see why.

"I am Mathieu Etcheberri, your cousin."

None of the women said anything.

I looked to Maria.

"You are Maria Mendia," I said. "I think we are second cousins."

Maria's face flushed. She glanced from side to side, looking for escape, like a sheep cornered by a coyote.

"Did I do something—"

A bump on my shoulder cut my sentence short. I looked around to see the hulking man's son standing there.

"*Pilota*," he said.

"What?"

He pointed toward the door.

"*Pilota*," he said again.

"Go away," I said and turned back to find that Maria and all the women had fled.

Jacques walked over.

"*Oui,* I tell you, Jean here, he want to do a game with you." The little man raised his glass of wine to me. "Jean he ruthless."

I was embarrassed and angry at the women and Maria and this Jean. What had I done wrong? Why wouldn't they even talk to me?

"*Pilota, Americano,*" Jean said and pushed his index finger into my chest. I knocked his hand away and said, "Fine—*pilota.*"

Jean nodded and headed toward the door. I followed—along with just about everyone else in the building. Outside, we walked around to where the court was. Only it wasn't like the handball court from home. On the ranch, my court was the barn wall and the hard-packed dirt marked with scratched-out lines. Here, the court had two walls and a slab of cement with painted white lines. The first wall was the side of the building we'd come out of. The second wall was connected to the first to form a corner.

This new arrangement confused me. A second wall added so many more angles. And then there was the cement: the ball's bounce would be higher than on dirt. For a moment, I thought of pulling out, explaining that I had to go to my aunt's for lunch. But Jean had already pulled off the white dress shirt he wore to church, and everyone from inside had lined up around the court to watch.

In his undershirt, Jean took his place on the court and tossed me the ball. He leaned forward with his hands on his knees like a lineman. And then he smiled at me kind of goofy like, how a kid would smile. And the way he had his hair cut short and the way his hands were all palms and the way his muscles knotted up around his neck turned him into Oxea from the picture of his wedding day. A big kid who didn't know what the hell he was getting himself into.

I bounced the ball in my hand. If Jean was like Oxea, he would be more strong than fast. And in *pilota,* speed was what counted. I smiled back at my opponent, tossed him the ball, and nodded for him to begin.

When Jacques had said Jean was "ruthless," I thought he had just used the wrong word. I soon found out that his "bad English" got it exactly right. And, unfortunately for me, speed in *pilota* also related to the ball. The velocity at which the first shot came caused me to stumble as I ducked to avoid being hit in the head by the ball.

"*Bat eta deus ez,*" Jacques announced. One to nothing.

The next point, the ball hit off both walls. And while I was able to react to it, the ball's bounce off the cement was higher than I expected. My hand slashed through empty air. People clapped and whooped.

"*Bi eta deus ez,*" Jacques said. Two to nothing.

On the third point, I finally made contact with the ball. But Jean was right on top of my shot and sent it back even faster. I was forced to dive for the ball and landed hard on the pavement. My right elbow scraped over the cement. There was scattered laugher, whistling, and yells of "Jean."

Jacques stepped forward to help me to my feet.

"*Oui,* I tell you ruthless," Jacques said. "Champion whole province."

"Great," I said, breathing hard. A dizzying heat filled my head. Blood dripped from the cut on my elbow.

I got back into position and focused on my opponent, who winked at me as I tried to catch my breath. So much for him being slow. He flipped the ball from hand to hand, casually resting his weight on one leg as he looked over at Maria and threw her a smile. It had no effect. Maria's face remained expressionless, as if she, Jean, and the game and the crowd around her weren't there, as if she were standing alone on a grassy hill, waiting for something to arrive that would give her a reason to smile.

That was when I knew I still had a chance. Not at winning. That was not going to happen. Not here. Not today. This was Jean's home court. And, for now, I was overmatched. I wiped the sweat from my eyes and flicked it onto the cement; it landed at Jean's feet. The only chance I had was to surprise my opponent—to do the unexpected. To embarrass Jean the way he was embarrassing me. And maybe, at the same time, to give Maria a reason to smile.

There was nothing complicated about my plan. I was simply going to wait for one of Jean's shots to drive me behind him. Then, instead of aiming for either of the *pilota* walls, my target would be the back of Jean's head. I imagined the feel of the ball making contact with my palm, sinking into my skin, pain racing up my forearm, the ball jumping from my hand to strike Jean's skull before flying off into the laughing crowd.

I nodded. I was ready.

Jean started the point. Keeping my steps small, I moved to the ball. Jean stayed right beside me. I tried to guide the ball, aiming low on the wall in an effort to force him forward. And when the ball did bounce short, Jean sprinted up and struck it with a heavy blow. The ball rocketed out of the corner to sail deep into the court. I raced after it. This was my chance. But then, as I went to hit the shot, I made a fatal mistake—I lunged.

My whipping arm nearly missed the ball completely; only my pinkie finger caught any part of it. So instead of a glorious shot to the back of Jean's head, the ball dribbled over the cement towards his heels. At the sight of my final failure, I let out a scream of rage that caused Jean to turn to look at me and not at the ball at his feet. When Jean stepped on the ball, his arms pinwheeled as his legs flew out from under him. For a moment, he seemed to float in the air like a weightless leaf; then he came crashing down to strike the court's cement with a solid thud.

Jean's fall was greeted by stunned silence. Then Jacques began to laugh and his laughter caught on. Soon the whole crowd was whooping and hollering. Jean scowled at me from where he lay sprawled out on the cement. I winked at him as I looked over to Maria and shot her a smile. She smiled back. And her smiling made this foreign town feel not so foreign. And I was glad I'd come. Glad I'd found these unknown family members. At least until my stomach knotted with pain and I doubled over and threw up a sickening mixture of red wine, eggs, and ham. Chucking my guts out in front of the entire population of Urepel put an end to the *pilota* match.

Jean shook his head in disgust as he got to his feet. He kicked the ball off the court and walked away. Jacques retrieved the ball.

"*Oui,* I tell you wine and *pilota* no so good together," Jacques said, and placed the ball in my hand. Then he led me off the court as some of the women threw buckets of water onto the cement to clean up the mess I'd made.

"I see later," Jacques said, and left me with a slap on the back that didn't help settle my stomach.

Humiliated, I slipped around the corner of the building and started toward Gorrienea. I just wanted to slink away unseen, but when I passed the building's door, I heard the two men who had been arguing earlier again attempting to converse in English.

"Why that Etcheberri boy here?" I heard the man from Biscaya ask.

I paused and listened. Now that the men had calmed down, their English was much more understandable.

"He come for home," the man from Zuberoa answered.

"Marcelino let him have?"

"No—never."

21

HOGEITA BAT

Aitatxi told me that he built the ranch house in 1932.

"Sure, no," he said. "I build up with own hand."

We were in the barn making the frame for a go-kart like the one Rich Clausen had. Rich got his go-kart from K-mart, already assembled. And his go-kart was made of steel, not wood, and had an engine that went over twenty miles an hour. To get my go-kart going, I'd have to push it up the hill behind the barn and let gravity supply the momentum for the bumpy ride down. And although my go-kart was not nearly as cool as Rich's, I wanted it, and so was willing to listen to whatever Aitatxi went on about.

Aitatxi and Amatxi arrived in America in 1931, two years after the stock market crash. I don't know why my grandparents left France to come to a country in the middle of the Great Depression. Or what the two-week ship voyage over was like: What did they eat? Where did they sleep? I could have asked Aitatxi how he felt when he first spotted the Statue of Liberty. Or what he saw on the train ride from New York to Arizona. But I didn't think to. And even if I had, I wouldn't have wanted to ask. I was eleven. And the only thing I wanted was for Aitatxi to finish my go-kart so I could be racing down the slope, wind in my face, barely in control. I didn't know that there would be other things I'd want later. My eleven-year-old world was made of right now. "Later" was a term that adults used to keep me from getting what I wanted in the present. And so I was unaware that something that happened before I existed could last longer than the go-kart I would later crash into the base of the pasture's oak tree.

Aitatxi removed the rubber tires from an old lawnmower and put them on the frame as he was going on about a cousin who'd run sheep down in

Tucson. This cousin let Aitatxi borrow some sheep to get his own flock started.

"I get land, no one they want," Aitatxi said. "Sure, no, peoples, they think land, it no good because it no flat and look like it no have water. Think I stupid man with my sheeps."

"I want it to go fast," I said as Aitatxi searched through a pile of tractor parts for something he could use for a steering wheel.

"*Baina* I dig well," Aitatxi said. "Find *urepel*—warm water just like home. And sheeps, they no care land no flat. They like climb. Make wool for shirt and pant—peoples they no like being naked all time."

Then Aitatxi talked about how he had to build an extra room on the house when Dad was born.

"Sure, no, he a bit of surprise."

"How come it's taking you so long?" I asked.

"I build right, for you," Aitatxi said.

"Does it have to take forever?"

"When I build house," Aitatxi said. "It take me ten month."

"You should have just bought a house that was already built."

"If I do that, it no be my home." Aitatxi pointed to the go-kart. I climbed inside. "How it is?"

"I can't straighten my legs," I said. "And the seat's all hard."

I got out, and Aitatxi used a pair of pliers to loosen a bolt and remove the seat. Then he wrapped it in a towel and used duct tape to cover the seat before repositioning it for more legroom. I climbed back inside.

"Steering wheel's too low."

Aitatxi adjusted the height.

I stretched out my legs, gripped the steering wheel, and bounced on the seat.

"Cool," I said.

"Sure, no," Aitatxi said as he oiled the go-kart's axle. "That because I make for you. You no can buy house is like that."

But I was no longer listening—already pushing the go-kart out of the barn, having gotten what I wanted.

As I walked up the slope toward Gorrienea, blood dripping from my elbow, I wondered if I would get what I wanted again. And if I did, would it be like with the go-kart—the thing I wanted ending up in broken pieces scattered over the dirt?

I told myself this was different. I was no longer a kid wanting something just because my friend had it. This time what I wanted was already mine. Artzainaskena belonged to me. But would Isabelle see it that way? The words of the two men I'd overheard talking quickened my pace. If they knew I'd come for the ranch, then Isabelle must know as well.

The house's green shutters were thrown open. The cow from the night before again stood with its head sticking out the ground-floor window. I walked inside and took the stairs two at a time. When I stepped onto the second floor, I again found Edita dancing in front of the fire.

"You late," Isabelle said as she chopped onions on a board.

And when I turned to answer her, I saw the hulking man sitting at the head of the kitchen table drinking red wine.

"This Marcelino—my husband." Isabelle dumped the chopped onions into a frying pan.

Marcelino looked at me and said nothing.

"*Errazzu 'egun hun,' mutikoa,*" Isabelle said to Marcelino. Say hello to the boy.

Marcelino let out a grunt and turned to watch Edita dancing.

"He not speak the English," she said to me.

The fact that Isabelle said her husband didn't speak English was strange. I remembered his words from the night before. "You just boy. Nothing but boy." She must know he spoke English. But then why was she lying? To spare my feelings? Make up an excuse as to why the man wouldn't talk to me?

"You bleeding on my floor." Isabelle walked over with a towel. She cupped it to my elbow and led me to the bathroom. Once inside, away from the presence of Marcelino, I found my voice.

"I know about the house," I said.

"*Ba,* we talk later," Isabelle said in a whisper as she used hot water to clean out the wound.

"We talk now," I said.

"It not the right time," she said as she dried my elbow and wrapped gauze around my arm.

"I'm not going to let you take—"

Isabelle pressed her hand over my mouth. The remnants of the onion on her hand burned in my nose.

"Marcelino he hear you, it no be good."

She removed her hand from my mouth.

"I thought he didn't speak English," I said in a hushed voice, the taste of onions on my lips.

"You no have speak language for know what said," she whispered back. "Wash face. It time we eat."

And with that Isabelle left, closing the bathroom door behind her.

As I ran cool water over my hands, I wondered how much Isabelle knew. Did she know Marcelino spoke English? That he would understand what I was saying? And if so, what did it matter? Why would it "no be good" if he heard? If those men in the bar knew why I was here, then Marcelino must also know. That still didn't explain his hostility toward me. After all these years, why would he even care about a house thousands of miles away in another country? And even if he did, what could he do to me? And then I remembered the men on the bus, the gun pressing between my shoulder blades. And what the men in the bar said: *Marcelino let him have? No— never.* This was not my country. I did not understand its people. Or know what they were capable of.

A crack ran through the bathroom mirror's cloudy surface. I splashed water on my face and watched as it dripped off my pointed chin.

"*Nola ziste?*" I heard Jacques's voice say through the closed bathroom door. How are all of you?

When I stepped out, Jacques had a foot up on the seat of a chair, a glass of wine in his hand, and his beret tilted back on his head.

"Ah, here the great player his-self," Jacques said.

"I threw up on the court," I reminded him.

"*Oui,*" Jacques said, "but you do like champion."

"We eat now," Isabelle said as she set dishes of steaming vegetables and meats onto the table where Marcelino still sat. "Edita, *txauri jarzite.*"

I was facing the kitchen with my back to the fireplace and so was not surprised when Edita danced past me. But my face reddened with anger and humiliation when I saw that her trailing hand was interlocked with that of my *pilota* opponent.

Jean must have arrived while I was in the bathroom. Edita now escorted him to the table. Without a look in my direction, Jean took a seat next to his father. Edita sat on the other side of Marcelino, who placed his meaty hand gently over hers and gave what, for him, passed as a smile.

I went to the opposite end of the table in order to sit as far away from Marcelino as possible. Jacques sat between Jean and me. Then, after she had loaded the table with food, Isabelle took the seat to my right.

Jacques led us in a quick prayer, said in French, and then the business of eating got under way. Eating was something my family always did well. Back home, the first time I had supper over at Rich's house, I was shocked when there were only three dishes on the table: rice, salad, and meat. Even if it was only Dad and me sitting down for a meal, there would be at least six dishes. Not including the sourdough bread and cheese we always had for dessert.

In Gorrienea, there were dishes of steaming potatoes and white beans with chunks of ham, slabs of roasted lamb and links of blood sausage, chicken legs dripping with lemon and salad dripping with oil. The smells formed a comforting fog over the table, with the ever-present scent of garlic binding the meal together. Other dishes were passed my way, foods I'd never seen before. Not wanting to be rude, I took some of each of those as well.

I started off eating slowly, with the dishes I knew. I didn't want a repeat of what had happened on the *pilota* court. But as the familiar flavors filled my mouth, my hunger returned. The roasted lamb tasted of Easter dinner; the lemon chicken of a Saturday brunch eaten under the oak tree in the pasture; the sourdough bread a late-night snack on the porch with my father. I shoveled food into my mouth as if I could eat my way back to Arizona.

As I grew bolder, I tried the new dishes. The only thing I refused was the *arno gorria* that Jacques offered me. The mere smell of the red wine brought a momentary pause to my eating. I turned my empty wine glass upside down and waved the bottle away.

I was not alone in my eating. Everyone at the table seemed focused on what lay on their plates. Though Marcelino and Jean did take time between bites to throw glares in my direction.

Even though their dislike for me was obvious, I couldn't keep from watching the two of them. There was something about the silence between the father and son that was reminiscent of Dad and me. They hadn't spoken a single word to each other. And while it was true that Dad and I often spent whole days in silence, theirs was a different kind of silence. Our silence spoke of familiarity and comfort. There was nothing comfortable about this silence. Jean leaned away from his father, almost turning his back to him as he huddled over his food, as if he expected at any moment for Marcelino to try and take it from him. For his part, Marcelino never once looked in his son's direction.

The tension between father and son was made more obvious because of the interaction between father and daughter. Marcelino rested his right elbow on the table as he watched Edita give pretend bites of salad to her teddy bear. Occasionally, he would run a hand over his daughter's head—fingers playing through Edita's gray-streaked hair. When she dropped her teddy bear to the floor, Marcelino retrieved it, gave the bear a quick kiss, and then tucked it back into her arms.

With mouths full, no one could really talk—no one that is but Jacques. He carried on a running dialogue in a mixture of French and Basque, with a little English thrown in for my benefit. With his mouth full of lamb, he teased Isabelle about "how all Basque woman marry ugly men so they no leave them." While drinking wine he complimented her on being the "only Basque woman with brains I ever meet."

For her part, Isabelle treated both his teasing and compliments in the same way. She neither laughed nor frowned. And occasionally shot back a comment.

"*Oui,* I tell you, Isabelle, you open restaurant," Jacques said. "You be infamous."

Isabelle gave me a smile at the misused word.

"That just like man," she said, "always keep woman in kitchen."

"*Oui,* just like woman to no see what good at."

"And man no know what woman good at."

"*Oui,* I tell you, Isabelle, talk with you like dance with bear. I no watch out, I get me-self bit."

That got a crackle of laughter out of Isabelle.

"If I a bear I bite someone with more meat on bones."

"*Oui*, Mathieu, you see, the women of Urepel always have something say."

"Not Maria Mendia," I said.

And for the first time during the meal, Jacques was silent.

I turned to Isabelle and asked, "Did I do something to offend her?"

"You Etcheberri," she said. "That offense enough."

"I don't understand."

I looked over at Jacques, but he had his head down, having decided that now was a good time to give his full attention to the food on his plate.

"Why is being an Etcheberri a bad thing?"

Across the table from Jacques, Isabelle set her knife and fork down with a clank.

"Being Etcheberri no bad thing," Isabelle said. "Unless you Mendia."

"But why is that?" I asked.

"Because of past."

"What past?" I said.

Isabelle waved a hand in the air—as if she were shooing away a fly.

"Tell me," I said. "They are my family too."

"*Oui*, I tell you, he make good point about—"

"Jacques!" Isabelle said.

"I shut the up now," Jacques said.

"Please," I said. "No more secrets."

Isabelle closed her eyes and sighed.

"Helena Mendia ride bike down hill from house each day—wind in her hair, laughing. I wave from kitchen window."

"My mom?"

Isabelle nodded with a gentle smile, and I noticed that everyone at the table had stopped their eating.

"*Ba*, two year before your mother go for America Theresa Corretegia, she go and come back with two hundred dollar and fur coat. She wear coat at church each Sunday for one year. Then priest's dog, he get hold of coat and bury in the woods. Theresa, she cry. The rest of us, we bless dog. Then Mendias they want send Helena for America and see what she come back with."

"But she didn't come back," I said.

"Her parents know your *aitatxi* and *amatxi* from when they live in Urepel. They write ask for Helena come visit. Only after, when Helena gone, Mendias find box with letters under bed. From my brother—your *aita*."

"What?"

"They letters of love," Isabelle said.

"But Dad told me he didn't know my Mom until she came to America."

"She know him," Isabelle said. "Helena no come back. Mendias say Etcheberris take daughter. Helena only child. When parents pass, Mendias lose family home."

"What do you mean, 'lose'?"

"The house Helena's," Isabelle said. "Only she no here for take."

"But aren't there other Mendias?" I asked. "Why didn't one of them take the house?"

"They no can take what no theirs," Isabelle said.

"So what happened to it?"

"No one pay taxes, government take—they never have problem taking from us Basques. After few year, house tore down. Now only green hill."

"But that was thirty years ago," I said. "The Mendias can't still be mad about—"

"Your *aitatxi,* he born in Gorrienea."

"Uh, okay, I don't—"

"His father, he make table we eat at. And his father carve wood over fireplace."

"What does—"

"In hall, they picture of each person who live in house for two hundred year," Isabelle said.

"But that—"

"Who I?" Isabelle asked.

"Is this a trick question?"

"I table, I wood, I pictures," Isabelle said. "I lose Gorrienea, I lose me."

And with that, the silent spell was broken. Isabelle's chair grated over the wooden floor as she started clearing the table. Jacques jumped to his feet to help her.

"*Oui,* I tell you, Isabelle, you should most defiantly open restaurant."

Edita went to dance in front of the fire. And Marcelino moved to a nearby armchair, lit a cigarette, and watched her. Jean watched Edita too, but only for a moment. Then he slipped from the table and without a word went down the stairs. I heard the door latch click as he left.

For my part, I remained where I was sitting, my hands resting on the table that my great-grandfather made. And while I understood the importance of family heirlooms, a table could be moved, a mantle taken down, pictures rehung. A house was only walls, a roof, and a floor. I was not the porch that Aitatxi built or the barn Dad and I raised. I was no more Artzainaskena than Isabelle was Gorrienea. Only she couldn't see that.

"*Oui*," Jacques said as he put a hand on my shoulder. "I must go to my house now. You walk some with me."

"Sure." I followed Jacques to the door.

Outside, the little man started off at a quick pace. I hurried to keep up. My cheeks tingled in the crisp air, and I thought of Edita dancing before the warm fire.

"*Oui,* I tell you, walk after meal, good thing." Jacques headed across the pasture toward the line of trees at its border. "You know, I never once hear her talk about what happen before now."

"Isabelle?" I asked.

"She no never talk about that thing."

"I don't understand why the Mendias are still mad."

"*Oui,* I no think they understand they-self no more," Jacques said. "*Etxea* always be problem for Isabelle. She have and no have—like husband."

"Marcelino?"

"*Oui,* I tell you, she good to that man even after all what he make."

"What did he make?"

"Edita," Jacques said. "And Jean."

We reached the line of trees on the far side of the pasture. They were covered in small green apples. Jacques picked a couple off a low-hanging limb. He wiped them on his shirt, bit into one, and tossed the other to me.

"Apple good with walk," Jacques said as we stood beneath the shade of the trees. "Jean, he good boy. If he no have Marcelino for father and mother still live."

"Isabelle isn't Jean's mother?"

"*Ez,* Jean mother she die many year ago."

"How?"

"Broken heart."

"You can't die from a broken heart," I said.

"*Oui*, you very young, you wait, you see," Jacques said.

"Marcelino reminds me of the Mamu," I said. "Big, hairy, and ugly."

"Marcelino he worse than Mamu," Jacques said. "He wolf."

"Is that why Marcelino doesn't live in Gorrienea?"

"He have own house—Odolenea." Jacques pointed to a house that appeared too small to contain the hulking Marcelino. The gray stone structure was no more than ten feet away from the rock wall that marked the border of Isabelle's land. I could have thrown a stone from one house to the other.

"That doesn't make any sense," I said. "Why would he have—"

"What you house name in America?" Jacques asked.

"Artzainaskena."

"*Oui*, the last shepherd," Jacques said as he started walking again. "We see."

As we continued up the hill, the apple trees gave way to other trees. Some, like pines, I recognized. Others appeared to be oaks, but I wasn't sure they really were.

"If Marcelino doesn't live with Isabelle, why are they still married?"

"Because of Gorrienea," Jacques said. "Marcelino, he think he get home one day. So he no free Isabelle. Then you come."

"What does my being here have to do with Gorrienea?"

"You Etcheberri," Jacques said. "You come, you take what for you."

And I thought again about what the man in the bar had said. *He come for home.* And I stopped and pointed back down the hill and across the pasture to Gorrienea.

"That home?"

"*Oui*, I tell you, only one home."

22

HOGEITA BI

In the Arizona desert, heat blurred the landscape, turning everything brown. Here, in the Pyrenees, water blurred the landscape, turning everything green. Green trees, green grass, and green shrubs dissolved into each other. And I got the sensation that where I was, where I had been, and where I was going were all the same place.

"I own Gorrienea?"

"*Oui,* your *aitatxi,* he no want Marcelino to get so he leave to your *aita,*" Jacques said. "Now yours."

We had just reached the crest of a steep hill.

"But what if I don't want it?"

"Want or no want, Gorrienea belong to you," Jacques said. "Here where I go to home."

"Good-bye," I said, and made a quick turn to start back the way we'd come in an effort to avoid the whole kissing thing again.

"*Gelditu,*" Jacques said. Wait.

"I better get back—"

"You have come this far, Mathieu, you should see the pew."

"You mean view?"

"*Oui,* I tell you, it take breath far away." Jacques pointed up the mountain. "Top mountain—you see whole world there."

"I'm not sure I want to see the whole world just now."

"Maybe see Mamu," Jacques said, and was off down the hill before I could point out that that wasn't funny. I watched as he cut across a meadow covered with yellow flowers and disappeared into the trees.

Stupid Mamu.

When he was gone, I gazed up at the mountain. The thighs of my legs were still tight from my *pilota* match, and I was having trouble getting a good breath in the thin air. I told myself, I should just go back to Gorrienea. I could rest there. Sit by the fire. Watch Edita dance. But what if Marcelino still sat in the armchair? And what about Isabelle? What if she wanted to talk about the house? How much truth did I owe her? What kind of lie would I tell? So much for no more secrets. Since I had no answers to my questions, I started to climb.

As I hiked up the mountain, thoughts swirled in my head. If I owned Gorrienea, then I could use it to get Isabelle to sign the quit deed for the ranch. A simple trade. And then I could go home and start my new life. But what if Marcelino wouldn't allow it? Jacques had said he was a wolf. But then Jacques's use of English was confusing at best. He had described Jean's *pilota* play as "ruthless." And it was. But then he had used "pew" for "view." Which made no sense.

I wondered what my father would do in my place. Of course, he was the cause of me being in this place, but blaming him wasn't going to get me the answers I needed. I waited for Dad's voice to provide me some guidance, but instead heard Aitatxi saying, "*Mendia heltzen da urrats bat aldian—* Take the mountain one step at a time."

"What other way can you take a stupid mountain?" I said aloud and kicked a rock that was in my path. It sent a sting up my leg that caused me to limp for several yards.

I shook my head to get Aitatxi out and again waited for my father. Only he never showed up. My chin jutted forward. Dad's voice had gone silent ever since I arrived in Urepel. And I knew why. He wanted me to figure it out for myself. Which only made me madder.

Clouds covered the top of the mountain I was climbing. When I moved into them, the world became unclear. Shapes came and went in the mist—a pointing finger curled in, a horse arched its neck in an unfinished gallop; the profile of my mother's face flickered by, her eyes looking off to the side, not seeing me. In Oxea's stories of the Mamu, this was where he lived— hiding and lurking and waiting.

I was about to give up and head down, figuring that with all these clouds there would be no view. What could I possibly see? And besides, instead of the climb helping me sort things out, it had jumbled them up even more. I had no idea what to do or how to use my owning Gorrienea to my advantage.

Slowing my pace, I started to turn around when I heard the crack of a breaking branch. A dislodged rock tumbled along the slope. I stopped and leaned toward the noises that came from below. The thudding of my heart was in my ears as I tried to see through the shifting clouds. I thought I caught a glimpse of something dark and large moving toward me.

Marcelino? Did he already know about the other house? Was the wolf hunting? Was I a lamb being led to slaughter?

Not waiting to find out, I rushed up the side of the mountain. I stumbled over broken rocks as I scrambled forward. The trees closed in around me. I forced my way through. Branches whipped my face. Thunder cracked, and in it I heard the growl of some great beast.

An *irrintzina*, shrill and high, cut through the mist. The Basque cry was like a thrown rope; it wrapped around my body and pulled me to a stop. A breeze blew over me and washed away the clouds to reveal that I was standing on the edge of a cliff. One more step and I would have gone over.

Sweat burned my eyes as I exhaled. My breath floated out into the emptiness.

Below me, the clouds pushed up against the face of the cliff like sheep against the wall of a pen. And I thought, *I am not here. I have gone back to Gorrienea. I am in the attic, lying on the bed—asleep. And all of this is only a dream. In a moment, I will wake up.* Then, as if the gate had been thrown open, the clouds rushed forward to reveal another shelf a hundred feet below me. Racing over the open grass, the clouds flew past Maria Mendia. She stood at the edge watching the clouds leap into blue sky.

Sunlight fell over Maria, who still wore the red shawl from church. Only now it was around her shoulders. Her hair was loose and blowing in the wind.

I was about to call out to her when I again heard the *irrintzina* of my dreams. The cry rose as a dark figure broke from the tree line below and moved toward Maria. I wanted to yell a warning. But Maria had already turned and seen the approaching figure.

She smiled.

And I watched as Jean ran to Maria, gathered her into his arms, and kissed her.

23

HOGEITA HIRU

On the plane to Europe, even though I told myself I wasn't going to, I took out my journal and wrote about the day of my father's funeral. I didn't put down how particles floated in the church's air like dust kicked up behind a tractor or how the words of the eulogy became notes to a song that Aitatxi hummed in my head. Instead I wrote about Jenny kissing me.

My hands are heavy at my sides, palms tingling as if I'd spent a day clearing a field of large stones. And now, as the last stone is dropped, blood rushes into my fingers, life returns to my limbs. The tingle of a breeze brushes my forehead. Jenny's breath smells of coffee and cinnamon. Lemons are in the air as the beat of my heart catches, changes, falls into rhythm with hers.

That was, until Mr. Steele interrupted us.

Still, I ended up filling three whole pages with something that lasted less than a few seconds. I could have written another ten pages, but when I looked over what I'd put down, the idea that someone might find and read it stopped my pen. Later, waiting for the bus that would take me as far as Aldudes, I again wrote in my journal. This time about what happened in the alley. Only I revised it.

Now, I know that the day of my father's funeral, Mr. Steele interrupted Jenny kissing me. And I know that that day in the alley, she punched me in the stomach when I tried to kiss her. But it didn't have to be that way—not in my journal.

Jenny was still in the alley, leaning up against the garbage bin, crying, calling me an idiot, and me being one. Her brown hair still danced in the sunlight. My chest was still tight as I stepped through that back door into the alley. A car horn still honked in the distance. Jenny's eyes still brimmed with tears. Her lips still glistened with moisture. And the heat of the sun was still on my neck as I leaned forward, closed my eyes, and moved to kiss her.

But here was where things changed—where the two moments became one.

A car horn honks in the distance as the tingle of a breeze brushes my forehead. The heat of the sun is on my neck as I lean forward, the beat of my heart catching, changing, as it falls into rhythm with hers. Lemons fill the air. My lips find Jenny's. And our kiss stretches out into forever.

In this version, there was neither a sucker punch nor a Mr. Steele. And so the kiss went on and on.

I was thinking about my revised version of that moment as I watched Jean brush a lock of Maria's hair from her face; she held his other hand to her breast and whispered into his ear. He laughed and kissed her again. This moment didn't need any revision. It was perfect. And because of that, I hated it.

Jean and Maria's real moment made my fictional one feel cheap and stupid and embarrassing because I hadn't kissed Jenny in the alley and our kiss hadn't stretched out into forever. But theirs could. Because their moment didn't have a sucker punch or a Mr. Steele to ruin it, that was up to me.

"Stop!" I yelled.

The lovers turned. And when their eyes met mine, the thing in me that wanted to destroy their moment together—because it didn't belong to me, felt like it could never belong to me—changed; it became a shame that made me shiver.

Maria pulled her red shawl over her head as she broke free from Jean's arms and ran. Jean didn't run after her. Instead, he kept his focus on me. And dropped into a crouch as if getting ready to spring straight up the cliff's wall. The fingers of one of his hands grazed the grass. He lips curled back to expose white teeth. And I knew I should flee. But I couldn't move. I was held frozen by eyes that, even from that distance, I could see held nothing but hate. I was the lamb. He was the wolf. And there was no escape.

But then Maria called Jean's name, and at the sound of her voice I was forgotten. Jean's muscles went soft as he cocked his head to the side and stood up straight. Maria called again to him from the trees, and without hesitation he bounded after her. When they were gone and I was alone, I slipped away to hide, trembling, in the green cover.

For a while I just sat there beneath the boughs of the trees, arms around my knees, rocking back and forth, going over and over what had just happened, trying to make sense of why I had yelled. Why didn't I just leave them alone? But then, what were they doing meeting on the cliff? Maybe they just wanted to keep their relationship private. But if it was all so innocent, why had Maria run? Which brought me back to why the hell had I yelled? Which kept me gnawing at myself like a coyote with a leg caught in a trap.

Then I recalled what Isabelle had said about the bad blood between the two families. Did that include Marcelino's son? If so, then their meeting was secret. Which meant my interrupting it was the right thing to do. In truth, I had done Maria a favor. Jean was a wolf, like his father. She shouldn't be sneaking around with him. Her parents wouldn't approve. Of course, I overlooked the fact that these were the same parents who would not even speak to me.

After a few more minutes of revising the facts, I stepped vindicated from the shadow of the trees to see the clouds were gone. I was back in the light of day. As I worked my way down the side of the mountain, I thought about Jean. I knew his secret. That brought a mean smile to my face. He was probably worried—afraid I would reveal his affair. Which was exactly what I planned on doing once I returned to Gorrienea. What would Marcelino do to his son when he found out Jean had disobeyed him? I pictured straps of leather being whipped through the air and something involving sheep shears.

I too could be a wolf.

I was so busy imagining the details of Jean's punishment that I didn't see Maria until I almost ran into her. She was waiting for me at the base of the mountain where Jacques had turned for home. She stepped toward me, the fingers of her right hand touching my forearm.

"Please, do not say about us," Maria said. "There is love."

Then, before I could think of how to speak against her love, she hurried away, red shawl trailing over the grass behind her. And as she went, Maria took all my meanness with her. She loved Jean. She had asked me, *please*. And even I, the beast that I was, couldn't refuse her. Oh why had I come to this country? How had this happened? This one day feeling like forever. This place seeping into every corner of my life, changing who I was.

Then I thought about Jenny. I didn't want to. I just did. What would Jenny say to me if she were here? Would she shake her head and call me an idiot? Or would she be too ashamed of me to even call me that?

With slumped shoulders, I continued down the hill toward the house that was not my home. A drizzle of rain began to fall. The moisture made the scrapes I'd gotten while crashing through the trees burn like welts from the strap I had imagined Marcelino beating Jean with.

And then there was Jean, cutting across the field in front of me. He didn't see me. His head was down, probably full of thoughts about what had happened. I could have called out to him, apologized for what I had done, and promised not to say anything. But I didn't. I just watched as he walked to Odolenea and went inside.

When I stepped onto the road that led first past Marcelino's house and then on to Isabelle's, the ring of a bell startled me as a bicycle rode past. On it was a skinny man in a blue hat and matching uniform. He had two leather sacks strapped to the rear fender of his bike.

"*Bonjour*," the postman called to me as he pedaled to a stop in front of the gray stone house of Marcelino and Jean.

Now, it was true that I had only ever been to Colorado before. And as Mr. Steele pointed out, "Colorado's not exactly a foreign country." But I was still surprised to see a postman delivering mail on Sunday.

The postman leaned his bike up against the wall and went to the door. He knocked and waited. As I got closer, I saw that the sacks on his bike were empty. He held a single white envelope in his hand as he knocked again. But Jean was not answering. With a sigh of disappointment, the postman wedged the envelope into the frame of the door. Then he retrieved his bike and rode back in the direction he had come.

I stopped at the gate of the house's yard. Jean was in there—angry, worried I was going to reveal what I had seen. But I wasn't. He would figure that out soon. But he probably wouldn't know why I was keeping silent. And I wanted him to know that it was for Maria—not him.

I walked up the pathway to the front door. Unlike the postman, I would knock until Jean answered. Then, as I raised my fist to pound on the wood of the door, I saw the return address on the envelope wedged into the door frame: *Mr. Thaddeus Steele, Esq.*

24

HOGEITA LAU

When I pulled the letter from Mr. Steele off Marcelino's door, I found that it was not addressed to him but to Isabelle *Odolen*. And when I saw that, I found myself nodding. Of course Mr. Steele would contact the person whose name was on the deed to the ranch. Of course he would write to her. Of course.

I found Isabelle out behind Gorrienea washing a pig. The animal's front and back legs were hobbled. And it had a rope around its neck. Isabelle held the rope with one hand while with the other she used a wet brush to scrub down the pig.

Coming around the corner of the house and seeing Isabelle with the pig didn't distract me from what I was determined to do. Everything was going to spill out now—about Gorrienea and my ranch and Mr. Steele and her lies. But before I could say a single word accusing Isabelle of deceit, she shoved a bucket into my hands.

"Take," she said.

"I don't want to—"

"Be ready," Isabelle said as she pulled a knife from the fold of her apron and jammed it into the pig's neck.

For a moment I thought the pig's wail of shock was my own. Then Isabelle tightened the rope around its neck and told me to catch the blood. Which wasn't that easy since the pig was thrashing and blood was spraying all over the place. My fingers were slick with blood, and I couldn't get a good grip on the bucket that kept slipping in my hands.

"Hold tight," Isabelle said.

It was not like I hadn't seen blood before. Each spring back home, Dad and I castrated lambs and docked their tails. And there was blood. And it was messy. But not like this: surging, gushing, spurting blood. It covered my hands, body, and face.

As the first bucket filled with blood, Isabelle handed me a second. She did this while keeping a firm hold on the struggling pig. Then came a third bucket. When it was about half full, the pig gave a final grunt, collapsed to its knees, and rolled onto its side.

I dropped to my knees as well, panting with exhaustion. Isabelle wiped her bloody hands on her apron and again took out the knife.

"You're not going to butcher this thing right here, are you?"

"Do not be silly," Isabelle said. "The butcher, he here soon take body."

"Then what are you—"

Isabelle thrust the knife into the pig's belly; its intestines spilled out onto the grass. I covered my mouth and nose against the smell of rotting vegetables that mushroomed into the air.

"We need intestines for blood sausage," Isabelle said.

As I remained on my knees and watched my aunt pull out the pig's guts, I thought about Aitatxi and how he loved blood sausage. Only I'd never seen him make it. Aitatxi must have known that if I'd witnessed the process I wouldn't have eaten the dark links he cut up on a plate and served with slices of sheep's milk cheese. I felt foolish now that I'd never realized that blood sausage was made of just that—blood. But then, at a young age I had learned that a word for something and what it really was often had nothing in common—especially with things having to do with being Basque.

"Wash," Isabelle said, and pointed toward the stream running past Gorrienea.

I went over and kneeled down in the grass that grew along the stream's edge. Every stone in the bed was visible, the water so clear that it was like looking through a window with no glass. I plunged my hands through that glassless window, expecting to feel the warmth of the town's name, Urepel. But instead my fingers went numb at the touch. Was this what these people thought of as warm? In Arizona, warm meant comfort, not the loss of feeling. Blood trickled off my hands and flowed in red ribbons down the stream. I splashed water over my face and shook off the droplets.

"Why didn't you just tell me about my owning Gorrienea when I arrived?" I said, and there was no sting to my words.

"I thought your father, he tell you," Isabelle said as she wound the pig's intestines into a neat pile on the grass.

"Well he didn't," I said. "And he didn't tell me about you either."

Isabelle gave me her combo smile—both amused and annoyed.

"Your father, he like his parents," she said. "Talking no something they like do."

"They were your parents too."

"Dominica and Mathieu Etcheberri no more my parents when they go for America."

"Wow," I said. "We Basques really got this holding a grudge thing down."

"They forgot me," Isabelle said. "I forgot them."

"Is that why you sent back—"

"Enough of past," Isabelle said as she went to the water pump and washed clean her hands. "We have blood sausage for make."

"I don't understand," I said. "You can't forgive your own parents but you can forgive Marcelino?"

Isabelle picked up two of the buckets of blood and lifted them onto a nearby table.

"Jacques, he always like talk," Isabelle said.

I got up and took the remaining half-full bucket of blood to her.

"He said Marcelino is a wolf."

"*Ba*, he wolf that love daughter."

"So you let him do whatever he wants?"

"You talk about Jean's mother." Isabelle poured the buckets of blood into a large copper pot. "We no together then."

"Are you together now?"

"Wood," Isabelle said as she opened the front of the black stove that sat up against the house. I grabbed some wood from the woodpile. She jammed it in and lit a fire. "Marcelino, he no leave when Edita born. Even when she special."

"Why didn't he?"

"He sorry I think."

"Sorry for what?" I asked.

"*Ba,* maybe Jacques not talk so much," Isabelle said. "Put pot on stove."

"Now what?"

"Your family never make the blood sausage?"

"Aitatxi did," I said. "But not with me."

"*Ai-ai-ama,*" Isabelle said as she handed me a large stick. "Keep stir blood until boils. If not, it no good. Then put spices. After cool, stuff intestines for make links."

"I am never eating blood sausage again."

"We see." Isabelle went to a nearby bench and sat down. "Stir."

As I stirred the blood, the afternoon light deepened and a flock of doves flew over, whirling and diving before disappearing beyond the top of the house.

"*Uso zurria errazu, nora joiten ziren zu,*" Isabelle sang softly as she watched the doves go.

"*Espainiako mendiak oro elhurrez bethiak dituzu,*" I sang, and Isabelle gave me a surprised look. "Amatxi used to sing that song to me when I was little. But she never told me what it meant."

"White dove tell me where you go. In Spain the mountains full of snow . . ." Isabelle's words trailed into silence. Then she said, "We in Spain when happen. Go San Sebastián for honeymoon."

"You and Marcelino?"

"*Ba,* we argue."

"What about?"

"Always same—Gorrienea," Isabelle said. "Marcelino, he no understand why now we married, my father no give Marcelino what his."

"Why wouldn't he?"

"He hear story about Marcelino—how he take guns over border from Spain."

"Was it true?"

"Keep stir," Isabelle said.

I stirred. A few bubbles broke on the surface of the blood as it thickened.

"Back before, thing they happen in España," Isabelle said. "Change. Marcelino, he not afraid. He do what he need for get what he want. Thing I love about him. Thing parents no love."

"Was he in ETA?"

"ETA no exist then," Isabelle said. "But if it do . . . then, *ba*, Marcelino, he ETA. My parents say I no can see him. So I marry when they go on boat for America. When they learn . . . well . . ."

"Is that what Marcelino is sorry about? That he married you without your parents' blessing?"

Isabelle came over and checked the boiling blood.

"Now add spices," she said. She pulled out a jar and had me pour the spices into the pot. "Stir. Scrape bottom. I big with Edita then. Marcelino, he yell—want have Gorrienea. He not look at road. No see bus. Blood everywhere. I no know where blood it from. Then I see—blood, it from me. Edita come early. Stay six month in hospital."

Isabelle wrapped a piece of cloth around the pot's handle and had me move it off of the fire.

"Is that why Edita is special?" I asked.

"*Ba*, maybe," Isabelle said. "Or maybe way God want her."

"Why would He want that?"

Isabelle gave me her special smile, and I was embarrassed but not sure why.

"Gorrienea belong you, Mathieu. But no matter what you do with, someone, they ask, 'Why he want that?'"

I pulled the letter from Mr. Steele out of my back pocket and handed it to Isabelle.

"I read it," I said. "I shouldn't have, but I did."

Isabelle drew the letter out of its envelope and looked at it for a long moment.

"What it say?" Isabelle asked.

"You should read it yourself."

"I no can," Isabelle said.

"Huh?"

"I speak English," Isabelle said. "But I never learn read—write."

25

HOGEITA BORTZ

Dear Mrs. Isabelle Odolen,

Thank you so much for your return correspondence. I do believe under the circumstances that we can arrive at a mutually profitable agreement concerning the property here in the United States of America. I will be sending further details and a contract for your signature shortly. Hope you are having nice weather. It is hot as hell here.

Best regards, Mr. Thaddeus Steele, Esq.

The first thing I thought when I read Mr. Steele's words was that Isabelle's speaking English made perfect sense. That would be part of her plan. She would need the language to get her revenge on my family. She had known about me all along and been waiting for me to show up. Mr. Steele had probably been in contact with her even before my father's death. As I neared Gorrienea, the facts came together—the truth became clear.

Except that I got it all wrong.

When Isabelle asked me a second time what the letter said, I told her it was from Dad's lawyer informing her of his death. Isabelle nodded, said that she was glad he had died well, and it was time to stuff the sausage links.

We cleaned out the intestines as the butcher took away the slaughtered pig. By then, it was getting dark, so we lit lamps and in their flickering light Isabelle showed me how to stuff the sausage links that would later hang in the kitchen.

When we were finished, we had a cold dinner of bread and cheese, and Edita held my hand as Isabelle translated the story her daughter told. It was about how the Mamu chased her through the woods, trying to catch Edita so he could take her to his home. But Edita was too fast for the Mamu. And he let out his *irrintzina* in anger each time she escaped. Edita's story ended with her dancing with the *lamiak*.

While Edita danced, I asked Isabelle why she didn't learn to read or write English.

"It not part of program," Isabelle said.

"What program?"

Isabelle went to a cupboard and got down a faded blue cardboard box. The front of the box was labeled ENGLISH TRANSLATION MADE EASY. Inside was a black tape recorder, a series of cassette tapes, and a yellowing pamphlet that described a "world of opportunity" at having a career as a translator. I checked the back of the box and saw that it came from Newark, New Jersey.

"You want to be a translator?" I asked.

"*Ba*, that long ago," Isabelle said as she cleared the table, using her hand to sweep the breadcrumbs to the table's edge, and then brushing the crumbs into her palm.

"So you did think about going to America."

"Edita baby then," Isabelle said as she tossed the crumbs into the sink. "I no could do alone."

"But you wouldn't have had to—your family was there."

"Edita, *oraintxe buba,*" Isabelle said. Time for bed.

Edita got up, gave me a kiss on the cheek, and danced her way out of the room.

"You do not go where you no wanted," Isabelle said as she followed her daughter.

Later that night as I lay in bed with the light on, I went back through the day. I tried to understand what I had done and what had been done to me. I thought of Isabelle's words and Gorrienea and Jean and Maria and this place I was a part and not a part of. But the more I pulled at the individual strands of the day, the more they knotted into a ball of wool I couldn't untangle. Maria was my cousin who was in love with my other "sort of" cousin who was the son of the man married to my aunt who lived with her "special" daughter in a house that I owned.

Only a month earlier, before I learned about Isabelle and the ranch and Gorrienea, my life was so much clearer. All I had wanted was to go to the university. One decision to be made. Yes or no. Now my life was made up of maybes: Maybe Isabelle would sign the quit deed, maybe Marcelino would let her, maybe I would give Gorrienea to Isabelle, maybe Marcelino would take it from her.

Finally, I gave up sorting out the "maybes" in my life and reached to turn off the bedside lamp. That was when I noticed the scratch across my right palm. The dried blood was black under the lamp's light. There was no pain, and I didn't remember getting the scrape. I traced the scratch with the index finger of my left hand. It started at the yellowing calluses along the base of my fingers and cut through the soft purple bruise I'd gotten from the *pilota* match. I turned both my hands over; tiny scrapes covered the skin bunched up around my knuckles—the skin so loose that it appeared there was room for the bones of my fingers to grow another two inches. They were my father's hands. Hands he had used to stretch fence around the border of our ranch. And before that, they were Aitatxi's hands that he used to build Artzainaskena. And before being Aitatxi's they were my great-grandfather's hands. His name would have been Ferdinand, like my father. The name of the firstborn son went back and forth through the generations—Mathieu, Ferdinand, Mathieu, Ferdinand. They were the hands that made the table where I had earlier eaten dinner. And my great-great-grandfather Mathieu's hands that carved the mantle over the fireplace in Gorrienea. God's hands. Which Aitatxi said were not "so good for grabbing a thing. But one time they get hold, they no let go." And now they were my hands.

I used those hands to take out my journal and began writing down everything that had happened since I arrived in Urepel. I wrote about the rain and the woman who smelled of stinky cheese and rose water and the other that smelled of anchovies and rose water. I wrote about Edita dancing in front of the fire and Marcelino saying, *You just boy. Nothing but boy.* And about church and Maria, and *pilota* and Jean. And about all my ancestors that died well and Joseph who didn't. I wrote about Jacques and climbing the mountain. And what I had seen. And what I had done.

And I wrote the truth, even though I didn't always want to. I wanted to not have yelled at Maria and Jean, and to not have thrown up on the *pilota* court. To not have accused Isabelle of writing a letter she couldn't. And to not have lied about what that letter said.

I didn't understand everything I wrote, or even why I wrote it. Understanding, I hoped, would come in the morning when I reread what I'd written. Then I would try and make sense of my sentences—try and see the meaning hidden within my words.

Still, even if I wasn't revising my actions, that didn't mean I couldn't clean them up a bit. I wrote that I didn't tell Isabelle about her owning my ranch because of Marcelino. I was protecting her from him. The same way Aitatxi had protected his daughter by putting Gorrienea in his son's name so that Marcelino Odolen couldn't take it. But then I had to write that that really wasn't true, since Marcelino must already know that Isabelle owned the ranch. He had to be the one who answered Mr. Steele's letter, pretending to be Isabelle.

I wrote what Isabelle said about not going where you are not wanted. And how I had. And about trying to figure out some way to give Gorrienea to Isabelle while keeping it from Marcelino. I filled ten pages in my journal before I clicked off the lamp and fell back onto the pillows of the bed.

Gorrienea was quiet below me. And I got the sensation that I was floating on a pool of still water. Beneath me the water stretched down into darkness. Something moved and sent a ripple up from the rooms below. I heard the shuffle of feet. I glanced to the attic's trapdoor and imagined Marcelino's head appearing. But then a cabinet clicked open; glasses clanked against each other. The faucet creaked and water spilled out.

Isabelle cleared her throat and I relaxed. A chair shuddered over the wood floor. And I wondered about Isabelle in this house for all these years, listening to English tapes, dreaming about a place that her parents had gone to, and feeling unwanted. Only it didn't make sense. I knew Aitatxi. He never would have left his daughter behind. No matter what she did. But then again, Aitatxi had never even mentioned Isabelle to me. Not once in all his rambling stories of the past did her name slip out.

I could hear Isabelle pacing. The firm, steady fall of her feet formed an image of her in my head. I saw the hard line of her jaw, the stiffness of her back. Then I heard something else—like the tip of a brush grazing over wood. And the sound caused the Isabelle in my head to change. She was limping. The motion so slight as to almost be invisible. Given away only by the scrape of her toe over the floor. And I realized what I was picturing was right; I had seen it earlier but not noticed. Only now, looking back, could I see it. Isabelle pacing the floor. Thinking about her parents. Thinking about her daughter. Thinking about the past, which weighed her down, causing her to limp toward an uncertain future.

That Isabelle was the one that walked me into sleep.

I was on the edge of the cliff again. The echo of an *irrintzina* fluttered up into a perfect blue sky as Maria and Jean ran hand in hand into the trees below. Across the chasm from me was another cliff. My father there. Calling to me. Three words. The wind picked up. But this time, instead of blowing his words away, the wind carried them to me: "You are etcheberri."

26

HOGEITA SEI

The day that Aitatxi showed up in my seventh grade history class to basically kidnap me and take me on the last sheep drive, he told my teacher, Ms. Helm, that our name, Etcheberri, meant new house. She said, "How interesting." And I wanted to die.

Ms. Helm had graduated from the U of A the year before, wore dresses shorter than any of the other teachers, and, I had learned, used the word "interesting" to describe anything that wasn't. When Mike brought a dead toad in a jar to class, she said that was interesting. Then made him throw it in the dumpster. And when Rich told the class how his dad could drink twelve beers in a row and burp the alphabet backward, she said that was interesting as well. Then scheduled an after-school conference with Rich's parents. So the day my name fell into the "interesting" bucket next to the dead toad and the burping father, I knew for certain that it wasn't.

I remember how Ms. Helm had wrinkled up her nose at the smell of sheep that clung to Aitatxi's black coat. But then Aitatxi told Ms. Helm about how each generation "flip-flop oldest son name—Mathieu, Ferdinand, Mathieu, Ferdinand." And she had said that was "charming," a word I'd never heard her use before. And when Aitatxi took off his beret and gave Ms. Helm a little bow, she sighed and said she "loved" it. And all the girls in class clapped.

Years later, when I was a junior in high school, Ms. Helm got engaged to a professional football player from Dallas. I saw her on the street a week before she was set to leave for her wedding. The floral print dress she wore was as short as ever but was no longer unusual, as the town's dresses had, over the years, risen to Ms. Helm's level.

"Hi, Mathieu New-house," Ms. Helm said with a smile.

I said hello and told her I hoped her wedding would be "interesting." Ms. Helm smiled, a little puzzled at my word choice as she walked on, recalling only a moment of a day whose every minute I would never forget.

Ms. Helm never returned to our town. She started a new life. Found a new home. And when I woke in Gorrienea's attic to the "baaing" of sheep, my first thought was not of Isabelle or Artzainaskena or Marcelino but of Ms. Helm. I wondered if her wedding had indeed turned out "interesting."

I tried to close my eyes and sink back into unconsciousness, but it was no use. I was still on Arizona time.

I turned on the bedside lamp and read over what I had written the night before. But no sudden insights came to me. I couldn't see anything but words and sentences that, while they told how things had happened, gave no hint as to why they happened or what should be done because of their happening.

My return plane ticket was folded in my passport and wedged in between the pages of my journal. I took it out and looked at the destination— Phoenix. I could go. Leave right then. Just walk away. I would be back in Arizona in a couple of days. Back on the ranch with the summer sun on my face. Jenny leaning her head on my shoulder. The smell of lemons in the air.

I put the ticket back in my passport and stuck it in my journal.

I climbed out of bed and searched for a place to hide the book, not wanting anyone to read my personal thoughts. I found a loose floorboard at the base of the room's far wall. I pulled it up and slid the book beneath it. Then I got dressed and grabbed the handball from the *pilota* match the day before. I bounced the ball in the palm of my hand a few times before closing my fingers around it and squeezing as I slipped downstairs and out into a cold morning.

When I reached the *pilota* court, I found it flecked with dew. The morning sun was creeping over the horizon and made the moisture shimmer even as it disappeared. I kneeled down, my thighs tight from yesterday's mountain climbing, and looked over the silent court. The two walls forming a single corner were the same, as were the court's painted lines. What was missing were the cheering spectators. The waiting opponent. I placed my hands flat on the cement. It was cool beneath my palms. Now it was only the court, the ball, and me.

I took my position and began to play. But like the day before, my shots didn't react the way I planned. I blamed the ball. Jean had made it and so it was probably defective. I blamed the second wall; it created too many angles. I blamed the cement; it caused a too-high bounce. I blamed my thoughts; they were scattered and unfocused.

As the ball sailed past me for the tenth time to roll off into the dirt, a woman with a chicken tucked under each of her arms walked by. Three sets of eyes watched me as I retrieved the ball, retook my position, and started again.

The sun rose higher. My muscles loosened. I got used to the angles caused by the second wall and the ball's higher bounce off the cement. I even, grudgingly, began to appreciate the construction of Jean's ball; it was tighter and had a harder core than any ball I'd ever made. Gradually, I began to anticipate the sharp angles and adjust to the tough bounces. And as I did, I pictured the shocked look on Jean's face as the ball sped past him. The image brought a tight grin to my lips. But, in time, Jean faded away. And there was just the ball. Which I struck again and again.

Thirty minutes later, drenched in sweat, I sat with my back up against the once foreign second wall, happy in a way that I hadn't been since before my father died. Somehow happiness for me had become something that lived in what-had-been and what-might-be. And not where I was. But on the *pilota* court there was no past and no future, only now. Happening moment by moment. And Dad was there. His voice steady within me.

One of Urepel's many Aitatxi copies tipped his beret to me as he passed. A group of girls in matching green and blue skirts giggled as they chanced quick glances my way. A young couple holding hands went by without noticing me at all. And I smiled at them just the same.

I was still smiling on my way back to Gorrienea when I spotted Marcelino. He was on his hands and knees in front of his house. The postman was there as well. He was demonstrating how he had placed the letter in the door's frame. I stepped into the trees and watched as Marcelino searched the dirt. Without looking up, he said something to the postman—his voice a rumble of unrecognizable words. Then he slapped the ground like a petulant child. A cloud of dust rose up around him. And my smile turned into laughter.

Marcelino got to his feet. The postman gestured with his hands and let out a flurry of words that appeared to be an apology. Only Marcelino didn't seem to be listening. He was busy hitting the front of his pants, beating the dirt out. The postman was still apologizing when Marcelino struck him in the face.

I choked on my laughter as the postman fell to the ground. Marcelino stood over him. And I wanted to call out—to stop Marcelino. Tell him that I had taken the letter. I was the one he should be angry with. But instead I stepped farther into the trees. Slid behind a branch to conceal myself.

Marcelino's anger was gone as quickly as it came. Without another word, at least that I could hear, he turned and went into Odolenea.

When he was gone, the postman scrambled to his feet and got on his bicycle. He pedaled down the road, right past me. Blood dripped from his right ear. And I knew I should stop him and apologize for what was my fault. But I didn't. I was too ashamed of the fear that swirled inside me at Marcelino's casual, sudden violence.

I stepped back onto the road and hurried home.

Links of blood sausage hung in the open windows of Gorrienea's second floor. Out the windows came a loud female voice, "I eat pancakes for breakfast, but not for lunch."

Inside, I found Isabelle at the kitchen sink peeling potatoes. Her translation tapes were spread out over the table. From the tape recorder a woman said, "I will have steak for dinner, please."

"I will have steak for dinner, please," Isabelle repeated.

I started to laugh at the scene, but then I saw that mixed in among the tapes was my journal. It was open—my words visible on the pages. My gut clenched at the memory of what I'd written the night before. Then I remembered that Isabelle could not read English: my secrets were safe. But just the fact that I had secrets that were written down made my face hot.

"Edita, she in the attic," Isabelle said as she reached over and hit the stop button on the recorder. "She bring this down. It yours?"

I grabbed my journal.

"I told her no go up there again." Isabelle cleaned her hands off on her apron. "So you write."

"Sometimes." I began to back out of the room.

"What you write?"

"Stuff," I said with one foot already in the hallway. "Things."

"*Ba*, read me some your stuff-things," Isabelle said and took a seat at the table.

"What?"

"Sit down," she said. "Read."

But I didn't move. I was too stunned by the request. No one had ever asked me to read anything from my journal before. Dad never had, and he'd seen me writing in it on the porch in the evening and out under the oak tree and while riding in the truck. Dad never once said, *read me some your stuff-things*. He wouldn't have. He knew what I wrote was private. Jenny had never asked me either. And she asked me all kinds of private things. Like how many kids did I want to have? And if I remembered how my mother smelled? And why didn't I cry when I found Oxea hanging from the oak tree?

I shifted my weight from one foot to the other, thinking about making a run for the attic. Time stretched out. Isabelle sat at the table, hands folded in front of her, waiting. I looked down at the journal in my hands. And then I realized there was something in my journal I could read—something for Isabelle.

I found the page titled *Amatxi*. I'd written it two years earlier. Before I'd known I even had an aunt. And yet, now I knew that I'd written it for Isabelle. The lettering was blocky, done back when I was more comfortable printing than writing in cursive. It was on a Saturday. Dad was in town. I was in the living room lying on the couch. Hungry. Thinking of apple pie. And the apple pie took me to Amatxi.

I began to read.

"Amatxi bakes on Saturdays. The smell of cinnamon draws me to the kitchen where she rolls out the dough. Flour hangs in the air, gathers in her hair, sprinkles down over me. Peeled apples bob in a bowl of water. She cuts a slice off one and hands it to me. Then bakes me a piece of sugar-coated crust. I eat it greedily. While it is still warm. And Amatxi calls me Gaixua, a word whose meaning I don't yet know. And sings to me in Euskara— *Badakit badela etxeat hemendik urrundena*. And picks me up and dances with me around the kitchen. And I laugh and love her without knowing that that is what I am doing."

I stopped reading and looked up to see Isabelle at the table. Her hands clenched together. Eyes staring across the room.

"I'm sor—"

"Ama bakes on Saturdays," Isabelle said. "I forget. She have me gather apples from trees. And she sing that song."

"I know it's about home, but I don't know what it means."

"*Badakit badela etxeat hemendik urrundena*," Isabelle sang quietly. "There a home I know that faraway. *Noizbait joanen niz etxe hartarat*. I will go some day for home. *Etxe urrun hartarat*. For home of faraway."

"Home of faraway," I repeated.

Isabelle sighed and got up from the table.

"Now you read something for me," I said.

"But I no can read—"

"Hang on." I jumped up and went to the attic. I returned with an unopened letter in my hand.

"What this?" Isabelle said.

"It's for you." I held out the letter posted February 10, 1933.

Isabelle did not take the envelope.

"Your name is on it," I said, which caused her to lean forward and read the front of the letter.

"It from Ama," Isabelle said. Mother.

I pushed the letter into her right hand. She looked at the envelope as if it was something she'd never seen before and, therefore, possibly dangerous.

"Sit down." I took my place at the table. "Read."

Isabelle sat back down. She opened the letter and unfolded the page within. For a few moments she read in silence. And I let her. When she was ready, she translated it into English.

"Gaixua, why you no answer my letters? My heart starting worry. Your father, he not sleep at night. He sorry you stay behind. I pray you safe and on way America. We find new home here—place called Arizona. It strange that place have Basque name. It good place. Come soon—please. We wait for you. Love, Ama and Aita."

Isabelle let her hand holding the letter drop to the table's top.

"Where you get this?" she asked.

"Amatxi saved it after you sent it back unopened."

"I never see before," Isabelle said.

"There are more."

"More?"

"Dozen," I said. "I can go get—"

Isabelle's chair grated over the floor as she pushed herself away from the table. Without a word she walked with the letter in her hand down the stairs. I heard Gorrienea's front door open and close.

Edita stepped out of her bedroom.

"Ama?" she said as she started toward the stairs.

I stopped her.

"*Ez orai. Egon hemen*," I said. Not now. Stay here.

Then, taking Edita by the hand, I led her to the kitchen window and looked out.

Isabelle was walking across the pasture toward Marcelino's house. Her back was stiff and her stride sure, as if she knew exactly where she was going. The white sheet of paper fluttered like a handkerchief in her hand.

"Ama," Edita said and pointed, her finger tapping against the glass.

As if hearing her daughter, Isabelle stopped and stood motionless. A breeze rippled through the grass. And as it passed over her, something in Isabelle's body seemed to break. She collapsed forward. Shoulders shaking as she wept.

27

HOGEITA ZAZPI

Of all the Basque tales Aitatxi and Oxea told me, the one that made the least sense was about the *lamiak*—the little people who came into houses at night and tried to clean up the messes left behind by the humans they dreamed of being. But always the *lamiak* would break something, their hands too small for the things of humans. And they would run crying into the night. What I couldn't understand—what made no sense—was why the *lamiak* wanted to be human in the first place.

"I would rather live in the wild than a house," I told Aitatxi and Oxea as we sat on the porch. Oxea was talking about different Basque creatures. He'd already told all his Mamu stories and was now onto the *lamiak*.

It was late autumn. Streams of cool air slid through the warm dusk. Dad was in Detroit. He had called before I left for school that morning to tell me he wouldn't be home for a few more days. And so I set fire to the oleanders out behind my sixth grade classroom and was expelled for a week.

"You live in wild," Oxea said, "you be in coyote belly by morning, Gaixua."

"Don't call me that," I said. "And I would eat a coyote."

"*Ez*, no taste so good," Oxea said.

"You ate a coyote?" I asked.

Oxea just laughed.

"Sure, no, why you want to be *lamia*, Mathieu?" Aitatxi asked.

"It would be better than being human."

"*Lamiak* no know how a use match," Oxea said. "Maybe you *lamia*, it better for all."

"How about you—"

"Tell me," Aitatxi interrupted my comeback, "why you no like being human?"

"I don't know," I said. "Because . . ."

And then the last of the day's light slipped away and darkness fell, so that when I turned from where I sat on the porch steps, I could no longer see Aitatxi or Oxea's faces. But I could feel heat coming off of them, like from the fire I'd started earlier, as if it were still burning, flames licking my skin, pulling up the anger in me from its dark hiding place.

". . . because humans are stupid." I looked out toward the pasture where the oak tree stood in the moonlight. "And they lie and they are full of things that shouldn't be inside them—things they don't need, things that make everything worse."

"What things?" Aitatxi asked.

"Things, things, you know, organs, stuff—hearts," I said. And there it was. I had said it. The thing that I didn't want to have. A heart.

"Your *aita,* he will come home soon," Aitatxi said.

"What do I care? He can stay gone forever."

"He will come back—"

"I hate him," I said. "I hate every—"

And then I was grabbed from behind. Heavy arms wrapped around me.

"What the—get off—let go!"

But Oxea wouldn't let go. The smell of sour sweat covered me as the rough stubble of his face scratched my cheek. I kept struggling to get free, but Oxea held me firmly to his chest. The pounding of his heart filled my head. There was no escaping him. I quit struggling. Started to cry. The fire in me went out. Oxea's arms went soft. He kissed me on top of my head.

"There, Gaixua," Oxea said, "now you human for always."

As I stood looking out Gorrienea's kitchen window at Isabelle holding a letter from her mother sent almost fifty years ago, I was again puzzled by the desire of the *lamiak* to be human. It didn't make any sense. Not when humans had hearts that were so easily broken.

When Isabelle returned from the pasture, neither the letter nor the fact that she had been crying was visible. She went to the stove and began preparing a lunch of blood sausage and potatoes. But her hands trembled as she cut the potatoes into quarters and dropped them into a pot of water. And her fingers were drawn over and over to the letter whose corner peeked from the pocket of her dress—like an open wound she couldn't help but touch. And even though I was burning to state the obvious—that someone had sent the letters back without her knowing and that someone was Marcelino—I didn't. I had given her the letter. What Isabelle did next was up to her. Still, the quiet in the kitchen that day reminded me of an approaching monsoon. The air tightening into a fist before flying open with a force that would take your breath away. A storm was coming. But since it hadn't arrived yet, I decided to enjoy the calm of the before.

For the next few days Isabelle didn't leave the house. It was if she were afraid of the world beyond the walls of Gorrienea, a world that had been changed forever by words on a page. She busied herself in the kitchen, baking pies and making preserves from the apples she had me pick from the trees growing along the far end of the pasture. She only spoke when she needed to. Her sentences were short and to the point: *Dinner ready. Bed now. Need more apples.* And each time Isabelle sent me to get another basket of apples, I had to walk past Marcelino's house. But I never saw him. Or Jean. The door to Odolenea was shut. The shutters closed. The house looking abandoned.

During Isabelle's self-imposed confinement, I took up the daily outdoor chores. One of them was milking the cow whose name Edita had changed to Mathieu, even though there were obvious reasons why that name was not appropriate.

Each morning as I was milking, a pair of cats would show up for breakfast. I would squeeze milk straight from the cow's teat into the cats' mouths. Well, somewhat in their mouths; the milk kind of got all over them. The cats didn't seem to mind in the least, and it made Edita dance in laughing circles while she called out the cats' names—both of which she had also changed to Mathieu.

Mathieus seemed to be filling up Gorrienea.

When Jacques stopped by, I told him about the letter and what had happened. He pushed his beret high up on his head and nodded.

"*Oui,* now we wet," Jacques said.

"You mean 'wait,'" I corrected him.

"That also," Jacques said as he went inside and told Isabelle he could smell the pies baking from mountains away. She handed him a piece and told him to sit down and fill his mouth with something other than words.

The only time I left the area around Gorrienea was in the morning. Before it was light, I would go to the *pilota* court to hit the ball for an hour or so. Each day, my shots became more sure as I grew familiar with the court. I worked out strategies to wear down my imaginary opponent and catch him off guard. Most of the time that opponent was Jean. I humiliated him with my play again and again—each game ending with his throwing up on the court. Other times, my opponent was Marcelino. Speed was the key with him. He lumbered around the court, and all I had to do was stay clear of his heavy shots. But even as I danced around him, I was trapped by the boundaries of the court—there was no escaping Marcelino. His angry face was always close. Once in a while my opponent was Isabelle. I had trouble working up a solid desire to beat her, as I still wasn't sure if we were opponents or allies. My battles against Isabelle were gentle.

On Thursday, after an imaginary whipping of both Marcelino and Jean on the *pilota* court, I returned to Gorrienea to find Isabelle sitting on the bench out front. It had been three days since I gave her the letter and this was the first time she'd come out of the house.

As I walked up, I could hear Edita singing from inside. "*Tun gulan bat, tun gulan bi.*"

Isabelle's hands were folded on her lap. Which was surprising; I couldn't recall ever seeing her hands without a bowl or bucket, a spoon or fork, a knife or gun in them. Isabelle's hands were always full of things. Always doing something. But now they were just lying there, palms up, fingers spread wide—empty.

The other surprising thing was how calm her face was. It was like she didn't have a care in the world: no house to clean, no beds to make, no pies to bake. And it worried me.

"You okay?" I asked.

Isabelle didn't say anything. And I thought, *she's had a stroke.* That was the only thing that could explain the way she looked.

"Aunt?" I said.

"Call me Ttanta," Isabelle said. "Ants things of ground."

"Okay, Ttanta," I said. "You feeling all right?"

"*Tun gulan hureran, er-or-i.*" Edita's voice floated out the kitchen window.

"You have *neska*?" Isabelle asked.

"A girl?"

"You must. You very *edera*—handsome."

I gazed down at the ground, embarrassed: it was one thing for me to brag about myself and a totally other thing to have someone do it for me.

"*Ba,* I see America Basque men same as here," she said with a laugh. "You say nice thing and they look like you punch in stomach."

"I don't understand her," I said as I raised my eyes.

"Does 'her' have name?"

"Jenny."

"You no worry understanding her, Mathieu," Isabelle said with a nod. "That come later. First, have her understand you."

"How can she?" I said. "I don't even understand myself."

Isabelle looked at me for a long moment and the hint of a smile came to her lips.

"*Ba,* I wrong," she said. "America Basque men, they different."

She patted the empty space on the bench beside her and I sat down.

"When I girl, *aita* sit with me here. We look at pasture and mountains and sky. And everything same as now. I still here. Fifty year like never happen. Then I look at hands—they twisted—wrinkled. Time it catch me."

There was no bitterness in her words. And for the first time since I'd arrived, I saw my father in his sister. She was simply stating how things were. Like my father had done when he told me he couldn't sell the ranch. Brother and sister accepting what they could not change in a way I didn't think I ever could.

"Why did they leave?" I asked. "Aita and Oxea?"

"Because this." Isabelle held up her hands to take in everything around us. "It never change."

"And that's bad?"

"Always enough from sheep for buy things that needed, but no enough for more. Then one year wool price high—more than ever before. Aita and Oxea Martin, they take money. Go America. Want more."

"Oxea did not die well," I said.

"*Ba,* I know," Isabelle said.

"How?"

"Even ocean no can stop hearing bad thing," Isabelle said.

A boy using a long stick to drive a cow came up the road. The cow's bell clanked. The boy waved as he passed and said, "*Egun on.*" I repeated his words as I waved back.

"You know what word they mean?" Isabelle asked.

"Hello?"

"Good day," Isabelle said. "You be my nephew, you no just speak the Euskara, you need know what mean."

"Cool," I said, and Isabelle laughed.

"*Ba,* Aita say everything better America. And he right. You here—you better."

"No, I'm not," I said.

"You come all way no knowing if anything here for you," Isabelle said.

"That's called stupid," I said.

"That call brave."

"You're wrong about me," I said and squeezed the ball I was still holding in my hand until pain shot up my arm. "You see, I had to come to Urepel— I had no choice. The ranch—my ranch—it's not really mine. It's yours. Your parents left it to you. So that's why I came—to get you to give it to me. So I can sell it. Go to school. Because I too want more."

Isabelle clasped her hands together as if praying. And I thought she was going to get up and again walk into the pasture. That I was again going to have to watch as her shoulders slumped with sorrow. But instead, she reached out and took my hand in hers and said, "Thank you, Mathieu."

"For what?"

"For giving me back Ama and Aita," Isabelle said. Then she let go of my hand and said, "You know Basque word for 'ranch'?"

"Uh, no."

"*Baserria,*" Isabelle said. "Beautiful word. Much better than English word for same thing. But Basque word for hope—*itxaropena.* I no like. It be good we pick best word from both language—make new one."

"I'm sorry I lied to you," I said.

"You no can lie about thing I know, Mathieu," Isabelle said.

"What?"

"I know about America ranch."

"But how?"

"*Avocat* tell me," Isabelle said.

"*Avocat?*"

"In English you say lawyer."

"You have a lawyer?"

"*Ba,* Jacques," Isabelle said as she got to her feet. "Go now house. I like see more letters you bring."

28

HOGEIZORTZI

"I sorry, Gaixua," Aitatxi said the day before he died. "I trick you, me both this time."

By then, the sheep were starting to lie down from the heat. The hidden spring Aitatxi had been counting on for water turned out to have gone dry. And we were halfway up the mountain, miles from civilization. Still, I wasn't worried. I had left a note for Dad, telling him we were headed up to the *etxola* on Aitatxi's secret trail. He would come for us—come for me. But then Aitatxi explained that the "secret" trail we were on wasn't the one I had thought.

"*Zure aita,* he thinking we go other *etxola,* one Oxea and me go before. *Baina* he go look at other secret trail."

"Dad's not coming to save me?"

"No Mathieu, no save."

And so it turned out that for three days I had been driving the sheep with my *aitatxi* along a trail whose end I thought I knew. Only to learn that I had never really known where I was going at all.

I felt that way again now as I came downstairs with the bundle of letters to find Isabelle and Edita waiting for me at the kitchen table. I still needed to get Isabelle to sign the quit deed so I could sell the ranch and go to the university. But how was my showing her the letters from the past helping me achieve that? What if the letters made her want to keep Artzainaskena for herself? And why was I getting so involved in the life of someone who a month earlier I hadn't even known existed? As I plopped down the bundle on the table, I realized I no longer had any idea where the trail I was on was leading me.

Isabelle untied the string binding the letters; they spilled out over the tabletop. Edita ran her fingers over the envelopes, her eyes wide as she touched each one as if it were a brightly wrapped Christmas present.

I gathered up the letters and put them in order by date while Isabelle poured coffee into mugs for her and me, and hot chocolate for Edita. It had taken awhile, but I was getting used to the bitter taste of the brown liquid. Besides, once Isabelle decided I should drink the stuff, there was no going back.

"Start here," I said as I handed her an envelope posted March 15, 1933.

Isabelle opened the letter and began to read.

Over the next three hours, I listened to three decades of my family's history. I learned that Oxea's wife, Pascaline, had been found dead in the apartment of the guy who delivered grain to the small ranch Oxea bought in Colorado. Pascaline called Amatxi when she left Oxea six months earlier, saying that if she had wanted to live on a ranch, she would have stayed in France. The grain guy was making a delivery in Idaho when Pascaline died. She had been dead for a week before he found her. By then, the coroner couldn't determine the cause of death. Oxea buried his wife, sold the ranch, and came to live in Arizona. The night he arrived at Artzainaskena, Amatxi wrote, Oxea got drunk and cried for hours. In the morning, he went out with Aitatxi to shear sheep and never spoke of his dead wife again.

Isabelle made us bread and cheese sandwiches, and as we ate them I learned that Amatxi had heard from a cousin in Saint-Jean-de-Luz that Isabelle had a baby girl. But the cousin didn't know the baby's name. Amatxi was sure it was something beautiful. Edita went to dance in front of the fire, and I learned that at the moment the car struck my mother, Amatxi was weeding her garden. The day went dark. And the sheep lay down in the pasture. The eclipse lasted ten minutes. When it was over, the phone rang and Amatxi was told that my mother was dead.

In all the letters there was no mention of Marcelino—or of Isabelle being married. Each letter ended the same way, *Otoitz egiten dut zu eta zure alaba jinen zistela gureganat fitexko. Izan ontsa, Ama.* I pray that you and your daughter will come to us soon. Be well, Ama.

I had to wonder at Amatxi not giving up. Even though all of her letters were returned unopened, she kept writing, carrying on a one-sided conversation with a daughter who, for all Amatxi knew, didn't want anything to do with her. What had kept Amatxi writing? Did she think that she could wear down Isabelle's silence? Or maybe it was just that hardheaded Basq-oh trait coming through. I pictured Amatxi sitting at the kitchen table back home, writing the letters I was now listening to. What had she been thinking as she moved her pen over the paper? What would I think if I was writing to someone I loved in another country? How could I stand not knowing if that person was alive? What would I do to find out? And then I knew. I knew what I would do and what Amatxi had done. She didn't write the letters in the hope that they would be read. Amatxi wrote the letters in the hope that they would be returned. Each returned letter was a signal that her daughter was still angry, still alive.

But the signals had been false because Isabelle wasn't the one who had sent back the letters. It was Marcelino.

When Isabelle had read all of the letters Amatxi had written, she opened the one addressed to her in Aitatxi's childlike scribble: September, 12, 1963.

How are you, Gaixua? We just buy fifty more sheep. Our flock now over 500. The land big. A flock of 1,000 my dream. Your mother died last Spring. She had the pneumonia. She cleaned the house before she lay down and no get up. Ferdinand's wife gone two year. This country seem hard on women. Sometime I wish we not come. Sometime I wonder what happen if I had make you come when we leave Euskal Herria. But you say you come soon. But that all gone now. Ferdinand's boy, Mathieu, three. He tall. He strong. He make good shepherd. Oxea say hello.

Be well, Aita.

When Isabelle was done translating the letter for me, I found I could no longer keep silent. Even though I was sure Isabelle knew Marcelino was to blame for all her lost years, it needed to be said out loud.

"You know this is all Marcelino's fault, right?"

Edita had fallen asleep with her head on her folded arms. Her hair spilled over the table. Isabelle gathered her daughter's gray streaked hair and tied it up with the string that had bound the letters.

"None of this would have happened if it weren't for him," I said.

"I make something for eat." Isabelle took a bowl of tomatoes from the counter and placed it in the sink.

"You and Edita could have come to Arizona to live," I said. "You were wanted."

Isabelle didn't turn on the water to wash the tomatoes. Instead, she leaned on the sink and looked out the window at the line of trees across the pasture. The sun was setting, and as it sank into the trees, they glowed.

"Always I like morning best," she said. "Everything new. But now . . . there something nice about end of day."

She placed the tomatoes on the cutting board and chopped them up.

"Aren't you mad?"

"At who?"

"Marcelino of course."

"There another letter." Isabelle put the chopped tomatoes into a bowl and sprinkled them with salt and pepper. She set the bowl of tomatoes on the table. "You bring letter I write?"

I swallowed, then reached into my back pocket and pulled out the open letter I had found in the box labeled *Dominica*. I hadn't given it to Isabelle. And I wasn't going to, not after I realized that the writing smeared at its bottom was not caused by spilled water but by Amatxi's tears. I put the letter on the table beside the bowl of tomatoes.

"Read," Isabelle said.

"My Euskara is not very—"

"I help."

"But I can't—"

"Read." Isabelle sat down in the chair beside me.

I could have kept arguing, but there was something about Isabelle that reminded me a bit too much of Aitatxi. Arguing with him had always been frustrating, not only because I usually lost but because so often I wasn't even sure we were arguing about the same thing. Right then, Isabelle was her father's daughter.

I opened the envelope and pulled out the worn and creased sheet of paper. I smoothed it flat on the table and looked at the letters that formed words and sentences that made no sense to me.

Agur Ama eta Aita, ezkondia niz orai. Badakit eztela ziek nahi betzala, bainan hola nahi nin nik. Marcelino gizon huna da. Ez niz jiten ahal Amereketarat. Ene bizia hemen da harekin. Itxaropen dut ulertzea. Iragana ahatziak da. Ene bizia berria da orai.

Izan ontsa, Isabelle.

Isabelle worked me word by word through what was written. And I learned that a *z* on the page had the sound of the *s* in "yes." And that *tx* sounded like the *ch* of "change." Some of the words I knew, others I had never heard, like *ulertu*—understand and *ahatzia*—forgotten.

Isabelle was patient and corrected my pronunciation, having me say the words over and over, stringing them together into meaning.

After I'd figured out the first sentence, I went up into the attic and retrieved my journal from its hiding place. I had continued to put the book under the loose floorboard even though it was no longer secret from Edita. It just didn't seem right to leave my journal lying around, even if there was no one who could understand what I'd written. I wrote down the first sentence of the letter in my journal. I continued to do that with every line as it was translated. When we were done, I read Isabelle's letter again. This time in English.

Hello Mother and Father. I am married now. I know that is not what you wanted, but it is what I wanted. Marcelino is a good man. I cannot come to America. My future is here with him. I hope you understand. All that has passed is forgotten. My life is new.

Be well, Isabelle.

"I should have write *forgiven,* not *forgotten,*" Isabelle said as she ran a hand over the back of the still sleeping Edita. "Tell them I sorry, even if not. Maybe then things different."

There was a knock on the door downstairs, followed by, "*Oui,* you are there?"

Jacques came up the stairs. In his hands, he held his beret full of chestnuts.

"I bring the *gaztainak,*" he said and plopped the beret onto the table. Several chestnuts rolled across the top and onto the floor.

"You want *arno sagara*?" Isabelle asked. Apple wine.

"What *gastainak* without *arno sagara*?" Jacques said.

"Wine there shelf, Mathieu." Isabelle pointed to a shelf as she got to her feet. Edita, still half asleep, was slumped against her mother.

While Isabelle took Edita to bed, I helped Jacques cut holes in the chestnuts before putting them into a blackened barrel. The barrel fit between two posts in the fireplace. I added some wood to the fire, and Jacques used the handle fitted onto the barrel to rotate it. The chestnuts clanked against the metal with each spin.

I poured out two glasses of apple wine and handed one to Jacques.

"*Zure osagarriari,*" he said as we clinked glasses. To your health.

The taste of the wine was new but familiar—like a tart apple dipped in sugar.

"*Oui,* I tell you, Isabelle, she make the first prize *arno sagara.*"

"To you, everything she makes is first prize," I said.

"*Oui,* I tell you, she first prize," Jacques said.

The smell of roasting chestnuts filled the air as the apple wine floated along the top of my head and the heat of the fire warmed my face. Jacques had stopped turning the barrel. But his fingers still rested on the handle as he gazed off into space, as if seeing a different room—or at least different people in the same room, with different relationships.

"Have you told her?" I asked.

"No is my place." Jacques motioned for me to come over and help him lift the barrel from the fire.

"Why not?"

"*Oui,* I tell you, very compliment," Jacques said as we dumped the roasted chestnuts onto a cloth spread across the table.

"You mean complicated," I said.

Jacques began cracking open chestnuts. He stacked the shells in one pile and the nuts' caramel-colored meat in another.

"Isabelle, she change now." Jacques poured out some more wine, and I began eating the shelled *gaztainak*. The meat was soft and buttery and reminded me of Christmas when Dad and I roasted chestnuts in the stove.

"*Oui,* I tell you, you good for she, Mathieu. Maybe you stay."

"Here?"

"This house it yours."

"This is Isabelle and Edita's home," I said.

"You give Isabelle—Marcelino he take. So why you no just keep?"

"Because it's not mine," I said, and thought about all those letters and that past that could have been and the future that could have come from it.

"*Oui*, I tell you, you go, soon it be no ones," he said and popped another chestnut into his mouth.

As I watched Jacques chewing *gastainak* and drinking *arno sagara* with his beret tilted back on his head just the way Aitatxi used to wear it, I wondered at all the trouble Aitatxi had caused me. If it wasn't for him I would have been sitting in a classroom at U of A working on math problems that had set answers instead of family problems that did not.

Sure, no, Aitatxi seemed to whisper in my ear. *I make great adventure for you, Gaixua.*

Yeah, a real great adventure—mil esker, I wanted to say to Aitatxi. *Thanks a lot. And don't call me that.*

I also wanted to ask him what he had been thinking when he left Artzainaskena to his daughter and Gorrienea to his son. It didn't make any sense. At least it didn't make any sense to me. It did however make perfect Aitatxi-sense. He'd spent his whole life tricking people into doing the things he believed they should. Aitatxi must have believed that sooner or later Ferdinand or Isabelle would need to cross the ocean separating them to get what they wanted.

Only Aitatxi was wrong. In the end, the journey to Urepel was left to me.

But what good had it done? I still hadn't gotten Isabelle to sign the quit deed to Artzainaskena. And I couldn't give her Gorrienea in exchange for signing because Marcelino would take the house. Now Mr. Steele was in the picture, and I had no idea what he and Marcelino were up to. On top of all that, even though I'd discovered a family I hadn't known existed, half of them wouldn't acknowledge me because of a feud that started before I was born.

Trying to make sense of it all gave me a headache.

It's your choice, son, I again heard Mr. Steele say. *What's it going to be?*

But what choice should I make? What choice would lead me to the end I wanted?

Nothing from the start of my journey had gone the way I planned.

Every choice I'd thought through—that I was sure made perfect sense—had turned out different than I'd expected. I needed help. And so I started to think about what Dad or Aitatxi, or even Oxea, would do in my situation. But then I stopped. They weren't in my situation. I was. This was my choice to make. And so instead of looking for answers from them, I looked for an answer from myself. I quit thinking and listened. And what I heard was the beating of my *bihotza*—heart; its steady rhythm led me back to a mirage on the horizon. And as I ran toward that pool of warm water, I found floating on its surface a choice that made no sense at all.

"You a first prize lawyer, Jacques?"

"*Oui,* I tell you, best in France."

"Can you meet with me tomorrow morning?"

"You come by office," Jacques said. "But how come—"

"Why you go Jacques's office?" Isabelle asked as she walked into the room.

I pressed an index finger to my lips to keep Jacques quiet.

"He want see me work," Jacques said.

"*Ba,* Mathieu, you no blink or you miss," Isabelle said.

And I laughed. In that moment, I was happy, by the fire, listening to Jacques telling Isabelle her eyes were like "shiny peas" and she telling him his eyes were full of apple wine. And I wanted it to last, even though I knew it wouldn't. Since the day of the accident, I had learned that the future was full of mirages and unseen cliffs. And tomorrow I planned to leap off one of those cliffs.

29

HOGEITA BEDERATZI

The Basque flag is red with a green X cut through it and a white cross on top of that. Oxea told me that the red was for wine, the green for grass, and the white for sheep's milk cheese. I was eleven at the time, and we were sitting on the dirt in the barn playing marbles.

"That's the ugliest flag ever," I said as I looked at the dusty and torn cloth nailed to the barn wall. Time had made the red pink, the green limey, and the white anything but.

"You ugliest flag ever," Oxea said. Which didn't make any sense, but was understandable since I had just won Oxea's favorite yellow cat's-eye, and he had called me a cheater and I had told him he was a baby and he said he didn't want to play anymore. But of course he drew a new circle with his sausage-like index finger and dropped his marbles inside it.

I asked Aitatxi about the flag while he was changing the tractor's oil. He said that the Basques called their flag the Ikurrina, and that it was the symbol of Euskal Herria, the Basque Country. The white cross symbolized the Catholic faith. The green stood for the Holy Oak of Guernica, and the red was the blood that was shed for independence. When I pointed out that there was no Euskal Herria anywhere on the world map in Ms. Helm's classroom, Aitatxi said, "Sure, no, it there. You just no know how a see."

"I have twenty-twenty vision," I pointed out.

"You no look with *behotza*—heart." Aitatxi put his flat palms over his chest.

"That's impossible," I said.

"You try, you see."

"I'm not going—"

"Close you eyes," Aitatxi said.

"What for—"

"Close *orai*," he said. Now.

"Fine."

"What color was your *ama*'s hair?"

"What?" I said, opening my eyes.

"Close." Aitatxi used his open palm, smelling of oil, to cover my eyes.

For a moment, I didn't see anything.

"Stop twenty-twenty vision," Aitatxi said and placed his other hand on my chest. "*Bihotza*." I could feel my heart beating against his palm. "She here."

And then she was. My mother's blonde hair caught in the wind, whipping all around me, brushing over my face. I reached out to touch her soft skin but instead found the stubble of my *aitatxi*'s unshaven beard.

I stepped away from Aitatxi, and he smiled at me.

"Sure, no, you use *bihotza* you see all kind thing—map or no map, Gaixua."

"Don't call me that," I said, but there was no power to my words.

Later, while sitting out under the oak in the pasture, I thought about the Basque flag. We were Catholic, so I was okay with the cross meaning faith. I had never even heard of Guernica and didn't know why they had a Holy Oak. But we had our own oak tree in the pasture, so I thought of that for the green. As for the red being blood shed for independence, well, that didn't make sense because the Basques weren't really independent since they didn't have a country on Ms. Helm's world map, no matter what Aitatxi said. The sun was setting. And as I watched it change from yellow to orange to red, I realized that the same sun was also setting on Aitatxi's Euskal Herria. The sun connected them—map or no map. So I closed my eyes and looked with my *bihotza* and let the day's last light spread over my face and become the red of my Basque flag.

The next day, when Dad picked me up after a three-day trip to Albuquerque, I asked him what the Basque flag meant. He said it didn't mean anything.

"Anyone can have a flag," he said and pointed at the gold flag hanging from the McDonalds arches as we turned in for dinner.

But that was when Dad still worked for John Deere and before the summer we moved back to the ranch and Dad remembered the past. The following fall when I asked him again about the Basque flag over a dinner of meatloaf and baked potatoes, he said, "The flag means hope."

"Hope of what?

"The future."

I didn't ask my father to tell me what he meant by *the future,* because at the time *the future* to me was that moment with him, on the ranch, us, together. I couldn't think to hope for more. Now, as I was walking to Jacques's office to sign away a home that a month ago I didn't know I owned, I thought about how the hope of *the future* had changed. *The future* was so much larger than when I was thirteen; it held things and people I hadn't even known existed. And, right then, I wasn't sure if that was good or bad.

Jacques's office was located in a storeroom above the bar. There was a Basque flag covering the wall behind his desk. The red, green, and white crisp and new.

"*Egun on,*" I said as I took a seat in a chair that was more comfortable than it looked.

Jacques was busy shuffling through a stack of papers. When I had walked him out of Gorrienea the night before, I told him what I was going to do.

"*Oui,* I tell you, Mathieu, you either genesis or crazy," Jacques had said.

"Can you draw up the papers?"

"I do," Jacques said. "But first, I find passport. This thing no work, I leaving country."

"Remember, I don't read French," I said.

"I make in English."

"You write English?"

"*Oui,* I tell you, much more easy than talking," Jacques said as he walked off into the dark.

Now, as Jacques slid in front of me the contract I'd asked him to draw up, he said, "You sure you want do this thing?"

I nodded.

"Okay, I make nice funeral for you." Jacques handed me a pen. "Sign bottom, both."

Before I signed, I read over what Jacques had written. The sentences were clean and clear. The paragraphing simple and direct.

"It's so clear," I said.

"*Mil esker,*" Jacques said. Thank you.

"But you aren't," I said. "You're like my *aitatxi*—I could never be sure what he did or did not mean to say. Or even why he said things sometimes."

"Mathieu a good man," Jacques said.

"You knew my *aitatxi*?"

"One time he catch me try sneak in house to see Isabelle."

"What happened?"

"He take by neck—"

"No," I said. "With Isabelle. Why didn't you two end up together?"

Jacques pursed his lips and rubbed his stubbled chin. His eyes moved to the window, as if he were seeing again what happened and thinking about why. The clock ticked. Someone walked through the room downstairs. Dust hung in the air, swirling with each of Jacques's breaths.

"No know," Jacques finally said and smacked his lips. "Sign."

"That's it?"

"What else you want?" Jacques said. "I tell you, I try and use all right words with Isabelle. And it no work. Marcelino, he grunt, she in love."

"What words?"

"*Oui,* I tell her she beautiful, wonderful, super, nice, good, pretty, stupid, re—"

"I hope you meant 'stupendous.'"

"*Oui,* I tell her all words I know for girl," Jacques said. "It no good. Now I use all wrong words and she like me just right. Women."

"Girls." I laughed as I thought of Jenny and the right and wrong words I'd used with her and how she punched me in the gut. And how that memory was now kind of nice.

"Sign," Jacques said.

I only hesitated for a moment, realizing that any advantage I had over Isabelle would be gone with a stroke of the pen. Then I signed the papers transferring the title of Gorrienea. And in doing so, leaped over the cliff's edge.

Jacques took one copy and handed me the other.

"Now what?" I said.

"I take this to Saint-Jean-de-Luz and give to court. Your copy, keep safe. Just in case."

"In case of what?"

"In case."

"You're worried about what Marcelino will do when he finds out what I've done with his Gorrienea."

"Plenty worry," Jacques said.

I got to my feet, folded up the document, and put it in my back pants pocket.

"That day when you sent me up the mountain to see the whole world—you knew Maria and Jean were up there, didn't you?"

Jacques shrugged.

"You knew I would see them."

"And you no say anyone what you see," Jacques said.

"I wanted to."

"But you no do."

"No."

"You know why you no say?"

"Because I'm stupid-endous," I said.

"Because you good shepherd."

As I walked down the stairs from Jacques's office, I thought about what he'd said. If I was a good shepherd, what did that make Maria and Jean—sheep? Part of some Basque flock? Back home, Father Bill's homilies contained both shepherds and sheep. Sheep were lost, found, and saved. A shepherd knew his sheep. A shepherd took care of his own. And then there was Father Bill's favorite: *They were like sheep without a shepherd.*

Outside the building the air was thick with the smell of wet grass. The light of the morning sun glistened off the pasture. A few sheep turned to look at me as a goat walked by, the brass bell around its neck clanking. Beyond the goat was Jean. He was leaning up against one of the *pilota* court walls, flipping a ball up and down in his right hand, as if he'd been waiting for me. Our eyes met. The muscles of my body tightened, and as I walked over, Jean tossed me the ball.

I took my place alongside him on the court. This time when I stepped onto the cement, I did not feel like I was stepping onto a foreign land. Over the last week I had become familiar with the court's extra wall. I had learned the angles it created. Adapted to the height of the bounce.

Jean again put his hands on his knees like a lineman. He again gave me his goofy kidlike smile and again reminded me of a young Oxea. But he was not Oxea. And this time, I was ready. Without a word, I pounded the ball against the wall.

I don't know how long we battled. I fell, got up, fell again. I don't remember the score. Jean fell, got up, fell again. Or even who won. But I do know that afterward as we sat shirtless with our backs up against the wall, bodies covered in sweat, the reopened gash on my elbow bleeding freely, Jean's right eye swollen and black from where the ball had hit him, that we were no longer enemies and something like friends.

And we never spoke a word to each other.

30

HOGEITA HAMAR

I took Jenny up to our summer *etxola* only once. It was mid-July and Dad was busy on the ranch. Jenny knew I was going to drive alone and so asked to go along.

"You're not going to talk the whole way, are you?"

"Not to you," Jenny said.

"Since I'm going to be the only other person in the truck, that means it will be good and quiet."

"Maybe I'll just talk to myself."

"Oh this is going to a real joyride," I said, but was glad Jenny was coming. I never liked to drive alone. On the ranch, I spent whole days off by myself fixing fences or plowing fields. And I didn't mind it at all. But in the closeness of the truck's cab, my being alone crowded me. Even with the windows down so that air whipped through the truck's interior, the aloneness didn't blow away. With Jenny in the truck, the chance of me feeling alone was pretty much zero.

She talked nonstop the whole way up. About school—she was going to be a senior next year and that was a whole new world. And Linda Carlisle—who was secretly seeing Matt Frederick who was supposed to be promised to Nancy Pruitt who was the nicest girl ever. And the diner, which her father totally needed to gut and then paint blue because that color was scientifically proven to make people hungry. Jenny went on and on, and I listened and nodded along and was grateful that she had insisted on coming.

Up at the sheep camp, after I dropped off the supplies, Jenny wanted to go on a hike before returning down the mountain.

"You ever spend the summer up here?" Jenny gathered pine cones from the needle-covered ground.

"I spent a week once," I said. "It was bo—"

"—oring," Jenny finished my comment. "Is everything boring to you?"

Before I could answer, a high-pitched "baaing" rose from the bottom of a nearby ravine.

"What's that?"

"Just a lamb," I said and started down the slope toward the sound.

"It sounds like a baby crying." Jenny followed me.

At the bottom of the hill, I found a sinkhole. I gazed in at a splash of white.

"What are you doing in there, Knucklehead?"

The lamb gazed up at me and kind of did look like it had been crying. Brown streaks ran from its eyes and down its face.

"I bet he's scared because he's all alone." Jenny dropped the pine cones and kneeled beside me to look in at the lamb.

"He's too stupid to be scared." I got on my belly and reached into the hole. I grabbed the lamb by the scruff of his neck and hauled him out.

"Poor baby." Jenny scratched the lamb's head.

The lamb nuzzled its wet nose into the crook of my neck as I checked its leg to make sure no bones were broken.

"Cool it, Knucklehead," I said.

"Don't call him that."

"It's his name."

"How do you know?"

"I named him," I said as I placed the lamb on the ground. "Now go find your flock, Knucklehead. And stay out of trouble."

When I let Knucklehead go, he jumped and kicked with joy at being free.

"You're welcome," I yelled after him.

Jenny rested her head on my shoulder. I breathed in the scent of lemon that now mixed with the pine and didn't move. We stayed that way until the light stretched into long shadows over the ground. The only sound was our breathing and the distant "baaing" of sheep.

"We should get going home," I finally said.

"We are home," Jenny said, and even though it didn't make any sense, it made me want to smile and spit at the same time, and made my gut cramp and my palms itch as I suddenly felt taller.

I started up the slope.

"Wait up, Etcheberri," Jenny called after me. "I don't want to get lost."

So I waited for Jenny, and she slipped her hand in mind, and we climbed up together.

I was climbing alone now, up the hill toward Gorrienea, dabbing at the fresh blood from my *pilota* match with Jean, and recalling again what Jenny had said. "We are home." But of course we hadn't been. We were in the woods, with nothing but trees around us. No floor or walls or roof for shelter. Still, with her head on my shoulder, Jenny'd called it home.

I was thinking about Gorrienea and Artzainaskena, and wondering what made those houses into places my family called home, when I spotted Edita.

She was running over the grass barefoot, darting in and out of the trees on the far side of the pasture. She had on the same charcoal dress from my first night in Urepel. A bunch of yellow flowers were in her hand. Her streaked black and gray hair flew in a tangle behind her as she glanced over her shoulder—as if she were being pursued—and screamed.

"Edita!" I called to her as I ran across the pasture and into the woods.

The wind picked up. The leaves of the trees chattered. I again called to Edita, but my voice flew back into my face. I caught glimpses of her through the tree trunks. Flickers of black and gray. A flame of yellow. One moment, she seemed so close that my fingertips could almost graze her hair. The next so far ahead that she was only a shadow in the forest. I passed her bundle of flowers discarded on the ground. Tried to quicken my pace, but my legs felt rubbery—their strength spent on my *pilota* match with Jean.

Despite the wind, Edita must have heard me calling. She must have known I was chasing her. And I realized that this had become a game to her. And in this game, I had become the Mamu.

The trees grew thicker, the trunks pressing together. Edita slowed as she searched for a way through. And as the distance between us closed, I could see smudges of black on her dress and smell the smoke in her hair. I almost had her. A few more strides. A grin spread across my face: I was the Mamu.

But then, as I stretched my hand to grab her, the world disappeared beneath my feet. And I fell. Down and down. With nothing to hold onto.

The world returned with a jolt. A shock of pain shot up through my body. Blood filled my mouth as I bit my tongue. My left leg twisted under me as I collapsed into a pile of damp leaves.

When I got my bearings, I realized I had fallen into some kind of sink-hole. Around me rose sheer rock walls. Above was a small opening through which I could see the sky. I swallowed the blood pooling in my mouth and worked my left leg out from under me. My already-swelling knee spiked with pain and pressed against my pant leg like an overstuffed sausage. I groaned.

Sunlight fell through the opening above, and I was thinking how lucky I was that I hadn't hit my head and killed myself when I saw that the wall in front of me was covered with crude charcoal drawings of animals and men. I recognized deer and rabbits. A hulking man and his son. And, of course, the towering figure of the Mamu.

"*Zer egin duzu?*" Edita called from above. What are you doing? And I looked up to see her leaning over the edge of the hole.

"*Deus ez,*" I said. "*Eta zuk?*"

"*Zuri behatzen dut,*" Edita said, and I managed a dry laugh at her response to my asking her what she was doing—Looking at you.

Then Edita disappeared.

"Edita?"

A pieced-together rope ladder tumbled in and Edita climbed down.

"*Egun on,*" Edita said when she reached the bottom.

"Hello to you too."

Edita picked up a piece of charcoal and, after studying me sprawled out on the ground, began drawing on the wall. The thick lines came together with just enough detail to the jaw line leading to a pointed chin to be recognizable as me.

When she was finished, Edita wiped her fingers on her dress, adding more black smudges to the fabric. Then she stepped over and helped me up.

I winced as I got to my feet. While I didn't think I had broken anything, my twisted knee couldn't hold my weight. With lots of stops and some scary moments, I managed to climb up the rope ladder to the forest above. Once there, Edita found me a walking stick. Leaning heavily on it, I began the trek back to Gorrienea.

"*Mamiain etxea sen hurn?*" I asked Edita as I hobbled along. Was that the Mamu's house?

Edita laughed as she bent down to gather a fresh bunch of yellow flowers.

"*Ez, haren etxea ainitz haundia da,*" she said. No, the Mamu's house is much bigger.

Baina, zer hura da? I asked. Then what is that?

"*Ene etxea,*" Edita said. My home.

But since *etxea* could mean either home or house in Euskara, Edita could have meant "my house." A playhouse? Like that of a child? Where she went to escape the world? To be alone?

My Euskara was not good enough to ask Edita the difference between a home and a house. Or to understand any answer she gave me. So I decided to wait until we got back to Gorrienea to ask Isabelle in English.

By the time we reached the line of apple trees that marked the edge of Gorrienea's pasture, the sun was already two-thirds across the sky. I stopped and pulled off a couple of apples. I offered one to Edita, but she shook her head.

By then, my swollen left knee would no longer bend. So I pressed my back up against a tree trunk and worked my way into a sitting position. I bit into an apple; sweet juice filled my mouth.

Edita began placing the flowers she'd picked into her hair. Once she was done, she arched her arms out and started turning in practiced circles. Slow and methodical. To some unheard music.

As I watched her turn left and then right, I heard something. I cocked my ear—the faint trill of a *txistua*? The flute notes floated down like leaves from the tree above me. I blinked. The steps of Edita's dance fell into unison with the notes. Then, from somewhere deep in the forest, the boom of a *danbora*—drum. Deep and resonating. It filled my body. And as the drum quickened, Edita's dance matched pace. Her dress flared out. The drum grew louder, the flute more urgent. Edita spun in dizzying circles. Swirling, legs kicking, arms flying—as she wrapped herself in the music. Then, with one last booming beat of the *danbora* and one last shrill note of the *txistua*, the music ended at the same moment as Edita's dance. Only then did she look at me, breathing hard, black and gray hair about her face, flowers falling from the locks, smiling, knowing that I had finally heard her music.

I was about to say something to Edita about the music—ask where it came from, where it went—when beyond her I saw Isabelle step out the door of Gorrienea. She was drying her hands on her apron, looking across the pasture toward Marcelino's house. Then, as if coming to a decision, she pulled off her apron, dropped it to the ground, and strode in a straight line toward Odolenea.

I got to my feet, forgetting my damaged knee until it gave out under me. I clung to the tree trunk for support, keeping my eyes on Isabelle.

Why was Isabelle going to see Marcelino? Could she know what I had done with Gorrienea? Had Jacques told her? Gone to see her while I was busy playing *pilota* and chasing after Edita?

At the thought of what Marcelino might do at the news, the apple in my mouth turned sour. I grabbed my walking stick, sent Edita home, and limped across the pasture, leaning on the stick that I knew might have to double as a weapon.

31

HOGEITA HAMAIKA

Whenever I went shopping with Aitatxi, I always walked several paces in front of him, hopeful that strangers would think we weren't together. Aitatxi always had on his beret and oversized black coat and smelled of sheep and sour milk. Being seen with him was like being dunked in a pool of embarrassment. No matter how I tried not to, I always got soaked. For his part, Aitatxi never asked me to slow down. He just went about his shopping, paid, and then met me back at the truck for the drive home.

The night before he died, Aitatxi embarrassed me one last time.

A storm had exploded and scattered the sheep. Rain fell in sheets of white. Aitatxi leaned on me for support. We were lost. And then I found the cave, and thought we had just gotten lucky. That is, until I saw the drawings on the walls. Drawings of Oxea and Aitatxi and a young version of Dad. I made a fire, and Aitatxi told me how my father had used charcoal to scratch the drawings onto the stone.

"What are we going to do once we get to the *etxola*?" I asked Aitatxi, because he was shivering and kept mistaking me for my father and calling me "Ferdinand." I wanted him to talk about the future, like it was a promise that once said had to be kept.

"Go home," Aitatxi said.

"That's it? We've done all this just to go home?"

"Home place always going."

"Home's boring."

"Then maybe you make no boring—make new."

"And how do I do that?"

"You are *exteberri*," Aitatxi said.

It wasn't until years later that I realized that was exactly why Aitatxi had taken me on the sheep drive—so I could go home. To an old house and find a way to make it new.

That night in the light of the campfire with the rain falling over the mouth of the cave, sealing us off from the rest of the world, Aitatxi told me about how when Dad was ten he broke his arm jumping out of the hayloft, and how Mom only rode horses bareback, and how he had to teach Oxea how to say "I do" in English on his wedding day. The last thing Aitatxi said was, "I no forget your birthday, Gaixua. I know just what I going a give you."

And I was embarrassed and told Aitatxi I didn't want anything. But I had. I wanted the chance to walk beside and not in front of him. To make right the past. It was a chance I never got.

Now I had another chance to make right the past. And I was determined not to waste it.

I didn't knock when I reached Marcelino's house. I just pushed open the door. The room was dark. All the windows closed. Light spilled in around me and onto the fireplace. There, Marcelino kicked a smoldering log. Flames leaped up. Smoke curled to the ceiling and gathered in a dark cloud over the only other person in the room—Isabelle. She stood opposite Marcelino at the hearth, their eyes locked on each other, fire burning between them.

"*Etxea enea da eta nahi dut,*" Marcelino said to Isabelle. The house is mine and I want it.

"*Zertako egin duzu?*" Isabelle said to Marcelino. Why you do this?

"He speaks English," I said. And only then did the two of them glance in my direction. "Writes it too. He's been sending letters in your name to Mr. Steele back in the United States."

Isabelle stepped in front of the fire so that flames danced around her. "What kind of man you?"

"I you husband," Marcelino said as he spit into the fire.

"You take what mine," Isabelle said.

"What you have mine."

"*Ez,*" Isabelle said—no—and she pulled her wedding ring from her finger, and threw it into the fire.

Marcelino moved as if to retrieve the ring from the flames, but Isabelle stopped him by pressing her hand flat against his chest.

"For now until always, what I have mine," Isabelle said. "You give back everything you take."

"I never do that thing."

"Then when you die," Isabelle said, "it not be well."

Marcelino took a step back, as if he had been struck. Then he turned from Isabelle to face me.

"Give me Gorrienea," he said. "Or I never let her free."

"Jacques was right," I said. "You are a wolf."

"Give me what mine."

"Gorrienea is not yours."

"Artzainaskena no yours," Marcelino said and smiled. "Mr. Steele he tell about you. We no so different."

"I'm nothing like you," I said.

"You come Urepel for take what yours. I do same. You play *gaixua,* but you *otsoa*—wolf like me."

The truth of what Marcelino said pushed into me. Was the ranch mine like Gorrienea was his? Something I wanted but had no right to? How could I be like him? I leaned on my walking stick to keep from falling.

"Give him Gorrienea," Isabelle said. "I no want no more."

"I can't," I said.

"Edita and I, we make new home."

"You don't understand—"

"Mathieu, please, just—"

"I don't own Gorrienea," I said. "I signed it over to Maria Mendia."

And the moment the words left my mouth, Marcelino let out a growl and lunged toward me. The memory of him striking the postman was in my head as I raised the stick to beat him back. But it wasn't necessary. I was not the wolf's intended prey. He pushed me aside and dashed out the door.

"What you do?"

"I did it to make right the past," I said. "For everyone."

"Marcelino, he no stop until he have Gorrienea."

"But Maria won't give it to him."

"*Ba*—so he make trouble for all Mendias—more stones in wall between us."

"But I was only—"

"I wrong, Mathieu," Isabelle said. "Maybe it better you no never come Urepel."

And at Isabelle's words, I was thirteen again, back in that silent cave, with my head on Aitatxi's chest, listening for the beat of his *bihotza*, powerless to bring him back, alone in a world I didn't understand.

I stumbled out the doorway and into the day's failing light.

32

HOGEITA HAMABI

Arizona has violent sunsets.

Each day ends in fire as the sun crashes into the desert. Colors explode. Flames shoot up through clouds that have spent the day wandering like lost sheep through a sky more white than blue. The clouds bleed red.

The Basque land has no desert.

And so the sun I watched as I limped from Marcelino's house back to Gorrienea sank gently into the line of trees across the pasture. Light filtered through leaves like flicked matches, momentary sparks unable to start a blaze.

Darkness fell. The night went cold. My breath rose in tiny ghosts to trail behind me. I stopped and looked back at Odolenea. What had happened? How had everything changed so quickly? But then I should have known. That was the way the world did change. Not in years but seconds.

I thought of Oxea and the day he died. I had just turned thirteen and believed that fact alone would change my world. But it hadn't. What did change it was Dad selling the last of our flock without realizing that Oxea could not live in a world where he was not a shepherd. And so he hung himself from the oak tree in the pasture, and I found his body swinging from side to side, ticking off seconds to a birthday that was over before it started.

Had I now made the same mistake as my father by giving away Gorrienea? By trying to make right the past without understanding its hold on the future? Not realizing that maybe Isabelle could not live in world without her family home.

A sheep "baaed" in the night. Instinctively I started toward the sound.

But then I stopped. I had heard the "baaing" of lost sheep all my life. And I had always come to their rescue. But what if I hadn't? What if I just let their cries for help go unanswered?

When Aitatxi died, the flock was scattered. I was left alone to get the sheep up to the good oak. And somehow I had. I gathered the flock and found the narrow way up the mountain to the *etxola*. And once the sheep were penned, and I thought everything I needed to do had been done, I heard the "baaing" of one last sheep. I recognized the cry; it was the sheep I'd named Gaixua. I went to find the lost sheep in a night so dark I had to feel my way along the side of the mountain, unsure of each step and where it was leading me until I arrived. Gaixua was huddled at the base of the trail. I gathered him in my arms and carried him to safety.

The sheep was still "baaing." Lost somewhere in Urepel. Waiting for me to save it. And even though part of me wanted to let the sheep remain lost, the shepherd in me couldn't.

"All right!" I called out. "I hear you—I'm coming."

And the moment I said that, the "baaing" stopped and the dark night grew lighter—too light. A warm glow seeped around me and up into the sky. I turned. Gorrienea was on fire.

My heart took one deep beat. And then I was running the best I could toward the burning house. The doors of surrounding houses flew open. Flashlights bobbed in the dark. White aprons fluttered like the wings of startled birds. All of Urepel rushed toward Gorrienea.

The smell of smoke was thick. People darted all around me, bumping into each other, yelling in Basque and French. I searched the crowd for Edita. But I couldn't find her. Not in the chaos. Was she in the house? Had she gotten out?

The front wall of Gorrienea's second floor collapsed. Through the flames, I saw the mantle of the fireplace. For a moment, the dark wood beam seemed to be untouched by the fire. But then the carved faces of my ancestors grew red and their ember eyes glowed as the mantle cracked down the middle and crumbled.

The roof of Gorrienea caved in and the fire leaped higher, illuminating the whole countryside. And for a moment everyone stopped—gazed at the flames rising toward the stars. Then, without a spoken word, men and women formed a bucket line from the stream. Water was passed up and thrown onto the burning house.

On the far side of the line, I spotted Edita. She was with Isabelle. The two of them huddled with the cousins from the church. The women clung to one another as if they were being beaten by waves and had only each other to use for anchors.

Jean and Maria ran past, hand in hand. I watched as they grabbed shovels and began throwing dirt onto the blaze.

I started forward, wanting to join in the effort to put out the fire. But before I could take a step, I was grabbed from behind. A club of a hand slapped over my mouth. The tip of a blade pinched my neck.

"I kill you here you no come," Marcelino whispered into my ear as he dragged me backward. I lost hold of my walking stick. Couldn't get my footing. Pain spiked up through my twisted knee as Marcelino pulled me from the light of the fire into the dark line of the trees.

There, he stopped for a moment, and I tried to sort out what was going on. Did he really say he was going to kill me? Marcelino took hold of my right wrist and, with an ease that at another time would have been embarrassing but was now only frightening, yanked my arm behind my back. His breath was thick with wine as he spit onto the ground and turned me from side to side, searching for a way through the trees.

"What do you want?" I managed to ask as he started to push me forward. "I don't own Gorrienea anymore."

Marcelino marched me uphill.

"Let me go." I tried to break free, but that only caused him to wrench my arm harder. The knife bit into my skin to send a warm trickle of blood down my neck.

"You set Gorrienea on fire, didn't you?" I said, not expecting or getting an answer.

I stumbled as we went uphill. He was half carrying me now, moving with a strength I couldn't resist. We passed the pasture where I had seen Edita running through the trees, and the spot where Jacques had turned for home and sent me alone up the mountain, and the rock Maria had been sitting on, waiting to tell me of her love for Jean. And I realized Marcelino was taking me to the cliff where I had seen Maria and Jean kissing. I also understood that I would not be returning. Isabelle and the others would think the stupid American had gotten lost in the dark and fallen to his death. They might even think I had burned down Gorrienea. And I would not be there to tell them otherwise.

"You could have killed your daughter," I said, and this brought Marcelino to a momentary stop.

"I never hurt Edita," Marcelino hissed in my ear. "She no in house when fire come."

"So you did start the fire."

"I no can have Gorrienea, no one have," Marcelino said.

"Now you have nothing."

"I have Artzainaskena."

A coldness foreign to the desert of Arizona slid through my body. I shivered as I saw a future with me gone. Marcelino would offer Isabelle her freedom in exchange for the ranch. And to be free of him, she would give it. He would leave this place—take the same plane I had back over the same ocean—and arrive at my home. Laugh as he spit on the ground of Artzainaskena. Drink wine as he tore down the barn Dad and I raised. Curse as he kicked open the door to the house Aitatxi built. Marcelino would rip my mother's cross from the wall and toss it aside. He would pull down Amatxi's plates and shatter them on the floor. Gather up the boxes in the cellar—full of my family's pictures and letters—and make a bonfire to burn my past as if it were nothing but junk to be discarded. And lastly, Marcelino would cut down the oak tree in the pasture, the tree with Aitatxi and Amatxi's initials carved into the bark, and sell the land to Mr. Steele. And thus, finally have his revenge on the family that had never accepted him.

Marcelino pushed me on. When we finally reached the cliff's edge, Marcelino and I nearly walked off it together. In fact, when my foot stepped into the nothingness, Marcelino pulled me back. I didn't waste time being grateful. I knew that he had only postponed my death. Did not want my end to come too soon. He wanted it to have meaning. To not be an accident.

I tried to back away, but Marcelino's grip was stone. I couldn't move. My swollen knee was now useless. The knife he held to my neck cut deeper into my flesh. I tried not to swallow, afraid that the motion would slit open my throat.

I was going to die. The thought seemed impossible. But then it had always been that way for me. Oxea dying was impossible. Aitatxi dying impossible. Dad impossible. And now I was going to do the impossible as well.

And I thought of my mother and the song she sang to me when I was a baby—"*Tun gulan bat, tun gulan bi, tun gulan hureran, er-or-i.*"

I could hear it now. As clearly as if she were there singing it to me. And then Marcelino heard it too.

"*Nor da hor?*" Marcelino called into the dark as he turned me to face the sound. Who is there?

"*Aita, egon ene beha,*" Edita called as she stopped singing. Father, wait for me.

"*Edita, zaza etxerat,*" Marcelino said as his daughter took shape out of the night. Edita, go home.

But instead of obeying her father, Edita reached out and took hold of my free hand.

"*Mamian etxea hurbil da,*" she said to me. "*Hogei. Eramanen zitut harat.*" The Mamu's home is close. Come, I will take you there.

"*Zaza!*" Marcelino knocked her hand out of mine. Go!

He pushed her so that she fell to her knees. Edita started to cry. And at the sound of her crying, Marcelino's grip momentarily loosened. The edge of the knife went slack. And when it did, I threw my head back into his face. I felt his nose break under the blow, his warm blood on my skin as the knife clattered onto the stones at my feet.

And then I was on the ground, scrambling for the knife. But my fingers came up short as Marcelino grabbed my bad leg. I yelled in pain as he dragged me forward. White clouds rolled up from below the cliff's edge, silhouetting my attacker. Only he was no longer Marcelino but the Mamu. And I was no longer in the mountains above Urepel but on the cliff of my dreams. There the Mamu I had turned from was angry and wild as he threw back his head and let loose his *irrintzina:* "Ai-ai-ai-ai-ai-ai-ai-yaaaaa!"

And that cry was met by another; Edita's dark figure flew past me and into the clouds.

Marcelino lunged for his daughter. The two of them disappeared over the cliff's edge.

I was left alone with only the wind whispering in my ears: "*Tun gulan bat, tun gulan bi . . .*"

I crawled forward to find Marcelino clinging to a rock with one hand. From the other dangled a singing Edita.

Marcelino turned his face up toward me. All I could see were his eyes. And in those eyes he was and wasn't the Mamu.

"Take," he said.

"No."

"Take Edita."

"I'll get some rope."

Then, with the same strength that he had earlier used to overcome me, Marcelino raised up his daughter.

"Take."

I grabbed onto Edita as the rock Marcelino clung to broke loose and his eyes became two more stars as he fell away into darkness.

33

HOGEITA HAMAHIRU

I started to say "No" when Isabelle asked me to be a pallbearer for Marcelino's funeral. But then Edita took my hand as she sang, "*Tun gulan bat, tun gulan bi, tun gulan hureran, er-or-i.*" And I thought of my own father's funeral. There had been no pallbearers. I couldn't even remember how his casket got into the open grave. Just that it was there and I was looking down at the sun reflecting off the shiny wood, and Father Bill was saying something about a shepherd calling his lost sheep home as the smell of fresh-cut alfalfa hung in the air. Edita squeezed my hand. Whatever Marcelino had done, in the end he was still Edita's father. And now he was gone. So I said "Yes"—for her.

Jacques met me at the church.

"*Oui*, I think maybe you want," Jacques said as he pulled my blackened journal from his pocket.

Even though the outside was scorched black from the fire, the paper inside was still white and undamaged.

"How did you get this?"

"Edita," Jacques said. "She find."

I flicked through the pages that held not only my words but my passport and plane ticket home.

"*Mil esker,*" I said. Thank you. Then I slipped on the coat I had borrowed for the funeral. Jacques handed me a tie. I closed my eyes as I put it on, letting my father's hands guide me, flipping the tie over the top then down through the middle before tightening the knot.

All of Urepel was crowded into the church. The men in white shirts and black coats leaned over the balconies and nodded to me as I entered. The women huddled in the pews, black shawls drawn up over their heads.

Isabelle and Edita were at the front of the church, surrounded by their female cousins. They were all crying and hugging each other, and while I knew it was from grief, from which grief I wasn't sure: Marcelino's death, the burning of Gorrienea, or all the lost years spent looking through instead of at each other.

Maria was there, holding Edita's hand. She had given Gorrienea back to Isabelle. Even though all that was now left was the house's concrete foundation. The gesture was enough. A home lost, a home returned. Now the wound between the two families could heal.

Along with me, the pallbearers were Jean and Jacques—and two other men who Isabelle said were from Spain and whose real names she did not know and did not want to know. Isabelle asked me to give the eulogy so that I could recount to everyone how Marcelino died. Jacques translated what I said into Euskara.

Marcelino Odolen was a shepherd and a husband and a father who sacrificed himself for his daughter. His last word was "take" as he placed Edita into my hands. When he fell, he did not cry out in fear. Marcelino was not afraid to die for what he loved. And so he died well.

I thought it best not to mention how Marcelino, Edita, and I got into the precarious position on the cliff or the knife to my throat and his trying to kill me. I decided to stick with just the end because, even if the end is just a small part of the whole story, it tends to be the part people remember.

Marcelino was buried in the Etcheberri section of the cemetery, and in that way was finally accepted into the family. I stood with Isabelle while Edita placed flowers on her father's grave. Maria and Jean were nearby. He had his head on her shoulder as she stroked his hair.

"*Atsoen otsoa biharen bidotsa,*" I whispered to Isabelle and motioned toward the couple. Yesterday's wolf is tomorrow's lamb.

"*Ba,*" Isabelle said. "Your Basque no so bad now."

"Thanks to you."

I took one of the flowers from Marcelino's grave and placed it on Joseph's. I imagined the birth date cut into the stone changing from 1928 to

1960. Imagined Joseph walking up the road to Artzainaskena with his James Dean swagger, hopeful and sure of himself—time and a strange country not yet taking that away from him. He would come and work on the ranch. We would be friends. He would not be alone.

"Will you put flowers on his grave for me?"

"*Ba,*" Isabelle said. "It time Joseph come home."

Isabelle looked in the direction of the black remains of Gorrienea.

"What will you do now?" I asked.

"Make new house."

"But you lost everything."

"*Ez,*" Isabelle said. No. "I find everything."

"We are *etcheberri.*"

"*Ba,* we make new home," Isabelle said. "*Baina,* no animals inside. And bigger bathroom, I think."

"Does that 'we' include anyone besides Edita?"

"Do not try and be clever, Mathieu," Isabelle said and smiled, but that smile had lost the sting it had when I first arrived at Gorrienea.

"I only hope Jacques knows what he's getting into."

"You men never know," Isabelle said as we started walking toward the cemetery gate. "Edita *txauri.*"

As we exited the cemetery, I placed a hand on Isabelle's arm and gave her my journal.

"Jacques can help you read it," I said. "And then, when your written English is 'no so bad,' maybe you can write me a letter."

Isabelle held the book in her upturned palms as if offering it back to me.

"Mathieu I no can take."

"Don't worry; I tore out the pages with embarrassing stuff."

"*Ba,* how you know what embarrass me?"

"I wasn't thinking about you," I said.

And Isabelle laughed and tucked the book under her arm.

After the funeral, everyone gathered in the large white building downtown. French, Spanish, and Euskara bounced off the walls and filled the air. And even though I couldn't understand most of what was being said, I caught Marcelino's name again and again. People were talking about the way he died. How he sacrificed himself for his daughter. Repeatedly, I heard: "*Odo bizitzea gogorra da, ondo hiltzea gogorrago.*" Living well is hard, dying well is harder. Marcelino's "dying well" had changed everything. His whole life rewritten by its ending. The dark moments forgotten, weaknesses explained away, wrongdoings undone. And even though I had been there when Marcelino died and had felt his knife against my throat, I too looked on him with gentler eyes. Marcelino said "take" and I had taken.

But it wasn't just Marcelino's death that filled my head that day but Oxea's. I couldn't help but think of Oxea's ending. It wasn't fair that people back home remembered him only as the man who hung himself over a flock of sheep. There was so much more to his life before that final chapter. And so I promised myself that I would write about the things Oxea had done, so people would know that for him it was not about how he died, but how he lived.

The bar in the corner was set up like before. And Jacques was there. Again drinking a glass of red wine. He handed me a glass as Edita danced by singing, "*Tun gulan bat, tun gulan bi, tun gulan hureran, er-or-i.*"

"I've learned a lot of Euskara, but I still can't understand what that song means," I said. "Something about falling and water?"

"You know what *urepel* it mean?" Jacques asked.

"Warm water."

"*Oui,* I tell you, *urepel* is the water," Jacques said. "*Tun gulan bat*—you fall down once; *tun gulan bi*—you fall down twice; *tun gulan hureran, er-or-i*—the third time you fall, you fall into water. You in the *urepel* now, Mathieu Etcheberri."

Before I could ask him to explain what he meant, Isabelle came over with a dozen female cousins, and I was showered in tears and kisses, and told over and over, "*Zuri amaian begiak dituzu*"—You have your mother's eyes.

After I had met all my mother's relatives, and increased the size of my family by thirty plus, I told Isabelle I needed to get going. There were no tears with her. Just a single kiss on each of my cheeks and the words, "*Ondo ibili.*"

"You travel well too," I said.

I took off the black coat, dress shirt, and tie I had borrowed and laid them on a table. My backpack and all my clothes had been lost when Gorrienea burned. So I was leaving with only what I wore, my passport, and my return plane ticket. As I took a last look over the family that I'd never known I had but now planned on keeping, I breathed in the smoke that clung to my T-shirt from the night of the fire and touched the patch Isabelle sewed over the rip in the knee of my jeans from my fall into the sinkhole and stretched my neck against the scab from the cut of Marcelino's knife and smiled and was glad I had come.

I headed toward the building's door. There, just before I exited, Edita ran up. She wrapped her arms around me, pressed her face to my chest, and repeated what she'd said to me that first night in Gorrienea, when I stumbled in from the rain to find her dancing before the fire.

"*Zu hemen zira. Banakin jinen zinela. Aspaldian hemen nintzan.*" And then in an English I did not know she had, "You are here. I knew you would come. I have been waiting for you forever."

With that, Edita danced away into the crowd. And I stepped through the doorway and started down the hill toward home.

As I walked, I thought about Aitatxi and Dad and their secrets. I might never know why they wanted to keep their *bihotz isilekoak*—secret hearts—from me. But now I at least understood those hearts a little better. I also knew why Dad saved the picture of himself, alone, sitting on the grass, with his back up against the oak tree in the pasture. He did it because of what he saw through that camera lens—the future. All the things to come both good and bad. And even though that future might not have been in perfect focus, I like to believe it was clear enough to make my father want to look through that lens again and again.

HOGEITA HAMALAUR

The law office of *Mr. Thaddeus Steele, Esq.* seemed shabbier than I remembered. Mr. Steele smaller. The darkness not as dark.

"Well, son, you back from your a . . . a adventure?" Mr. Steele said from where he sat behind his metal desk, again using a plastic spoon to eat a Dennis the Menace Peanut Parfait.

"I got home yesterday," I said as I went into the adjacent room, retrieved a chair, and sat down to face him.

"And did things a . . . a transpire the way you a . . . a planned?"

"Not at all," I said.

Mr. Steele chuckled.

"Life rarely does, son," he said. "Luckily everything is negotiable, and so I am a . . . a presuming you have a proposition concerning ownership of the ranch."

"Why do you think that?"

"Well, I'm guessing this ain't no social visit," Mr. Steele said.

I studied the giant black-and-white map of Phoenix behind Mr. Steele. Searched for a pattern in the green and red pins scattered over it.

"You have a red pin marking the ranch."

"Hoping to change that to green," Mr. Steele said. "Now what is it you want, son?"

"I want you to unfreeze my bank account."

"I'm talking big picture here," Mr. Steele said and scooped into his hand the peanuts that had fallen off his ice cream and popped them into his mouth. "You're more like me than you know, son. I never liked sheep either. Stupid animals. Don't know why God made 'em."

"Maybe it was to give shepherds a job to do."

"Maybe," Mr. Steel said. "But there's a whole world out there doing just fine without sheep or shepherds. Don't you want to start living in that world?"

And I did want that—to live in that other world, far away from sheep and ranches and fallow fields and small towns. To just walk down the road and never look back. Or at least part of me wanted that. Maybe it always would. But another part of me, the bigger part, well, it wanted just the opposite.

"I can't sell the ranch," I said.

"'Can't' is just a 'won't' prettied up."

"Artzainaskena isn't mine to sell," I said.

"So your aunt wouldn't sign the quit deed," Mr. Steele said as he tossed his ice cream container into the trash. "Decided to keep the ranch for herself—"

"Oh she signed the quit deed."

"Then you own the ranch, son."

"No."

Mr. Steele narrowed his eyes.

"Then who does?"

"An owner who can never sell it to you."

"Don't be too sure about that." Mr. Steele chuckled. "When I want something, I can be mighty persuasive."

"I know," I said. "That's why I made sure the new owners couldn't be persuaded."

"Everyone can be persuaded."

"Not everyone—not sheep."

"Sheep?"

"Isabelle gave me Artzainaskena," I said. "And I gave it to the flock."

"What are you talking about?"

"I had a lawyer in France draw it up," I said. "As long as there are sheep on the land, it can never be sold."

For a moment, Mr. Steele didn't seem to have heard what I said. Then his face grew red and he began to breathe hard and spittle gathered on his lips.

"You son of a bitch!"

He started to get to his feet. And I tensed my muscle, not sure what he might do. I wished I'd made sure he didn't have a gun stashed in his desk drawer.

But then Mr. Steele's body went limp and he collapsed back into his chair and a funny, perplexed look washed over his face.

"Sheep?" Mr. Steele said, as if trying to understand how a stupid animal had undone all his careful planning.

Right then, I thought it was probably a good time for me to exit the law office of *Mr. Thaddeus Steele, Esq.* Besides, I had another appointment to keep.

When I got to the diner, I waited until the lunch crowd filtered out before entering. The clank of the door's attached cowbell never sounded so loud. Afternoon sunlight fell through the blinds of the front window and onto Dad and my's booth and the bull with a saguaro coming out of its rear. The smell of fried hamburgers filled the air. And Reba McEntire sang, *You lift me up to heaven.* Her voice tangled in the cloud of smoke drifting from the kitchen.

"What do you want?" Jenny asked as she stepped through the kitchen's swinging door.

"I came to pay the money I owe you." I placed a five-dollar bill on the counter.

Jenny wrinkled an eyebrow at the bill.

"It's a little more than that."

"I plan on paying in installments."

"You going to be around this *boring* place long enough to do that?" Jenny picked up the money and stuck it into her pocket. "Or will you mail me the payments from the U of A?"

"I've had a change of plans," I said. "I'm staying here."

At that, Jenny leaned her weight onto her hip and looked me up and down like I was a stranger she had just met and not yet decided to trust.

"Why should I care?"

"I don't know that you should."

"Then why are you here?"

"I told you—"

"Just go," Jenny said as she gathered a stack of plates into her arms and started toward the kitchen.

"Jenny." I took hold of her arm.

"Don't you touch—"

And when she tried to jerk herself free, the plates fell from her arms and shattered on the floor. But I didn't let go. Instead, I used my Basque hands for what they were made for—holding on.

"I know why you kissed me the day of the funeral," I said.

"Good for you."

"The same reason you punched me in the alley."

"I don't care—"

"It was because you were afraid," I said.

"I'm not afraid of you."

"Not me—the future."

Jenny stopped struggling.

"But the thing is—the thing I've learned—is that even if you make your own *pilota* ball and think you know the court, there are still going to be bounces you can't see coming and they'll send the ball off in directions you never imagined and you just have to be ready and adjust and keep trying. Because the future is like that. But you need it—and the past. Because without both of them, *right now* isn't worth living."

Jenny cocked her head to the side and bit the corner of her lip and there were tears in her eyes.

"You sound like an idiot," she said as lemons filled the air.

"I am an idiot," I said. "But I was kind of hoping that maybe I could be your idiot."

And this time when I moved to kiss her, Jenny kissed me back. And no one got punched and no one interrupted. And while our kiss didn't stretch on into forever, it did last a good five minutes.

"I have to go," I said when I finally pulled away.

"Where?"

"To the airport—to get my cousins."

"Cousins?"

"Jean and Maria—they just got married. You'll like them." I backed toward the door.

"They're coming here?"

"They're going to help me out on the ranch so I can take some classes at the community college," I said. "Sheep and the university might not be able to be on the same list—but I think I can make sheep and the community college work."

"What are you talking about?"

"The future," I said to Jenny as I pushed open the door. "Our future."

Outside, sunlight reflected off storefront windows as the familiar oily smell of asphalt rose to make my eyes water. I quickened my pace as I gazed up into a sky as blank as a white sheet of paper waiting to be written on. On it, I made my list: Pick up the truck I'd bought back from the mechanic who charged me a hundred dollars more than he'd paid for it; *bat*—one on list. Get Jean and Maria at airport; *bi*—two on list. Meet Luis and Diego arriving at Artzainaskena with flock; *hiru*—three on list. I would add more to my list; fill the sky with the things I wanted to do. But for now, this was enough.

Somehow, the sheep that had started out ruining my life had become its center, anchoring me to this world. And while I was happy about how everything worked out, in the distance I again saw a monsoon gathering on the horizon. Still hours away. But approaching.

A mirage obscured the highway. Today, the water seemed far away. Smaller. Just a splash of silver, evaporating in the very sun that created it.

And I thought of what Aitatxi had said about the last shepherd.

"Sure, no, last shepherd he be same as first—Mathieu. He man now. And as man he know he no can save all the sheeps. World a big. Wolves a many. But he save what can. And then funny thing, it happen. By saving sheeps, he save self."

"But what about the world he wanted to see?" I had asked Aitatxi.

"Sure, no," Aitatxi said. "World it still be there. But last shepherd, he need a take care of flock first."

And I would.

Oraindik nahi nin—I still wanted. And I knew that someday the water shimmering in the distance would again swell—become an ocean. And on that day the muscles of my thighs will tighten and I will sprint through the wavy lines of heat and dive into the *urepel* and swim through the warm water to that other world.